"Ghada Samman's rebellion in the middle of the twentieth century was a slap in the face of a conservative Levantine society that did not believe in freedom of women reaching beyond their drawn boundaries, and a slap to bourgeois society that refused a working or divorced woman. *Farewell, Damascus* is a new slap by the author to the 'barbarians' of Syria who want women to live like prisoners in a bottle" – **Maya al-Hajj – Al-Hayat Newspaper**

"Ghada Samman condensed her narrative, brimming with delight. This 200 page novel is full of ideas, opinions and attitudes, that are being expressed with the writer's usual calm, and only freedom has its unique and very special voice, within the symphony that aims towards a better tomorrow for the people." – **Zahra Mar'ae – Alquds Alarabi**

"At the core of Samman's writing is a cry for individual liberty… her work exhibits a boldness that defies restriction… her interesting blend of surrealism and verisimilitude, allows her to be simultaneously poetic and political in her prose writing… Samman's perceptive and creative works seem to function as literary wake-up calls for those willing to listen." - **Pauline Homsi Vinson - Al Jadid Magazine**

T0386556

Farewell, Damascus

Ghada Samman is a Syrian novelist and poet born in 1942 in Beirut, Lebanon. She worked as a journalist, broadcaster and translator, and began writing fiction in the early 1960's. In order to prevent censorship, she established Ghada al-Samman Publications to publish her own works including short-story collection *Your Eyes Are My Destiny* (1962). She later moved to Paris after events in Beirut, and wrote over 25 volumes of stories, verse, essays, drama and novels, including *Beirut '75* (1975), *Beirut Nightmares* (1976), *The Incomplete Works of Ghada al-Samman* (1978), *Love in the Veins* (1980), and *The Square Moon: Supernatural Tales* (1999). Samman's poetry collections include *I Declare Love on You!* (1976–83) and *I Testify Against the Wind* (1987).

GHADA SAMMAN

Farewell, Damascus

DARF PUBLISHERS
LONDON

Published by Darf Publishers, 2017

Darf Publishers Ltd
277 West End Lane
West Hampstead
London
NW6 1QS

Farewell, Damascus
By Ghada Samman

Translated by Nancy Roberts

Cover designed by Lorraine Pastré

Originally published as منشورات غادة السمّان) يا دمشق وداعا (2015)

Printed and bound in Great Britain by Clays Ltd, St Ives plc

ISBN-13: 978-1-85077-295-8
eBook ISBN: 978-1-85077-302-3

www.darfpublishers.co.uk

To my mother city, Damascus, who, though I may have left her, has never left me. The day we parted she cried, "Wherever you go, you'll always be mine!"

And to the beloved I could never betray: Freedom... Freedom... Freedom.

Chapter One

I'll have to slip out of bed without his noticing, get dressed *in a flash, and leave the house before he wakes up and either interrogates me or follows me. He mustn't know where I'm going—nobody can. If I'm going to take hold of my life again and escape the murder in disguise that's in store for crazy, disillusioned lovers like me, I've got to keep my secret all to myself.*

Once I'm there, I'll have to strip down completely. I can't even have polish on my nails. I've already been stripped of everything else, including moral support from family or friends. I haven't told my female cousins or Grandma Hayat, or the classmates I feel comfortable talking to. I haven't told Nabila, or Muntaha, or Afaf, or any of my other close friends. Confiding in others is a luxury reserved for people who are in physical pain. It's not something you do when you're agonizing over whether to commit a murder. Besides, we're born alone and we die alone, so I've got to face these things without help from anybody else. For weeks I've felt barren and dry on the inside, and there's a kind of red line between me and other people that I can't cross.

In order to survive, I've got to do this alone.

The only one in on Zain's plan was her owl, who'd been with her through thick and thin. She sat perched at the foot of the bed with her wide, mysterious eyes, making noises Zain didn't know how to interpret. Was she warning her, or encouraging her? She couldn't tell. For some reason the little bird's cries and chirps had never wakened Zain's husband. In fact, he'd never seen her.

Zain stole quietly out of bed to the steady rhythm of her husband's faint snoring. He'd never know about what she was going to do that day.

She tiptoed out of the bedroom, which was shrouded in semi-darkness by the drawn curtains. Her heart was pounding like a bongo drum, but nobody but she could hear it.

She headed for the kitchen to make the morning cup of coffee she couldn't do without. Then suddenly she remembered she was supposed to have been fasting since midnight. *Farewell then, coffee, and good morning, living death.* The night before she'd hidden some clothes under a stack of clean sheets so her husband wouldn't see them if he woke before she did. She threw them on. She'd chosen them with no thought for style. They only needed to be light enough for a balmy, early Fall day, and easy to take off.

Before leaving she crept up to the bedroom door to make sure her husband was still asleep. The owl's mysterious, penetrating gaze at Zain made her wonder whether she was egging her on, or warning her. Meanwhile, her husband's snoring got ominously louder.

The last thing Zain needed would have been for her husband to get up, brandishing the fancy diamond necklace his mother had told her he wanted to give her for her birthday. Since their wedding a year earlier on her seventeenth birthday, she'd endured a thousand and one years of sorrow and disappointment. She knew, of course, that if he did wake up, she wouldn't tell him what she was thinking. She would just make her getaway as fast as she could. After a week of indecision, fear, worry, silence and nightly crying sessions on the back porch, she knew she had to take charge of her life. Zain's elderly neighbor, a widow by the name of Mrs. Kotalli, would try to console her. For all Zain knew, Mrs. Kotalli had heard her whole story just the way all the other neighbor ladies had. Grandma Hayat—who'd always seemed as old as the stones in her brother's house, which had been built into the Damascus wall—had told Zain one time, "There's no such thing as a well-kept secret in Damascus. The houses would never keep a secret, since the people who live in them are like talking windows. Wherever you go, the walls might have ears. But in Damascus, they have lips too!"

Zain didn't plan to take any identification with her, but she put on her diamond necklace. Assuming she made it back alive, she wouldn't be bringing it home with her, since it was the price she'd have to pay for what she'd decided to do.

Before lying down the night before and pretending to sleep, she'd oiled the door hinges on the sly so they wouldn't creak the way they usually did. On her way out, her hands were trembling. Even so, she managed to turn the key in the lock without a sound. Then she took off running down the stairs.

As I was on my way down the stairs, a grouchy neighbor opened his door, shot me a dirty look and then slammed it shut again without a word of greeting. He didn't like me because he thought I was a bad influence on his sister Najiya. Najiya was a shy, docile girl, and the only time she ever perked up was when the two of us would mop down the stairs together. The place would be filled with the smell of the detergent we sprinkled on the stairs to make them spick and span. Sometimes we'd slip and fall on the suds and get the giggles, and I'd start talking to her about freedom. When her brother heard me say the word—which was an obscenity in his book—he said he wished he could burn my tongue with a hot coal. That was what a neighbor lady in Ziqaq Al Yasmin had done to her daughter one day because the poor girl had dared to use the word "love." "Love"? "Freedom"? "Rebellion"? They're all dirty words!

Once she was out in the street, Zain could run without worrying about her shoes clattering against the morning pavement. The exhilarating fragrance of a warm fall Damascus day wafted through the air. As usual, the baker next door had his radio on full blast, and she heard pop singer Fayza Ahmad crooning, *ana 'albi ilayk mayyal, wa ma fish ghayrak 'al-bal!* ("You've got my heart on a string, and I've got you on my mind!") As for Zain, the only thing on her mind was to get away from the person she'd once been crazy in love with.

The nostalgic fragrance of the Damascus autumn mingled with the aroma of freshly baked bread. People were on their way to work, and I was on my way to my own private ordeal. A guy that glanced at me as we passed each other on the sidewalk might have thought that, like him, I was almost late for work. If he'd passed me on some other day, when I was in my usual employee/student mode, he would have been right, since I would have been rushing to the library. But today was different. Nobody would ever have imagined what I was about to do. It was against everything I'd been taught all my life. It was even against the law, and if I were found out, I could be arrested. In fact, it went against most of the voices in my head and heart. But I didn't want that husband of mine to be the father of my son or daughter.

I didn't want any child of mine to be born into a broken home the way I had been. I wanted to place a full stop at the end of the sentence and start fresh on a new line. Is such a thing really possible? Whatever the case, I was as determined to separate from him now as I'd once been to marry him. I'd made a mistake, and I wasn't going to go back on my decision to take hold of my life no matter what it took. I'd let my life slip out of my hands, and had nearly been carried away by the current of the familiar and routine.

Voices in the street overlapped with the voices in Zain's head. As Abdel Halim Hafez sang, *ahwāka wa atamanna law ansāk* ("I'm in love with you, wishing I could forget you!"), she could hear her aunt shriek, "Love?! Heaven forbid! You're not allowed to get to know somebody before you marry him. You've got to sign the marriage contract first!" And that's what she'd done. *If they'd allowed me to get to know him first, what happened wouldn't have happened. Got a lousy marriage? Well, forget divorce! The only option for a respectable girl is to get pregnant and have a baby to distract herself from her misery. My husband had done his best to make that happen, and unfortunately, he'd succeeded.*

Does a girl want to marry a man she's in love with? That's a sin. Instead she has to marry someone the clan picks out for her and who would be a "suitable match." I'd committed the sin of marrying somebody I was in love with over my father's objections. It just so happened that the person I'd fallen in love fit my family's specifications. Yet even then they'd gone berserk. What?! Let a girl choose her own husband? Perish the thought!

The only family member who'd stood up for me was my dad, since he couldn't bear to kill my mother twice. And now I was about to commit a second sin, socially speaking. I'd decided that on my eighteenth birthday I was going to announce that I wanted a divorce. I'd made a mistake, and I wanted to correct it. When men correct their mistakes, the clan applauds. But when a neighbor lady in Ziqaq Al Yasmin dared to do the same, she'd gotten her throat slit. Males have a monopoly on the right to make mistakes. So since I'm a woman, I have to pay for my mistake for the rest of my life. My mistake is an unforgivable sin. As for a man's mistakes, they're negotiable. But ever since I was a little girl my father had told me, "Admit your mistakes, and correct them!" And that's what I was going to do.

Of course, her father might have been talking about something like breaking a water glass, something that could be fixed or replaced. But could she fix a mistaken marriage by getting a divorce? Could she correct one big mistake with another? After all, the people around her considered divorce a sin. So was she about to correct a mistake with a scandal that might scar her for life? *I'm not going to punish myself for wanting an abortion, damn it!*

She passed through the Arnous neighborhood. It was in the Arnous Library that she saw her husband for the first time, and she'd been smitten from the first glance. And here she was on her way to forgetting him in the building right next to it. The grocer's radio blasted out the words, "I once pledged you my love till death do us part. We had beautiful dreams, but they've fallen apart." She nearly teared up. Hesitating in front of the building, she stopped. *Nobody knows where I am or where I'm about to go. And nobody knows whether I'll come out alive. Maybe I should at least have told Grandma Hayat what I was planning to do. After all, she's good at keeping secrets.* From the radio in the butcher shop wafted the voice of Farid Atrash: "No matter how much you cry, don't cry to anybody else. No matter how much you complain, don't complain to anybody else. Whether people are true to you or not, keep your sorrows to yourself."

Her grandma was good at keeping little secrets—like not snitching on her grandchildren when they jumped on the bed, or the time when Zain broke the water jug. But could she handle a secret like this? Her father loved her dearly, and openly disliked her husband. But would he condone what she was about to do? And would Nabila, Afaf, Muntaha, or any of her cousins or her other friends be able to keep a secret like this one?

A beggar came up and started badgering her, saying, "May God protect your children—now give me some charity for God!"

"Listen, lady!" Zain nearly screamed, "I'm on my way to kill one of my children—the first of them! But here—take some charity anyway!"

But instead she just went on her way.

Zain walked into the building and up to the office door. She reached out and touched the doorbell. *Shall I ring it, or not? Maybe I should have left a note for Baba so he'd know where I went in case...* She stood with her hand on the doorbell. *There are certain decisions we have to make without leaning on anybody else, and we have to take responsibility for them on our own. I'd decided to marry my husband on my seventeenth birthday, and now I had to divorce him and get rid of his child. And on my eighteenth birthday, of all days. So was it a birth day, or a death day? In any case, it was the date the doctor had decided on, and I'd agreed to it. My birthday didn't mean anything to me or my family anyway, since it had always just been the day when we remembered my mother's first death. She'd been having a difficult delivery, as though I didn't want to come out and face the world, and I nearly killed her by forcing her to have a caesarean section. So am I crazy to be coming for an abortion all by myself? Well, who of us isn't crazy in one way or another?*

As Zain stood there agonizing over what to do, a voice inside her said: **You've got to get on with the amputation, then cauterize the wound!** It was a voice she'd started hearing when she began writing her first stories and poems. She'd written in secret, like somebody committing sin—fornicating with language. *And isn't it a sin for me to write? Maybe this was the offense my mother paid for with her life. She'd fallen out of favor with my father's family, and as she lay dying in labor with her second child, my father's brother refused to bring a doctor for her. Since she was a woman, no man (and every doctor is a man, right?) could be allowed to see her body even for purposes of medical treatment. The so-called "family honor" was more important than her life. When our cat had a litter once, it was this same uncle who threw the females against the Damascus wall and let the males live.*

The voice inside her said: **Knock! No door is going to open unless you knock on it! If you don't take life by the horns, nobody else is going to do it for you!** The voice deep down—the voice of the rebellious woman inside her—was getting louder and louder. *She claims to speak for me, but without caring what happens to me or to her after that!* She had once started dictating what sounded like part of an article in Zain's head. She said: **We have to go through a painful second birth. But as painful as it is,** *this is what will heal our wounds, past and future. It's the new birth that comes with the taste of freedom.*

As Zain wrote more "nonsense" in her head about the thrill of freedom, she felt pained and happy at the same time. She knew all she had to do now was knock on the door in front of her. But instead she kept writing inside her head: *I've been a silkworm that produces its precious, traditional treasure, and I was about to die of suffocation for the sake of someone who wasn't worth the price. But now I'm going to sprout wings and break out of my cocoon. Or maybe I'll fly away on the wings of an owl that floats about effortlessly like a ghost, or on the wings of an eagle, or on a glider like the one I used to go up on before I got married.* Her husband had told her to stop riding the glider, and she'd surrendered to his tyranny in the name of love. But now she was rebelling in the name of honesty and freedom.

But she hadn't told anybody. Her grandmother might have kept her secret. Then again, she might not have. The same was true of Zain's girl friends. *We don't know who other people are on the inside—in fact, we hardly know ourselves.* All she knew for sure was that her own voice had started to merge with the voice of the mad writer inside her. She had to start standing on her own two feet. She had to stop writing in her head like Hamlet, quit her useless chatter, and ring that doorbell!

Why didn't I tell anybody what I was planning to do? Well, whatever the reason was, I didn't, and that's that. Maybe it was because I knew nobody would be able to keep my secret. There's a story about a king who used to tell his secrets to the river frogs for fear that if he confided in anyone else, his confidence would be followed by a dagger in his back. I guess I want to be like him.

For the third time Zain made up her mind to ring the doorbell. But while she was still deliberating, the door was opened by the doctor's wife, who worked as his assistant. Zain suspected that the woman had seen her through the peephole and knew how long she'd been standing there since, as she opened the door, she said irritably in broken Arabic mixed with French, "We've been waiting for you. Come in." As if in hopes of winning her approval, Zain stepped inside with a cheery "Bonjour" instead of the more common *sabah al-khayr*.

The doctor's wife pointed to a chair near the waiting room entrance and, speaking to Zain in French, said, "Sit here. I don't know what made you stand outside our door that way without ringing the doorbell. Or is it not working?" Zain sat down, but pretended not to have understood what she said. When making the appointment, she'd posed as the semi-illiterate daughter of a dancer at the Siryana Nightclub. She'd told the doctor she'd been raped by her mother's lover and that although her mother didn't know she was coming to see him, it was through her mother that she'd learned about him since she had a record of previous abortions. *Will Baba be mad at me if he finds out what I've done? I've already caused him more than enough misery.*

As she sat down, wild stallions went galloping through her head. As if she were recalling the past in preparation to die—or maybe, in preparation to survive—her memory went on a free-for-all. She thought back on how, when she'd insisted on marrying somebody she was madly in love with, her father had been furious. He'd said she was just a teenager who didn't know what she was doing. *It looks like he was right.*

But actually, he'd been more sad than angry. He'd been sure the marriage would be a failure, but, starry-eyed lover that she was at the time, Zain hadn't understood why. She'd honestly thought she knew better than her forty year old father, and better than everybody else, for that matter. When he reminded Zain that she was just seventeen years old, she informed him that she'd grown up and understood the world now. He hit himself in the face, and it pained her. Then her beloved groom's upper crust family had intervened in support of the marriage, though all they really wanted was for him to settle down and stop giving them trouble.

I really put my father in an awkward position. Socially speaking, he couldn't refuse the family. At the same time, he couldn't say he approved of the family but didn't approve of the suitor because of what he knew about him. After all, there was bound to be a ready reply: Don't worry. Once he's married, he'll straighten himself out! *So my hard-working dad spent a fortune on my trousseau, including a top-of-the-line wardrobe. It was so top-of-the-line, in fact, that the cheapest items came from the ritzy Hayek's Department Store, which had opened recently in the building that overlooks the Barada River downstairs from the* Akhbar al Yawm *newspaper. The trousseau also featured embroidered nightgowns from Rahibat Tailor Shop, and a Christian Dior wedding dress like the one Cinderella wore in the fairy tales I'd studied at the Lycée Francais on Baghdad Street.*

When the women from the groom's family, who wore the highest heels on the social ladder, came to look at the trousseau in keeping with tradition, they oohed and aahed over my luxurious stash, since it was synonymous with my value to my father and, more importantly, the value of the groom's family. After all, the groom's father was a pillar of the famed Quartet Company.

My dad was a little boy when he lost his father, the owner of a corner store behind the Umayyad Mosque near our house in Ziqaq Al Yasmin. He'd spent his youth in poverty because some of his uncles had commandeered his share of the corner store in their capacity as his guardians. My grandmother had to work as a seamstress in order to provide him with an education. He worked hard too, and ended up studying medicine in Paris. It pained my dad to have high-class folks look down on us. Or, to be more precise, it pained him for me to be looked down on by my in-laws. So he tried to outdo them, and he would have managed if it weren't for the fact that the house they bought and furnished for us was in the upscale Hayy al-Ra'is, or President's Quarter, so named because, as my fiancé's mother informed me smugly, it was where then President Shukri Quwatli lived.

This string of events passed before Zain's eyes like a flash of lightning. But no, she wasn't going to back down. She had to go through with the abortion no matter what physical or psychological misery might follow it. She was terrified, of course. She imagined herself running scared toward the operating table through a jungle filled with crocodiles, snakes and huge tarantulas. But as scared as she was, she knew she had to erase this man from her life. She didn't want to give birth to a child who'd have to grow up without a mother the way she had. She knew only too well what that was like. She didn't want him to be the father of her child. She never even wanted to see him again, and if she did see him, she hoped she wouldn't recognize him.

Where is that doctor, anyway? Why does he keep me waiting like this, at the mercy of my fears and thoughts?

She knew she had to find her "second engine," the one her dad had told her about years earlier.

I was ten years old, and my dad and I had gone on a "farewell to summer" walk that took us from Bloudan, to Baqin, to Zabadani. As we hiked down dusty side paths on our way back, I started to give out. Even though I wanted to please my father, I collapsed beside a spring, exhausted and thirsty.

"Get up now," he said.

"I can't," I whimpered.

"Come on," he urged. "Start up that second engine of yours. It's something you do with will power. I know you've got it. For all we know, you might have a third one, a fourth one, or even more than that! Get up and run this time instead of just walking. Remember how strong you are."

I didn't understand a word my dad had said apart from the fact that I had to get up. So I did. I learned how to get up again. But later, when I made up my mind to marry Waseem, I used my second engine against him.

Zain had met Waseem for the first time three months before her seventeenth birthday at the Arnous Library, next to the clinic, and it had been love at first sight. Fueled by a million engines, her infatuation with him was fiery, fierce, and wild. Nothing could have stood in its way. On account of it she waged all-out war on her family. And her decision to leave him now was just as fierce and unstoppable as her determination to marry him had been before. When she realized she had to leave him, they'd been together a little less than a year. Some of that time had been

spent in a dreamy courtship between Mount Qasioun and the
romantic Candles Restaurant, and some of it in the throes of
bitter matrimony. Once their week-long honeymoon was over,
her days were spent rushing back and forth between the library,
the university, and the house, where she'd head straight for the
kitchen to cook, only to end up dozing off at the table from sheer
exhaustion. *I thought to myself: Is this daily and nightly frenzy
what they call marriage? If it is, then I don't want it, and I can't
take it. What I'd wanted was a home of my own where I wouldn't
be bothered by aunts, neighbor ladies, and the ideas they stuff into
your head in Ziqaq Al Yasmin. But all I'd done by getting married
was trade one form of oppression for another.*

These memories flashed through Zain's head as she waited
to be seen by the doctor. She didn't give the necklace a second
thought, but she did wonder momentarily: *Do I really want to do
this?* It wasn't long, though, before she realized she had no choice
but to cut every last tie with that awful mistake. She had to put
the past behind her and face whatever lay ahead. The last thing
she needed was a child that would end up being a battleground
between her and her husband.

In search of a solution, she had started by inquiring indirectly
about the different ways of getting an abortion. She'd claimed
she was asking for a friend of hers who'd gotten pregnant by a
coworker who already had two wives, and children, and had just
wanted to have a fling with her. *I can't believe how easily I make
up stories and scenarios about people who don't even exist.* By the
time she'd heard all the gory details about the things some women
go through to get abortions, she was quaking in her boots. She
could hardly imagine subjecting herself to that kind of torture.

She got the low-down on everything: from a method called the "mulukhiyah skewer" to hitting yourself in the belly with the big stone mortar people used to grind meat. Then finally, she caught wind of a rumor that a certain well-known doctor who taught in the Faculty of Medicine did abortions secretly in the clinic annexed to his house, and that his French wife, a nurse, was his assistant. The physician in question, Rahif Manahili, was somebody Zain had known since she was a little girl. The fact that he was a university professor inspired her confidence, as did the fact that given his social standing, he would be as afraid of a scandal as she was of bleeding to death!

So she went to see him. She didn't tell him, of course, that she was the daughter of his lawyer friend, Amjad Khayyal, for fear that he might refuse to deal with her. Instead, hoping he didn't remember her, she told him her father had died and that her mother was a dancer at the Siryana nightclub, but that she had a diamond necklace she could pay him with. She claimed to have stolen the necklace from her mother, who was sure to accuse one of her lovers of taking it.

His wife had made her an appointment, and now here she was. The doctor might have had some qualms at first. However, his wife had seized at the opportunity. And who could have blamed her? She was a foreigner fed up with life in Damascus, and probably wanted the money to improve her own lot.

There was no going back on her decision to divorce. She could still hear her sister-in-law's insults ringing in her ears. *I'd be rushing back and forth trying to get everything done and she'd describe me contemptuously as "a fireball in the street, a limp rag in the kitchen!" Well, I'm not going to be in his kitchen anymore!*

I'm going to devote full time to my studies and my clandestine writing projects.

The doctor came in and, in a reassuring voice, said, "You'll need to get undressed and put on this white robe. Don't worry. Everything will be just fine."

Taking off her diamond necklace, Zain offered it to him, saying, "Thank you. I'll rest a bit, and then get ready."

To her surprise, he seemed hesitant to take the necklace. *Does he recognize me as his friend's daughter, the one he used to hold in his lap when she was a little girl? My mother's early death made me grow up fast, or at least that's what people have always told me. And he always seemed happy to be able to have "grown-up" conversations with me. So maybe he does know who I am.* Just as the doctor seemed about to return the necklace to Zain, his wife walked in and snatched it. *So, does he remember me, or not? If not, then why would he have hesitated the way he did? On the other hand, he wouldn't have wanted me to know he recognized me, since if I knew, I'd be agitated during the operation.* Whatever the case, his wife grabbed the necklace, and when he reached out to stop her, she scolded him in French, thinking Zain wouldn't understand. She reminded him that they needed to save up some money before they moved to Paris so that they could buy a clinic on Foch Avenue. He said nothing.

I got the same feeling the first time I came to see him—the feeling that he knows who I am. But how could he? Did my father invite him to the big wedding bash they put on for me at the Orient Palace Hotel? Even if he did, I doubt he realizes I was the bride that day. Granted, it seems odd that he would have been reluctant to accept a diamond necklace that was worth a small fortune. But what if, as rumor has it, he's actually a good-hearted man?

Zain got undressed, slipped into the white, shroud-like medical gown, and recited a prayer of repentance her grandmother had taught her when she was a little girl who'd never stopped to think about her own death. As she went through the motions of undressing and putting on the gown, a collage of images, voices, sounds and scenes went running through her head, juxtaposed on top of each other as though somebody were projecting several films at the same time onto the same screen. Before putting on the gown, she sniffed it to make sure it was clean, and nearly burst out laughing at herself. *What an old-fashioned Damascene lady I am, wanting to make sure her burial shroud is clean! And am I really going to die? Forgive me, O my soul, for all the sins I've committed in the name of love!* The doctor's wife led her gently down a corridor and into a room lit by nothing but a lamp mounted over a narrow, elevated metal-frame bed with metal stirrups at the foot of it. She gestured for Zain to lie down and put her feet in the stirrups.

Zain was gripped with terror. The place bristled with scalpels, scissors, probes and sterile gauze. Never in her life had she seen such a torture chamber. Her panic attack was interrupted by the doctor's entrance. Taking her hand reassuringly, he asked his wife in French, "Did you remember to give her the tranquillizer?"

She replied. "I was afraid that if I gave it to her earlier, she might not have been strong enough to walk. She's been shaking like a leaf. I'll give it to her now."

She then proceeded to plunge a needle into the arm of a puny, fragile girl who was scared to death of shots.

Clearly wanting to put her at ease, the doctor explained, "This is a tranquillizer that will help the anesthesia work more effectively and keep you from feeling any pain. Don't worry. I'll take care of you as though you were the daughter of a dear friend."

If she hadn't been so panic-stricken, she would have paused to contemplate the meaning of that last phrase. But at that moment, all she could see was that he had laid her out naked on a Shakespearian stage to peals of thunder and flashes of lightning. *Or was I just delirious from the shot?* The doctor's wife placed a mask over her face, and a disgusting odor filled her nostrils. But in the woman's eyes Zain perceived an endearing tenderness. She heard a voice tell her in French to count down from ten to zero. She couldn't go on pretending not to understand, so she started counting out loud. She heard her voice echoing, and then little by little it faded out. Or rather, Zain herself faded in and out, in and out. She hurt, but she couldn't scream. She felt a hot skewer going through her. Then she went on fading out, fading out…

I'm walking through a raging storm surrounded by howling wind, flashes of lightning, and peals of thunder. King Lear is walking beside me, and as he curses his fate and his foolish ways, I hear myself saying with him, "Thou wilt break my heart!" Regretful for what I've done, I tremble with fright. I'm the one who cast myself into this wasteland, and I want desperately to run away. Is it all over? Why do I hear myself talking? Why can't I keep quiet? Why is my spirit as scattered as my thoughts? I hear the voice that I always hear when I write, the one that gives pep talks to the coward that lives inside me. A voice that sounds like mine—or is it the voice of my mother as she lay on her death bed?—says to me: Don't be afraid. Don't be afraid. *I listen intently, and the voice is all I can hear. Then, as my nose and mouth are covered again with the mask that gives off the nasty odor, I hear the doctor say, "More anesthesia. Give her more anesthesia," and suddenly I decide: I'm not going to be afraid! I'm not skinny and fragile! I'm a boulder on Mount Qasioun that isn't afraid of the rain, since it's the rain that washes me clean. I'm not afraid of the lightning and thunder, either, since they come out of me. I'm a boulder next to Qubbat Al Sayyar. No probe could ever penetrate me, and no lightning bolt could set me on fire. I'm a living boulder.*

As Zain repeated these things to herself, she heard the doctor repeat, "Give her more anesthetic," and her mother's soothing, "Don't be afraid" as she slipped away on her death bed. She was a little girl again, collapsed beside the spring along the path between Bloudan and Zabadani as her father admonished her, saying, "You're a big girl now. You're ten years old! Rev up that spare engine of yours!" She felt a searing pain in a sensitive part of her body. Was it the dreaded mulukhiyah skewer she'd heard horror stories about? What was going on? A voice echoed again, "Give her more anesthetic."

I alternately sink and float. I'm not going to scream or moan. I'm a boulder on Mount Qasioun. Nothing can crush me. The rain, the wind and the lightning bolts pass through me, but they can't shake me. For ages I've been a boulder next to Qubbat Al Sayyar. I hear myself moaning. No, I'm a boulder on Mount Qasioun that feels no pain. I'm not hurting anymore. I'm fading… I see myself laughing with my dad. Then I doze off. After a while I wake up to the sound of a voice reciting a Shakespeare sonnet: "To die: to sleep. No more, and by a sleep to say we end the heart-ache and the thousand natural shocks that flesh is heir to, 'tis a consummation devoutly to be wish'd." I realize it's my own voice I'm hearing and that I've got to be quiet. Even so, either my own voice or somebody else's repeats in English, "I am not dead. I am alive." I try in vain to keep my mouth shut. That mask with the stinky smell is about to suffocate me. I'll just give in to it and relax. I may be a boulder, but even boulders surrender to the storm. In fact, they embrace it, become one with it. I am the storm. The lightning and thunder are coming out of me, out of the boulder. I fade out. I wake up to the sound of my own moaning. I don't know how long I've been in this state. I keep floating and sinking. An earthquake is convulsing the Qasiounian boulder, which I see as separate from me.

Half in pain, half numb, half awake, half alive, Zain heard somebody's voice. It was her own voice. She heard herself reciting something. But what was it? What had she been blabbering about?

Whatever it was, she kept on, and couldn't shut herself up.

She opened her eyes. She saw a strange face. *Oh my God. It's the doctor.* She saw another face. The nurse is gawking at me in horror as though she just saw a landmine right in her path. Apparently I'm not a boulder anymore, since I see now that I've been raving deliriously and need to be quiet. But no: I'm not going to shut my mouth anymore. I'm going to say I'm in pain, that I'm miserable, defeated, and disillusioned. So, is it over yet?

Zain tried to get down off the operating table, but nearly fell, so the nurse helped her.

"Things went well," the doctor informed her reassuringly. "Don't worry, you'll be able to have children in the future."

Still under the effect of the anaesthesia, Zain said groggily, "I'll be going now," not realizing what had come out of my mouth.

"I won't let you leave yet," the doctor replied gently. "You lie down for a while in the next room. Then I'll take you home. Don't worry. It's all over."

"I can walk home," she insisted.

Half-chuckling, he replied, "You sleep now. Don't worry!" and left the torture chamber.

Zain fell fast asleep. After some time she woke up refreshed, but with a pain in her abdomen that went away after a while thanks to a dose of medication.

Ever so slowly she got dressed and, forgetting the earlier conversation with the doctor, decided to leave, though without knowing exactly where to go. She lumbered toward the door, trying to make her getaway. But before she made it out of the room, the doctor gently took her arm, saying, "Come. I want to measure your blood pressure."

She came docilely back. A few minutes later he announced, "You've got a strong constitution, and you're fine. Even so, I'm going to drive you home. You need to take it easy."

From the wall clock behind him Zain discovered to her astonishment that it was four in the afternoon. She'd been there nearly all day! Again she told him she could make it home on her own, but he wouldn't hear of it. Zain still didn't understand exactly what was happening to her. As she left the clinic with him, her will no longer her own, she kept quiet, trying to focus on revealing her identity. She told him she was living in the building across the street from the main entrance to Subki Park.

"So is that where you'd like to go?" he asked in a familiar tone, as though she were his sister or his neighbor. *So does he know me, or doesn't he? Does he know where I really live? Why should I lie to him?*

"Yes," she fibbed. "That's where my house is."

As Zain got ready to leave the house with the doctor, his wife suddenly asked her in French, "Who are you, anyway? When you were unconscious, you started quoting poetry that my husband said was from Shakespeare!"

Zain didn't say anything. She wished she could tell her the truth: that her marriage had failed and that she hoped her divorce would succeed. But she had to keep up the pretence, for the time being at least.

The doctor's wife hesitated briefly. Then, without giving Zain a chance to spout another lie, she stuffed a prescription into her hand and practically shouted in her face, "Neither of us believed you were the daughter of a nightclub dancer—especially my husband!"

Then she slammed the door behind them. For all Zain knew, the doctor had known from the start that she was lying, and was trying to pull the wool over their eyes with her clever scenarios. For all she knew, he'd suspected from the start that she was Zain, his lawyer friend's daughter. For all she knew, he'd sensed the tragedy that had come out of her crazy infatuation, her Romeo and Juliet complex, the kind of headstrong passion that thumbs its nose at social norms and family expectations. Maybe he'd seen pictures of her from the wedding party. Or maybe he'd even been one of the guests.

As she walked down the steps with him, leaning on his arm, he looked at her as if to say, "Do you really think I don't recognize you, Zain?"

Whether he did or not, all that mattered to her now was to keep going, to get out of the painful spot she'd gotten stuck in. She was so scared and mixed up, she was telling lies that contradicted each other, and there were things she didn't want to talk to anybody about, such as her feelings of defeat and all her mistakes. She was trying to extricate herself from the love net she'd spun in luminous, intense moments now past.

As she thought back on all the humiliation she'd endured in her marriage, she didn't feel as though she'd just taken an innocent life. In fact, she felt she'd come to its rescue. What she'd killed was the needless degradation this little boy or girl would have been subjected to now that a one-time sweetheart had turned into an executioner.

The doctor didn't say a word as he drove her to Subki Park. When they arrived, she got out of the car, went into the building she'd directed him to, and waved gratefully goodbye, bracing herself against the pain. She stood for a few minutes in the entranceway, praying that none of its residents would come in or out and see her skulking there. She waited to hear the doctor drive away, taking the day's events with him. Once she was assured he was out of sight, she walked over to Subki Park and collapsed onto a bench. Knowing she might be bleeding, she sat with her legs pressed together, trying to decide what to do and where to go.

Chapter Two

When Dr. Manahili dropped Zain off at the door, she staggered so badly that he didn't have the heart to leave her. He decided he had to take her to her actual house, wherever it happened to be.

He drove to Mt. Qasioun, where he parked in the square and sat waiting in his car. *She doesn't seem to realize I didn't believe her story about being the daughter of a dancer at the Siryana Club. The girl's a lousy liar, but she certainly is brave. She's the only person who's ever come for an abortion all by herself, and I know she can't possibly be her stated age of twenty-four. I've been around too long to fall for a claim like that. All the others have come with a husband, a sister, a mother or a girlfriend—in other words, with some sort of moral support. When she came to make the appointment, she was plastered with makeup to convince me she was the daughter of this imaginary nightclub dancer, but I was skeptical. Granted, some nightclub dancers care more about educating their kids than some high-society ladies. But that girl's no skid row kid. For one thing, the diamond bracelet she tried to pay me with is worth a lot of money. It's obvious that she comes from an aristocratic family and that the bracelet is an heirloom— unless she stole it, of course. Besides, nightclub dancers and their daughters know the value of the money they work so hard for, and there's no way they'd give up a diamond bracelet to pay a doctor like me. In any case, I'm charmed by her innocent gaffs, and I don't blame her for thinking she could buy me with a diamond bracelet, since I've got a pretty bad reputation around here. The fact is, sometimes I agree to perform illegal abortions for the sake of the unborn children. I'm not worried about the money. It's my wife who worries about that, since she's got her heart set on us settling in Paris and opening a clinic there. I don't want to see any child be born into a broken home and suffer the way I did. Zain probably suffered a lot herself from her paternal aunts in the big house in Ziqaq Al Yasmin, where I used to play with her dad when we were little boys. This is assuming, of course, that the mystery girl really is Zain Khayyal. When my wife heard her raving under the effect of the anesthesia, she jumped at the chance to ask her what her name was. She didn't exactly admit to being Zain Khayyal. She said a name I'm not sure I understood right, but that's what I think I heard. She was muttering so incoherently most of the time, she might have been saying something else.*

My wife asked her the question in French and she answered in Arabic, "My name's Zain... Zain Khayyal." At least that's what I think she said. Despite her valiant attempts to learn Arabic, my wife still doesn't understand it very well, and she asked me what the girl was saying. "Oh, nothing," I told her. "She's talking nonsense." When a woman is lying terrified on an operating table with a gas mask on her face and a needle in her vein, she has no idea what sorts of secrets she's giving away. When I hear the things patients say, I begin to hate some and sympathize with others. This girl's one of the ones I sympathize with. She was doing her best to keep her subconscious under control, but nobody can hold out against drugs like these. The prick of a needle in the right place and a few drops of the right drug, and the doors of the mind fly open like a bank's vault at the touch of a seasoned burglar.

He thought back on the various scenes subsequent to her arrival at his clinic. With every step she took and every muffled groan she released, she seemed to stalk his very thoughts. He remembered supporting her on his arm as she got into his car and asking her where she wanted him to take her. "To Subki Park," she'd replied mechanically. "To the house across from the park entrance." Hoping to catch her off guard, he'd asked, "Which entrance?" "The main entrance," came her curt reply. He could tell she was lying. He knew her father's house—if she was Zain Khayyal—was on Abu Rummana Street in the Sahat Al Midfaa neighborhood. So he figured she must be directing him to where she lived with her husband. *No, maybe she's still not telling the truth. But as bad as it is, I love the way she lies.*

Zain had pointed to a two-storey building across from one of the entrances to Subki Park. On the main door he had seen a sign that read, "Building for Sale."

"Here," she had announced abruptly with a wince. She seemed to have difficulty even lifting her arm to point to the place.

As Dr. Manahili got out of his car at Sahat Al Muhajirin, he was haunted by the memory of Zain's muted dignity and her amateurish fibs.

He paced up and down the square, trying in vain to get her out of his tortured thoughts. *I knew that wasn't her house. She's the worst liar I've ever met, which makes me feel even closer to her. Or maybe what draws me to her is her guts. I didn't mention anything about this to my wife, and I've hardly been able to admit*

*it even to myself. But in spite of all the problems here, I don't want
to move to Paris. I want to stay in Damascus. When I let her out
of my car, I was so worried about her I couldn't get myself to leave.
So I drove to the end of the street that runs alongside Subki Park
and pulled over for a while, not sure what to do. She's the type that
doesn't like other people butting into her affairs. That was obvious
even when she was still partly under the anesthesia.*

*If, as I'm inclined to believe, she really is Zain Khayyal, then
we're bonded by the fact that we're both orphans. We orphans
know by telepathy who loves us and who doesn't. We've learned
from bitter experience how to read people's intentions toward us.
We've also learned to support each other in secret, and openly too
sometimes. So when she claimed to be the daughter of a nightclub
dancer, I pretended to believe her. I kept telling myself that some
nightclub dancers are more cultured and warm-hearted than
some high-society ladies. I ought to know! Sometimes a celebrity
will come to me because she suspects she might be pregnant by her
dark-skinned lover and is afraid her blonde, blue-eyed husband
might notice that his child is half black. One woman, after getting
pregnant by a black waiter, came to me saying something ridiculous
about getting pregnant while she was taking a bath because the
maid hadn't cleaned the tub well enough!*

*My hunch had been right. In my rear-view mirror I saw her
leaving the building where I'd dropped her off. She'd hidden in its
stairwell, as I'd suspected she would, and had come out thinking
I was gone. She crossed the street and walked wobbly-legged into
Subki Park. I didn't spy on her after that. I knew she would collapse
onto a park bench to soak up some sunshine and recoup her
strength, then probably head somewhere else, though she hadn't*

decided where yet. I drove toward Sahat Al Muhajirin, a haven for Damascenes when their lives are in turmoil. When they're having a hard time, they tend to retreat into silence until they explode. About to explode myself by this time, I was tempted to follow her to Subki Park. I wanted to tell her, "I was careful to perform your abortion in such a way that you'll be able to have children in the future. Your courage is an inspiration to me, a cowardly orphan who was hurt as a child but never had the guts to speak up to his father."

Dr. Manahili paced up and down Sahat Al Muhajirin, looking out periodically at the orchards that stretched out below him. *This girl, who might be the Zain I know, has brought up sadness from my past. But what she did was a good thing. She had the pluck to abort a baby that would have ended up like me as a little boy, shuttling back and forth between two broken homes, subjected to insults, hatred, and even physical abuse. My stepmother seemed to take delight in me getting sick, since this gave her the chance to torture me on the pretext of taking care of me. And her remedy of choice: an enema! My father didn't object to her prescription. In fact, he used to thank her for taking care of me and would go off to work with his mind at rest. Torture by enema on the pretext of "treating" a child was common in those days. Raising the instrument of torture by a single centimeter would be enough to send waves of excruciating pain around the anus's tender periphery. So when she elevated the enema bag, the soap and water mixture would flow more forcefully into my innards, and I'd feel as though my gut was about to explode. But I wouldn't let myself cry. Then she'd raise it a little higher, hoping I'd cry out in pain and beg her to stop. My insides were being torn apart, but instead of* crying, I'd just flash her a defiant stare. When I'm in a lot of pain, I generally just scream and let it out. But I was determined not to give her what she wanted. Instead of begging and pleading, I looked at her with cold loathing. I knew better than to expect compassion from my tormenter, and I could sense with a child's subtle intuition that if I begged for mercy, she'd just want to hurt me even more. Sadists aren't out to kill their victims, since if they did that, they'd rob themselves of the pleasure of continuing to watch them suffer.

I feel sure this girl must have been subjected to something similar—if not physical torment, then the psychological variety.

As he paced his concrete platform overlooking the city, Dr. Manahili wished he could take Zain to the rustic cafe near Qubbat Al Sayyar. *Of course, she wouldn't be able to climb the dirt staircase that leads up to the highest section of the cafe. But she could have a cup of coffee at a table near the entrance. Wait - I wouldn't let her have even a cup of coffee now. She'd have to settle for some chamomile tea, mint tea, or... Oh, right, I forgot to tell her about that. But I did remember to write her a prescription... What's happening to me? Am I falling in love with this girl when I'm old enough to be her father? Or am I just taken by the fact that she had the courage to get an abortion all on her own despite her young age, the way I've always wished my mother had done? Isn't it true that I married my wife because I knew she was barren? Of course, she isn't barren exactly. She needs surgery on her fallopian tubes, and if she had the operation, she'd be able to have children. But out of selfishness I've never told her so. I'm no saint, that's for sure.*

When my wife wasn't looking, I put the diamond bracelet back on the girl's wrist while she was recovering from the operation. I was impressed by the fact that even when she was delirious from the anesthesia, she didn't say a word about her partner, as if she were determined to take sole responsibility for the abortion.

After downing a cup of black coffee, Dr. Manahili went back to Sahat Al Muhajirin, parked his car, and walked down Al Qasr Al Jumhuri Street along the railroad track, to his right the Presidential Palace and the Al Idlibi Family villa. He passed through Sheikh Muhyi Al Din, Al Jisr Al Abyad, Arnous, and Shaalana on his way to Subki Park. *I confess, I'm worried about her. I want to make sure she's all right. Where has she gone now? To her husband's house? To her father's house? And where would either of them be?*

Dr. Manahili decided to pay Zain's father a visit the following day. That way he could confirm whether she really was Zain Khayyal whose wedding he'd been invited to. *No... I'm not in love with her. But she's the daughter I would have hoped to have, and I'm going to support her. Or rather, she's the daughter I didn't want to have, but that I admire with all my heart! I love her. Yes, I love her the way I would have loved the daughter I was fortunate enough not to have. She's got plenty of faults, foremost among which is her weakness for trying to lie her way through hard situations and doing an incredibly bad job of it. At the same time, she's brave and defiant. She makes her own decisions and acts on them.*

I suppose I'm a liar too, but after so many years of practice, I've mastered the art of prevarication. Zain—if that's who she is—will never know I love her, and neither will anybody else. Love her? There goes the artist inside me babbling away like a lunatic... How could I be in love with somebody whose name I'm not even sure about? I'm just a crazy old man who needs to learn to keep his feelings in check! How could I be in love with a girl who's young enough to be my daughter? That's ridiculous... But whoever said love was rational? On the contrary, it's the irrational par excellence, or so it appears to be at this moment. My feelings for her are so confused. She's stirred up all the pain in my heart, and suddenly I'm remembering whole strings of events I thought I'd forgotten all about. It's as if she's aborted my ability to keep bad memories at bay.

He walked back to his car and drove to the Arnous neighborhood where he and his wife lived. He was afraid she might see him as she left their house on her way to the French Cultural Center and the elementary schools where she volunteered as a French teacher. The last thing he would have wanted to do was hurt her feelings. A goodhearted woman, she had agreed to come with him to a country she knew nothing about, and had worked hard to adapt to life without knowing anything about the tormenting thoughts that haunted him. Yet despite his worry that she might spot him, he hung around Subki Park to see what Zain—or whatever her name was—had done with herself.

My father, a government employee who was always getting razzed by his subordinates, used to beat me. I was his scapegoat, and he would take all his bitterness and frustrations from work out on my little body. As his switch seared my back he would hiss, "Why didn't you die? Your mother did everything she could to abort you. And now you're tormenting your poor 'Auntie'!" I was determined to survive despite all my disappointments, but when I went to my stepmother for comfort, all I got was a cold, disapproving stare. Meanwhile, she pampered her own little boy, the one she'd conceived with her new husband. After working for a while at a grocery store, I got a job working for a blacksmith who sharpened people's knives for them. Meanwhile I was sharpening my own knives, studying at night on the sly for my middle school certificate. Then I worked as an elementary teacher and managed to finish high school. When I was a teenager, my father avoided me. He wouldn't even look me in the eye. In fact, he was so intent on dodging me that he wouldn't go to the kitchen until he'd heard me turn on the light in the bathroom. Not realizing I was studying, he used to make fun of my interest in books, and he resented having to pay the bill for the electricity I used up by reading at night. So when he asked me what I was reading, I'd tell him I was reading the Qur'an, since nobody would dare scold his son for reading the book of God.

When my father found out I was in medical school, he was so furious that he told me to quit my stupid studying and do something I could make a living from. I told him I wanted to be a doctor. "What!" he scoffed. "A beast like you become a doctor?" "That's right," I told him. "Like other beasts, I'm struggling to survive."

Changing the subject, he groused, "You're living here rent-free, by the way." A classmate of mine had told me about a room for rent in an elderly widow's house, and the next day I moved out. I didn't say a word. I just disappeared from their lives, which was exactly what they wanted me to do. After I graduated I found out they'd been looking for me. And why? Because my father wanted to rake me over the coals for leaving, and my stepmother wanted to tell me how grateful I should be to her for wearing herself raising me!

She was good at making up stories about how she'd taken care of me when I was little, when she was the one who'd made me sick in the first place.

Have I forgiven them? I don't know. Forgiveness is an elusive sort of thing. Sometimes, when you're feeling serene, you stitch up old wounds; then along come the shadows of bitterness and resentment and tear the stitches out. In any case, I went to France on a scholarship to study obstetrics and gynecology. My aim: to be able to abort any woman who was carrying a child nobody wanted. A child that would come into the world only to be abused and degraded, then grow up without being able either to forgive or forget.

When I met the French nurse who later became my wife, I didn't tell her about any of this. The look of admiration in her eyes came as a thrill to this hardworking man who had felt so degraded and defeated. Here was somebody who, as she handed me the scalpel, looked at my hands with respect and appreciation. I was a sucker for her veneration, and when I came back to Damascus after graduating, she came with me.

Once you've tasted the water of Al Fijeh Spring, you'll be nostalgic for Damascus as long as you live. Ah, the memories of wandering through Bab Al Jabiyah, Bab Tuma, Al Salihiyah, Al Jisr Al Abyad, Sheikh Muhyi Al Din Mosque, Al Qassaa, the Umayyad Mosque, Souq Al Hamidiya, Al Marjah, Baghdad Street, Qanawat, Al Shaghour, Mi'dhanat Al Shahm, Qabratkeh, and on and on… They won't let you forget them. I came back to Damascus not to take revenge on the people who had humiliated me and who need me now. I came back because my love for Damascus won't let me go.

The city changed a lot while I was gone, as had everyone I'd known there. This kind of change goes on all the time, of course, and cities mirror the spirits of those who live in them. When I got back, everybody seemed to think I'd forgotten the abuse I'd endured during my childhood and adolescence, and when they came to the clinic for treatment, they'd make up funny stories about things I was supposed to have experienced with them when I was a little boy. All I could remember was maltreatment and humiliation. Somehow I managed to keep my mouth shut with a stupid, Mona Lisa-esque smile plastered on my face.

Maybe I get my calm resignation from drawing pictures of the children I've aborted. Before doing a drawing, I form an image in my head based on what I know of the parents' features, my impressions of their personalities, and the kinds of suffering that might have been in store for the child. I have a huge collection of drawings that people might think are of babies I delivered. Little do they know they're of children I euthanized. As for people who know what I actually do, they assume I do it for money, and I let them think whatever they please.

Tonight I'll go home to my wife, who doesn't know a thing about what goes on deep inside me, and plant a kiss on her forehead. Then I'll head for my clinic, which at night I turn into a studio, and draw Zain's baby. He'll be beautiful and mournful like his mother, who has no idea what sorrows she's stirred up in my soul. This is the first time a girl has come to get an abortion without support from anyone at all, and it's shaken me to the core. I go looking for her in Subki Park, but I don't see her. I wonder where she went.

The building Zain had asked Dr. Manahili to take her to had once been home to her friend Nayela. The two of them had attended twelfth grade together in Al Jisr Al Abyad neighborhood, and Zain had passed by Nayela's every day so that they could walk to school together. Nayela didn't live there anymore, and the building had been put up for sale. Even so, Zain plopped down on its front steps to rest for a while until the doctor was out of sight. She doused her neck with jasmine perfume from a Parisian crystal bottle she'd inherited from her mother. Jasmine perfume made her feel stronger, as if it were the scent of her ancestors' spirits.

The abortion was just the beginning. The worst part is still to come. My husband's been getting ready to celebrate my eighteenth birthday in full bourgeois style. But tonight I've got to tell him that it's all over between us.

Zain got up and left the building. She was afraid some resident might come out, find her sitting on the stairs and ask her what she wanted. She was too worn out to come up with a story about why she was there. Feeling more exhausted than ever, she decided to rest for a while on the bench nearest the Subki Park entranceway. She could hardly walk, but she had to decide what to do next. Now that she was homeless, whose house would she go to – her husband's, or her father's? And how would she get there? Would she have the strength to tell her husband what she'd decided to do that very day, or would she put it off until the next morning? Was that Dr. Manahili's car parked at the end of the street, or did it just look like his? As she collapsed onto a green bench, she regretted not having bought her scarf to wrap around her neck. Damascus's autumn sun was warm. It was hot, in fact. Even so, she was shivering. She felt panicky. She might start bleeding, and catch a cold, too.

I'm a boulder on Mt Qasioun.

Afraid one of her aunts might pass by and see her, she moved to a bench further from the entrance. On one bench lay a homeless man taking a nap. Then she spotted an empty bench across from a turbaned man with a rosary in his hand. When he saw Zain, his fingers started fiddling more rapidly with his beads as though she were an evil omen. Undeterred, she flung herself down on the bench opposite him, closed her eyes, and fell into a coma-like slumber.

She was wakened by the sound of children who had come to the park with their mother and were taking turns screeching. She was too tired to move to another bench, but she planned to pass by the Kaddoura Pharmacy to buy the medications the doctor had prescribed. She hadn't understood part of his instructions, so she'd decided to read the prescription later when she felt calmer and to ask the pharmacist about what she'd missed.

As she sat there engrossed in her anxious thoughts, in pain and on the verge of despair, she heard a voice speaking to her. It was vivacious and manly.

"Would you mind if I sat down here?" the voice asked. "All the other benches are occupied, as you can see."

"Go ahead," Zain replied curtly without a sideward glance. As she spoke, she picked up her purse and shrank toward one end of the bench. Meanwhile, she continued to wonder how she was going to get home when she could hardly walk, and whether she would go to the house she'd been sharing with her husband in Hayy Al Ra'is, or to her father's house in Sahat Al Midfaa. It was a reminder that she didn't have a house she could really call her own. At the same time, she couldn't bring herself to go to a hotel.

I wish I had a cave in the wilderness just for me, some place where I could argue with myself, and with the woman who lives inside me and who's started using my fingers to express her ideas.

She felt a terrible urge to go to the old house in Ziqaq Al Yasmin. If she just told her family what she'd done, maybe they'd take her in and give her the TLC she needed so badly. Then she realized what a ridiculous thought this was. *In your dreams, girl! Who do you think you're fooling?*

The stranger sharing the bench with her said, "I'm Ghazwan Ayed. What's your name?"

Looking over at him for the first time, she saw a slightly built young man of medium height whose face was adorned by a mop of thick hair, a pair of eyes that dripped with honey, and an exquisitely dimpled chin. She wondered if his mother had pressed a chickpea into it when he was little to make that lovely indentation. According to her grandmother, at least, this was how people got dimples in their chins. For a few moments Zain forgot all about her pain and the awful day she was having. At the same time, she drew her blouse more snugly around her as though to protect herself from an invasion. The stranger took off his suit jacket and, without asking her permission, draped it over her shoulders and tucked it fondly around her neck.

"There," he said simply. "You're so beautiful! But you're so pale and tired-looking. And you're shivering with cold even though it's warm!"

She said nothing, but made no attempt to resist his gesture. She really had begun to shiver despite the warmth in the air. She felt herself slipping out of consciousness again. In a voice she felt she'd known for a thousand years, he said, "I'm Ghazwan Ayed. I'm telling you my name again because I don't want you to forget it. And I want you to know that as drained as you are, I find you ravishingly beautiful without a drop of makeup. Are you a Palestinian refugee like me?"

Amazed by the steadiness in her voice, as though she were drawing strength from his presence, she replied tranquilly, "I'm a local refugee from no place and no time. I could tell you were Palestinian from your accent. I have a cousin who's a Palestinian refugee too. You're welcome here."

"Don't worry," he added amiably, "I won't be invading your house, or even your neighborhood! My family has a house here and I've got a job as a teacher in Kuwait. But I'm on leave now, since I'm also a student at the University of Damascus."

She cracked a smile for the first time since her miserable day had begun. She wanted to tell him that she was a university student too, and that they might even have a class together, but she couldn't get anything to come out of her mouth. Her nerves were a wreck, and she kept fading alternately in and out of consciousness.

"You're not much of a talker," he commented. "But your eyes speak for you. I can hear them. They've got a music about them, and they fill the sky with a rainbow of light."

Then he went quiet.

They sat pondering the colorful autumn leaves as they fell from the trees. Zain seemed to recall hearing of Ghazwan Ayed before. She'd read some short stories in newspapers by someone with that name. She felt as though they'd lived some previous life together. *Come on now. Don't go off on some romantic tangent. You've seen his picture in a magazine on literary criticism. No, it wasn't him. Yes, it was. Those eyes... that dimple. That handsome face...* **Chill out**, advised the sensible writer who lived inside her. **The anesthesia hasn't worn off, and you're still not rational.**

Ghazwan looked her straight in the eye for a long time. Then suddenly, and with utter seriousness, he said, "Will you marry me? If you've turned eighteen, how about we do the ceremony today?"

Zain burst out laughing. "But you haven't even asked me what my name is!" she said, "Or whether I'm married or not. Or pregnant, for example!" **Does every day bring a new love?**[1] she whispered to herself. His presence almost made her forget her pain and the tangled web she was struggling to break loose from.

"Well, girl, whatever your name is, I love you!"

So there it was: an outpouring of madness, Palestinian-style! And what a beautiful madman he was. She knew she'd never forget him. How could she forget a handsome young man who'd asked for her hand in marriage the very first time he saw her? But she wasn't going to get carried away by romantic fancies or "love at first sight." She'd tried that before, and now she was suffering the consequences.

If it hadn't been for a sudden stab of pain in her abdomen, she would have sprouted wings and flown away right there and then. The wave of pain and fatigue pulled her into the depths and nearly drowned her. She didn't really know whether she had seen that face in *The Critic* magazine or not, or even whether she'd heard the name before. Her mind was a total blur. She was so exhausted, all she wanted to do was close her eyes and sleep. She

---

[1] A line from a poem by Bisharat al-Khuri (1885-1968).

needed to lie down on a bed that wasn't an operating table, and without a doctor in a white lab coat standing over her.

"I've got to be going," she said to Ghazwan.

"What?" he said. "Are you leaving? Do you think you can run away from me or forget me? I love you, and that's that!"

Ghazwan had swept her off her feet, but her body wasn't up to the adventure. She felt about as energetic as a limp rag. In a tremulous voice that she could hardly bear to hear coming out of her mouth, she replied, "I'm going to the pharmacy to buy some medicine." What she didn't say out loud was: Then I'm going to my husband's house behind the pharmacy to sleep!

The writer living inside her, whose voice was getting louder by the day, said: *Spend one more night in your husband's house. You need rest before making the final leap. Besides, going to my dad's house would mean having to explain myself, and I'm too spent for that now. Okay then, one last night with my husband, and tomorrow morning I'll tell him goodbye.*

In a tone as serious as it was playful, Ghazwan asked her, "Now that I've proposed, might you do me the honor of telling me your name, Miss Mystery Girl?"

Her only reply was, "I've got a cold and have to be going…"

"I'll take you wherever you need to go. I've got my friend's car till ten o'clock tonight."

"To Kaddoura Pharmacy, please," she said. "I need to buy a bottle of aspirin, then go home."

"Very well, Subki Park girl!" he agreed.

"Let's go, then," she said. Ghazwan was enthused, thinking he'd find out where she lived. He didn't want to lose track of her. Something drew him to her, though he wasn't sure what it was.

When she gave his coat back to him, he nearly told her to keep it, but then he thought better of it, since it was the only one he had.

He never wanted her to go away. It surprised him to feel this way, since he usually took to women who were fans of his, who had read his stories and who knew him as a writer. *This girl doesn't seem to care about anything, as if she were living on some other planet. On the other hand, I think she really is sick. She must have a cold, or something worse.* Zain wanted to tell him she was married, that she'd had an abortion just hours before, and that this was why she was feeling so awful. But she couldn't get herself to say it. He drove off with her, wishing she could stay by his side forever in a car that would never stop, break down or blow up! Unfortunately, though, they reached their destination.

He pulled up in front of the pharmacy. Zain got out with a painful slowness that was inconsistent with her youth, giving him all the more reason to believe she was genuinely ill. She reached out and shook his hand. He took her hand in his, saying: "I'll wait for you." As he held her hand, he realized how a handshake can be the equivalent of a warm embrace. He didn't know what madness had come over him, but whatever it was, he wanted more than anything else in the world never to part with her.

At last she withdrew her hand from his with a smile and fibbed, "I'll be back after I buy the aspirin." For some reason he didn't believe her. Even so, he still expected to see her when she came out of the pharmacy. Little did he know that the pharmacy had a back door that opened onto the alley off the street she lived on. So after buying the medicine, she escaped to her house through the back entrance. Meanwhile, he went on waiting in his stopped car while a traffic policeman took his license plate number.

Once in the house, Zain fell exhausted onto the bed. It had been a long, long day. To her relief, her husband wasn't home. She drew the curtains and lay back down. In the dim light she saw a naked infant floating through the air. She felt the pain of the millions of people all over the planet who are miserable for one reason or another. She saw scissors, scalpels, tiny probes and terrifying needles floating all over the room alongside the baby. They went flying around in front of her face, in her eyes, inside her head. She took her head in her hands. She wanted to scream, but stifled herself, afraid that her husband might come home and see what was wrong. The minute she thought about him, everything vanished. She went out onto the balcony and tried to breathe, but the pathway between her lungs and her throat felt blocked, like a mountain road covered with rocks and dirt from a sudden landslide. She was tempted to take refuge in the sleeping pill the doctor had given her as she got out of his car. *He said, "You might need this tonight." What a thoughtful person he is. He's nothing at all like the rumors going around about him.*

She pictured Ghazwan's refreshing face as he said to her on the way to the pharmacy, "You've got your whole life ahead of you. The future is yours. Don't crawl into your shell. Poke a hole in it the way a butterfly does with its cocoon, and come fly with me. I love you. I love you!"

Zain swallowed the magic pill. Then she sank into a coma-like slumber. Some time later she was wakened by her husband's voice. "Get up, lazy bones! We're going to celebrate your birthday tonight. Have you forgotten? And why did you run off in the early morning before I got a chance to see you?"

She didn't reply. *It's as if I'm at the bottom of the sea, and voices come and go like waves along some deserted shore.*

"How can you sleep now?" he asked, his voice fading in and out. "I reserved your favorite table for dinner on Candles' second-floor balcony. We're going to celebrate your eighteenth birthday in style! And here's your present: a diamond necklace."

"I've got the flu," she said in a whisper. "I took some medicine for it, and it's the kind that makes you sleepy."

His tone suddenly sharp, he demanded, "So where were you all day, anyway? I didn't find you at the university, or at the library either!"

"I was at the doctor," she replied listlessly. "I've got the stomach flu, so it's better not to get too close to me. You go have a good time with friends or family, and we'll talk in the morning. I'm all doped up now. I feel like I'm at the bottom of a well."

Hoping to avoid sharing a bed with her husband that night, she decided to tell him she'd sleep in the library because she didn't want to give him the flu. The library gave her a cozy feeling. She would shut herself up alone there, let out her frustrations by dancing to the wild strains of Stravinsky's Firebird Suite, and study the rest of the time. But she was too weak to carry through with her plan.

After giving up on getting her to cuddle, he drifted off to sleep. She could hear his snoring. Amazed to be alive, Zain struggled to keep the day's grueling events from replaying themselves in her brain, but they kept running across her inner screen like a bad movie while she faded in and out of consciousness. Even so, she was grateful to be lying in a bed instead of being laid out in a death shroud.

The fog in her head was suddenly penetrated by the image of Ghazwan in Subki Park. *I've always dreamed of going to Hyde Park in London, Central Park in New York City, the Flower Clock in Geneva, and on and on. It never occurred to me that out of all these places, the one that would be branded into my heart would be good old Subki Park. And why? Because that's where I first met Ghazwan. I was in a sorry state, like an owl with a broken wing, but he was so good to me. If my mother, the closet litterateur I've never had the pleasure of knowing, had seen me, she would have understood, and she would have bent down to mend my wing. Grandma Hayat always says I'm "just a little bit of a girl – a half-pint." But I carry around the sorrows of a middle-aged woman.*

So what's going on with me? The minute I come out of one relationship, I'm in danger of getting mixed up in another. Like somebody swinging over an alligator- and snake-infested swamp, I let go of one rope and grab onto another one. Does every day bring a first love? *Is Ghazwan's love dangerous? The danger is to my mental health. How could I let him slip into my life when it's in such a mess?*

I think of the doctor's kind-hearted French wife, who had no idea what she was getting herself into when she came here. I'll bet people blame her for every mistake anybody makes. After all, not only is she a woman—she's a foreigner. So people accuse her of getting Dr. Manahili into the work he does. I'm thinking about her because I'm pretty sure I'll meet the same fate she has. I'll be stigmatized as an "insubordinate" woman, and my husband, who

*hasn't been able to break into my mind and spirit, is sure to use
that against me. But I'm a boulder on Mt. Qasioun.*

***

When Zain woke up the next morning, she ran her hands over
her body one part at a time, like a teacher taking attendance. To
her amazement, she wasn't in any pain at all. On the contrary, she
felt energized, and her bleeding had stopped. She voiced a silent
thank you to Dr. Manahili, who appeared to have taken top-notch
care of her. When she got up to wash her face, she discovered that
her diamond bracelet was back on her wrist. She was sure she'd
given it to the doctor's wife. So what had happened? And why
hadn't she noticed it on her arm until now? *Was I that out of it
from the anesthesia?*

She was more determined than ever to get out of her marriage.
She needed to end this chapter of her life, turn the page, and start
at the beginning of a new line. It was terrifying to be faced with
the unknown. She got out of her marriage bed for the last time
while her husband was still asleep and slyly drank her coffee. In
a small bag she placed the secret notebooks that held her stories
and poems, and in another she packed her school books.

*Ever since my husband started sweet-talking me ten days ago
about what we were going to do on my eighteenth birthday, I've
felt like telling him – and specifically on my birthday – that I don't
want to live with him anymore, and that it's all over between us.
I don't want to go on and on about it or have to justify it either
to him or to myself. No stinging reproach, no bargaining, no
calculating profits and losses. We're through, and that's that. There*

*are so many painful details to deal with, we could go on fighting
for hours.*

*But I haven't said a thing to him. I haven't told him I was
pregnant either, even though I'd known it for more than two
weeks when I had the abortion. I suddenly realized I couldn't say
anything to anybody, not even to my dear father, my nurturing
grandmother, or my girlfriends. I was going to have to make my
own decision and bear the consequences without any external
support. The only thing I could rely on was what my dad used to
call the second engine. I had to grow up, and I did.*

Her books and papers were all she planned to rescue from
the sinking ship. She'd leave her clothes and jewelry behind. Her
university textbooks were especially dear to her heart. Every one
of them represented some moment of indecision or transition,
such as the moment when she'd fallen in love with an author's
creativity, or with an idea. Each one contained her hand-written
impressions, and the Arabic meanings of words that had still
been unclear to her even after she'd looked them up. She'd really
communed with the things she'd read and studied.

Zain got dressed, but she didn't spruce herself up or even get
her makeup bag out the way she usually did.

She wasn't sure what to do next, though. Should she wake her
husband up to tell him she wouldn't be coming back? Should she
wait until he woke up on his own? Or should she leave without
saying anything at all, and to hell with the Damascene good manners
she'd been raised on? Remembering a notebook she'd hidden under
her side of the mattress, she sneaked in to get it, and decided to
leave right away without saying anything to her husband. She knew
he might call her or follow her to work to spy on her. If he did,

she would tell him from there that they were through: no blame, no regrets, no heated exchanges. When everything is over between two people, it's best to stop talking altogether.

She was tempted to take her pen cemetery with her. She never had the heart to throw pens away when they went dry, and her defunct pen collection was the final resting place for her dearest friends. But she didn't think she'd have room for it in her bag.

Like a wary owl, she slipped quietly into the bedroom to extricate the notebook. The mattress was heavier than usual. *Or maybe I'm still just worn out from what I went through yesterday. I haven't got time to be thinking about that, though. I must face today, which could get stormy when I tell him I want a separation— or rather, that we need to recognize the separation that started the moment we were married.*

No sooner had Zain drawn her notebook out from under the mattress than her husband got up and turned on the light switch. He peered at her groggily. "What time is it?" he asked with a yawn. "And where are you going if you're sick?"

With a cool, calm voice that she hardly recognized as her own, and which had merged with the voice of the rebellious author inside her, she announced, "I'm going to work, and I won't be coming back here this evening. It's all over between us, and I want a divorce."

She fled from the room before he could start shouting and cursing. She picked up her suitcase, repeating to herself over and over, "I'm a boulder on Mt. Qasioun. I'm not afraid. No, I'm not afraid. I'll speak my mind, and nobody is going to scare me from now on. I'm a boulder on Mt. Qasioun. A boulder doesn't tremble, and it doesn't cry." Her husband beat her to the front door and shouted, "All right. If you don't want to come back, so be it. But you'll have to wait until I get dressed so I can go turn you over to your father!" Then he locked the door with the key. She didn't try unlocking it with her own key for fear that he might get violent. He was a lot bigger and stronger than she was.

She sat waiting in the entranceway, pretending she didn't hear her husband pacing nervously back and forth and ranting and raving to himself as he put his clothes on. They got in the car and he drove like a maniac, as though he wanted to run over everybody he passed. She didn't reply to a thing he said on the way.

They walked up the steps to her father's law office. Her husband went in without her, and she heard him say, "I've come to turn your daughter over to you." The words "turn… over to you" exploded in her head *So he's "turning me over" like some spoiled merchandise he wants to return to the seller!*

"So," Amjad Khayyal retorted, "you're bringing her back to me a squeezed lemon!" The phrase "squeezed lemon" also went off like a bomb in her head. *A squeezed lemon? Right. Well, I've lost a lot of weight and I had an abortion yesterday. But I'm a human being, not a lemon that somebody squeezes and throws away. One of them wants to turn me over like a piece of merchandise, and the other one's decided the merchandise isn't usable anymore.*

She felt so degraded and furious, she couldn't say a word. Whenever the voice of the rebel inside her got louder and louder, she went silent: wounded, insulted, humiliated. The voice deep down, which she knew was her own, said, ***Don't start to cry now. This won't last. You won't let it. You're going to stand up to him. Remember: You're a boulder on Mt. Qasioun.***

She sat down on a bench next to the exit. *I hate arguments. And I hate violence disguised as polite clichés. That's why the people I reject are so taken off guard. I do it without warning, and with a composure as cool as a cucumber. I kill them in my heart with a silent, bloodless elegance. My husband is dead to me now, and all that remains is to list his name in my heart's obituary column. We never got into any arguments, since I discovered that trying to discuss things with him was a lost cause. I tried at first to draw him into conversations, but it never worked. I told myself it had been a good learning experience and all the usual things people say to make themselves feel better when they're let down. But something inside me had broken. I still feel insulted and defeated, but I'm holding myself together. So if this is what love does to people, then it isn't for me! This is the last time I'll let myself be ground into the dirt.*

Leaving her father and her husband to bicker over the squeezed lemon, Zain left and went to her father's house in Sahat Al Midfaa, where she could see Grandma Hayat, the only person who'd ever really welcomed her with open arms.

Seeing Zain in the doorway with a suitcase in her hand, her grandmother knew something big was afoot.

"I've left him," Zain announced. "We're through. I want a divorce."

"You're always welcome here, honey. Besides, nobody ever liked Waseem. You weren't right for each other. Your dad knew it from the start, but because he loved you so much, he went along with what you wanted."

"Well, it's over, Grandma. I'll tell you what happened to me…"

"Don't you tell me a thing," her grandmother interrupted. "I might open my big mouth and blabber to somebody about it! You shouldn't trust anybody with your secrets, not even me. The only person we should complain to is God. Like they say, 'Better a heartbreak in the kitchen than a scandal around the block.'"

The old woman's words came as a relief to Zain. She felt as though she'd been freed from a heavy burden. She'd learned from the time she was a little girl to keep her suffering to herself, mostly to spite the aunts who tried to keep her at their mercy. *Did all that really happen? Or am I just imagining it? So many memories are hazy.* Losing her mother as a little girl had been traumatic, and she wasn't sure she really wanted to get over it. Even so, she preferred to focus on the future rather than dwelling on the past. She recalled the outbursts of rage she'd endured as a child whenever she tried to assert herself, and the more she thought about it, the more she rebelled against the familial repression that masked itself as altruistic concern.

Grandma Hayat added, "A lot of people are going to ask you why you left Waseem. Some of them will want to gloat, some will be looking for something to gossip about at the reception,[2] and some will want to use your story to scare their daughters away from doing the same. If anybody asks you why you're getting a divorce after you were so in love, just say, 'It wasn't meant to be!' After all, everybody believes in fate."

---

[2]   The reception was a monthly women's gathering held in a neighbor's or relative's house.

Zain figured her grandmother was probably right. *Don't wear yourself out trying to explain things to other people, or even to yourself. Love was born. Love died. That's that. Beware of explaining the gory details to people who couldn't care less about you and your feelings, and who just want a scandal to wag their tongues about. What happened, happened. And you survived it. So don't let it destroy you now.*

In a resolute tone Zain repeated back to her grandma, "It wasn't meant to be!" Then she added, "Can I go to my old room, or is it being used for something else?"

"Nothing's changed," her grandmother assured her, "and we always keep it clean. I always expected you back. You know nobody in the house liked him."

Zain knew that, like a true-blooded Damascene woman, her grandmother knew how to keep quiet about something when circumstances required it. Her unspoken rule of thumb was: Tell people enough to help you in your future, but not enough to let them hold your past against you.

Fitna, a neighbor lady, came in. Seeing Zain back at her father's house at an unexpected hour, suitcase in hand, she'd picked up on the scent of some juicy gossip. With typical Damascene urbanity, she asked, "Well, what brings you here, dear? It's lovely to see you!"

"I've left my husband," Zain replied straightforwardly, "and I'm going to ask for a divorce."

"Oh, why would you do a thing like that, sweetheart?" Fitna probed, her appetite whetted.

"It just wasn't meant to be," Zain answered simply, her eyes meeting her grandmother's. She was pleased with herself for not saying any more than this to her neighbor, or even to her cousin. When her cousin telephoned asking if she could come by Zain's workplace, Zain was taken completely by surprise. It was the first telephone call she'd gotten from her in her life. *What's going on? Has word gotten around so fast that the whole family knows about it already? Or is this just a coincidence?*

"How did you know I was here?" Zain asked her.

"Oh," she said, "I called my uncle to ask for your number at the library, and he said you were at home today."

Zain went to her room, and her grandmother followed her. Despite her earlier advice to Zain not to tell her secrets to anyone, she couldn't contain her own curiosity. "What happened?" she asked anxiously. "Aren't you going to miss him? Are you sure about this?"

"Don't worry, Grandma," Zain replied. "He's given me no reason to miss him!"

* * *

Waseem sighed with satisfaction as he drove to his family's house for lunch. *Man, have I got it made! I'm getting rid of that shitty wife of mine, Zain Khayyal. And since she's asking for the divorce herself, it'll cost me a lot less. I was an idiot to marry her in the first place. On the other hand, though, it makes me mad that she was uppity with me, and that she's the one saying she wants out. In any case, I'll come out without any material losses to speak of. That damned lawyer-dad of hers set her divorce dowry[3] ridiculously*

---

[3] According to Islamic law among Sunni Muslims, a husband who divorces his wife is required to pay a sum of money which is agreed

high—it comes to nearly the price of a three-story building. It never occurred to him that if we split up, I'd make her waive all her financial claims against me before I agreed to a divorce!

I doubt if there's a man on earth who'd put up with a wife like her. Zain's unbearable. Sure, she's got a delicate, feminine look about her, but she's as tough as a man, and she's always trying to act like one. Instead of staying home and cooking for me and whoever I'm in the mood to invite over, she gets up at the crack of dawn to go to her job at the library, and then to the university. She doesn't even go to hair salons or doll herself up so that she'll be looking her best when I get home from work, from hanging out with friends, or from hooking up with other women. She's got no business knowing where I've been or who I've been with. Her job is to do what I say and be content with what she's got.

My poor mom likes Zain even though I've told her how awful she is. She even fixes food for us every day and either sends it over or has me pass by and get it. It doesn't even occur to Zain that her priority should be to set up shop in the kitchen and learn how to cook from my mom so that she can make feasts for my friends whenever I want her to. Instead, she thinks she's my equal, as if we had two men in the house. She goes to her job and comes home tired. Then she buries herself in her books and doesn't give a damn whether I stay home or go out for the evening.

So I'm ecstatic to be getting divorced! But the fact that she seems even more excited and happy about it than I am makes me mad. She might even come to the court for the divorce proceedings all by

---

upon at the time of marriage and written into the marriage contract. The minimum divorce dowry is four silver dirhams. If the wife initiates the divorce, however, no divorce dowry has to be paid.

herself. I suppose she won't feel intimidated by the judge, or bat an eyelid when I stand next to her. Those damned books of her are the real reason we're splitting up. They've ruined her mind.

The crazy girl used to chatter away to me about things I didn't understand, and were boring as hell. She would say, "The only person who doesn't make fun of me for getting engrossed in reading and writing is my dad. When I study Western literature and read the books my dad shows me from the Arabic tradition, I feel as though I find myself. I'm starting to understand the meaning of freedom, equality, and civilization – what it means to be a human being, and who I really am. You know, it's really important to write about what you think and not to hold back. So if anybody tries to keep me from swimming in my inkwell, I just write that person off."

The things she says are a pile of crap, if you ask me. All she does is try to show off how "cultured" she is. So even though I'm her husband, it looks like she's written me off, and the kisses we used to steal in the orchards outside her father's house in Sahat Al Midfaa don't mean a thing anymore. Even back then I remember her going on ad nauseum about books until I started to yawn. All she really wanted was a house of her own where she could spread out her books and papers and study non-stop. I'd come home drunk at dawn after a night of carousing in taverns and bars, and she wouldn't say a damned thing. She'd just go on getting dressed for work as if she couldn't care less what I did. At first it made me suspicious. I thought maybe she had a lover. So I had my driver start spying on her. After a month of following her around, he told me she really did just go to work and to the university, and that she holed herself up at the library every evening till it closed. And that made me madder than ever.

Damn it! No woman has the right to think she's my equal, and that her job is more important than whether I spend my nights with her or out on the town.

She doesn't care about money or threats or anything, and it irritates the hell out of me. Zain doesn't give a damn anymore. It's as if she doesn't even hear my voice. Like an idiot, I thought of asking her grandmother Hayat to talk her into coming back. A lot of good that would do! I doubt if she'd even ask Zain why it is that after raising hell to get married to me, she's raising hell now to get away from me.

Anyway, I'm not going to let her ruin my chance to get to know Lieutenant Nahi, who can help me bring in cheap merchandise from Beirut and sell it in Damascus for double the price.

A week earlier, Waseem's business partner Badee had told him he'd met with Lieutenant Nahi and that after a wild night out, they'd talked about money. They'd also discussed the businessmen who were afraid of Socialism and who were bitter over the nationalization laws instituted under Abdel Nasser when Syria and Egypt formed the United Arab Republic. He'd reassured Waseem that business would flourish thanks to people like him and that they'd make huge profits trading in basically everything. He also hinted at a huge cut he'd be getting off every deal.

***

After starting her shift at the Syrian University Library one day, Zain received an unexpected visit from her cousin Fadila. It was the first time anybody in her family had come to her work place.

Zain felt concerned when she saw the look of distress on Fadila's face. Still in distress herself over her abortion, she bypassed the usual niceties and asked Fadila straight out, "What brings you here?"

"Well," Fadila hesitated. "I wanted to talk to you alone. It's about Najm Rabi`ee, my first and only love. I need your encouragement."

Zain's features tightened. Misinterpreting the look on Zain's face to mean she objected to Najm because he was poor and from a village, Fadila quickly added, "Najm isn't poor, by the way! You may have read in the newspapers a few days ago that an uncle of his who's emigrated to Gabon left him a huge fortune. Maybe he did it as a way of thumbing his nose at everybody else!"

Appreciating the fact that her cousin had sought her out for help, Zain measured her words with the greatest of care. "Well," she began, "even if the news reports are true—and I doubt that they are—money isn't the problem here. The problem has to do with love itself. What I mean is that something changes after people get married."

"But I really do love Najm, and I need your support," Fadila pleaded. "You're the Ziqaq Al Yasmin Troublemaker, as the neighbor ladies refer to you, or the Ziqaq Al Yasmin Insurgent, as my educated Najm prefers to call you!"

The two of them burst out laughing. "Excuse me," Zain said. "Dr. Jean needs help checking out some books. I'll be right back. Wait for me here."

Hardly had Zain taken a step in Dr. Jean's direction when her coworker, Ikram, came rushing enthusiastically to the professor's assistance. Ikram was obviously smitten with Dr. Jean and determined to catch his eye. *Love… it bubbles up all around me in the faces of friends, relatives, and strangers alike. Love… that*

colorful, infectious sentiment surrounded by Beethoven's music to
Elise, and Chopin's tears dripping blood-like onto the piano keys as
he played for the hard-hearted George Sand. Chopin professed to
belong to Sand. She believed him, and so did the critics. But I don't.
Artists aren't faithful to anyone or anything but their craft. I know
it from my recent experience with words.

When Zain rejoined Fadila, the latter gushed, "I want to be
like you! So I've told people I'm in love with Najm and that I
don't want to marry Mutaa! But I need you to stick up for me to
other family members, since you led the way by telling people
how things were going to be and marrying the person you were
in love with."

Zain nearly weakened before her cousin's barrage of earnest
pronouncements. She was so impassioned, and her heart so on
fire for her beloved Najm. Zain felt ashamed not to be able to play
the role of the self-sacrificing heroine of movies and romance
novels. However, the owl came in through the window, perched
on Zain's shoulder, and said what needed to be said.

"Listen, Fadila," Zain confessed. "You know I love you. But
the fact is, I left Waseem a couple of days ago and I'm asking for
a divorce. Things didn't work out. I made a huge mistake. But
that doesn't mean every first love has to be a failure. It's just that
mine was a failure."

"Oh my God!" Fadila gasped. "I don't believe it."

"Life is unbelievable sometimes," Zain conceded. "But like I
said, my failed relationship doesn't mean everybody who falls in
love will fail the way I did. And it doesn't mean you're going to
fail. You're another girl, with another man, and the two of you
have your own story. I've lost hope in this love, but I haven't lost

hope in love itself. Go ahead with what you think is right for you, and don't be afraid. But just remember: There's no such thing as a 'love insurance policy.'"

"And why would you want to divorce him?" Fadila sputtered in an outburst of what seemed like personal hostility.

Remembering her grandmother's advice, Zain said evenly, "It just wasn't meant to be. Everything comes down in the end to what was, or wasn't, meant to be. It's a matter of destiny."

A student came up and requested help finding a book. Excusing herself momentarily, Zain accompanied the student to the bookshelves. But when she came back, Fadila had disappeared.

Once she was home, Zain holed herself up in her old room, the room where for so long she had sworn by Waseem's name and lit him love candles. She nearly cried. But the friendly owl that her mother always sent her in times of need landed comfortingly on her bed. She heard her mother whisper, as she had at the moment she died, "Don't be afraid of any of them. Don't back down. Don't give up your life for somebody who doesn't deserve it."

Zain stretched out on the bed, still exhausted from the abortion a few days earlier. *I made a mistake, and now I'm correcting it. I'm paying the price. I have to get a divorce no matter what if I'm going to survive. Then let come what may. I'll be rebelling against people's love for me, and that's hard. I'll also be rebelling against their rejection of me, and that's a relief! I'm a boulder on Mt. Qasioun.*

Chapter Three

Two clouds of rage had now emanated from Ziqaq Al Yasmin where I grew up. When I'd insisted on marrying Waseem, it had come from the older generation, and now that I was insisting on divorcing him, the younger generation was in an uproar. The telephone rang.

"Your cousin Hamida wants to talk to you," my grandmother told me.

Her voice trembling with rage, Hamida demanded, "How dare you announce that you want a divorce after the hell you raised to marry this guy! How could you do this to me?"

"And what does that have to do with you?" I asked, taken by surprise.

Her answer pained me. "When I announced my decision to marry Suhayl, the guy I love, I was following your example after what you'd done with Waseem. And now they're pushing back against me because your grand revolution flopped, and now you want a divorce. My mom told me the news and was gloating in my face. So, is it true?"

"Yes, it's true," I admitted. "I fell in love and announced it to everybody, and we got married. Then the marriage didn't work out and I announced that I wanted a divorce."

"How could you do this to me?" she repeated dolefully, as if she and Suhayl had already married and divorced.

Trying to reason with her, I said, "Just because this is happening to me doesn't mean it has to happen to you! Suhayl might be better than Waseem, or he might be worse. The point is, he's a different person. Every man has his own set of fingerprints, and no two relationships are the same. I failed. I admit it, and I'm trying to take responsibility for it. But neither you nor Suhayl has anything to do with it."

"You're the one who gave me courage," Hamida went on forlornly. "And here you are backing out and letting me down!"

"I'm not letting you down," I insisted. "On the contrary, admitting my mistake and retreating takes the same courage it took me to insist on marrying the guy I loved. And this is what I have to do, or I'll destroy myself. Regardless of what image you have of me, I have to live my own life. Besides, like I told you, the fact that I failed doesn't necessarily mean you will, or that love itself will fail. Life is pretty risky when the other side of the equation is an unknown, and you can't claim you know somebody for the simple reason that he says he loves you."

"Everybody in the neighborhood is gloating over you," Hamida informed me. I wasn't surprised. "Your Aunt Buran said the neighbor lady had done a good thing when she put a hot coal on her daughter's tongue for saying she was in love, and that your dad should have done the same thing to you. In fact, he should have done it twice: the first time when you said you were in love, and the second time when you said you wanted a divorce!"

Then she added with a note of satisfaction, "As you probably know, there's never been a single divorce in our family."

"You're right about that," I concurred. "We cover up our festering wounds for fear of what people will say. But what people *say doesn't mean a thing to me. All I care about is what my own mind, heart, and conscience tell me."*

When Hamida ended the call, I couldn't tell whether she was feeling braver than before, or more miserable.

After the call from Hamida, Zain thought to herself: Nobody's on my side. And nobody approves of the writing I do. But I'm determined to go on. No one has the right to stab me with his dagger. If I deserve a dagger in my chest, I'll put it there myself.

***

After her brother Amjad left Ziqaq Al Yasmin for the Sahat Al Midfaa neighbhorhood, Zain's Aunt Buran had become more outspoken and overbearing than before. One day she said to her daughter Fadila, "Mutaa Ribati's mother came by yesterday and talked to me about moving up the wedding date for you and Mutaa, and I agreed to it. The boy's father is excited about the idea, and he and his brother will be coming over to recite the Fatiha with your dad."

Fadila was stunned. How could her mother agree to let her marry a man she didn't know just because he was rich and had a respectable position on the Damascene social scene?

"No!" Fadila burst out. "I'm not going to marry somebody I barely know. I don't love him. In fact, I don't even like him! I'm not some rag doll people can buy and sell. I'm a human being, and I've got feelings. If I'm going to marry him, I need to spend time with him and get to know him first."

Horrified, her mother replied, "We'd have to write up the marriage contract before you could do that."

"All right, then," Fadila countered with unaccustomed decisiveness, "provided that I have the right to divorce written into the contract. It isn't fair for men to be the only ones who can initiate a divorce. And they shouldn't be allowed to subjugate their wives and demand their obedience. Those are things of the past, Mama."

Jumping as though she'd been shocked by a live wire, her mother shrieked, "Who told you wives could have the right to divorce?!"

"Zain did," Fadila answered simply. "I've been visiting her at the library lately. She told me she hadn't known about it before, either. But Islam gives women this option. She said Uncle Amjad had told her about it one day when she complained to him that Islam isn't fair to women. He explained to her that Islam liberates women in a number of ways. It started when the Qur'an forbade people's ignorant practice of burying their baby daughters alive. Islam gave women rights that, at the time, were quite progressive, including the right to divorce their husbands on their own initiative. Zain tells me that the purpose of Islam is to free women, not to oppress them the way society was doing before Islam came, and the way some people still want to do now. She says we have a duty to enlighten women about their rights, and she's been giving copies of an article she wrote, 'Liberated Girls,' to girls and women in the neighborhood."

***

Fadila's brother, who had been eavesdropping from behind the door, couldn't stand to listen to another word. After reading Zain's first article, which she had published in the Readers' Mail column along with her picture (*for shame!*), he had slit her owl's throat and put its carcass in her bed. He figured it would give her the scare of her life, and that she wouldn't dare do something like that ever again. Instead, though, she seemed to have gone even farther off course than before. When he stalked her with a rifle, he was sure she'd either die or shut her mouth for good. Dying would have been the preferable outcome, of course, as far as he was concerned.

He walked into the room, pretending not to have heard anything but the last part about copies of the article. "So," he asked his sister with feigned nonchalance, "did she buy copies of the newspaper and pass them around to your girlfriends?"

"No," replied Fadila. "She can reproduce documents at the library with a mimeograph machine and a stencil. That's how they make copies of test questions for all the students."

My, how times have changed! Buran thought to herself.

As she lay in bed that night, Buran thought back on how she used to put up with her husband's snoring without daring to slip out of the room to catch a few winks of her own. As moonlight poured through the window onto her face in magical streaks of liquid silver, she wondered: *If I'd been free to decide who I was going to marry, would I have chosen this man to be my husband? And if I'd ever dared to think of divorcing him, would I have stayed with him all these years? Didn't I deserve to live my life, too?*

She ran her hands over her body in the moonlight, exploring its cobwebbed recesses and the curves that had grown flabby without ever having been pleasured by her husband's lips, even on their wedding night. She rose quietly and went over to the mirror. She took a close look at her face, perhaps for the first time in years.

***

Nawal, who'd been visiting her uncle in Aleppo, got back to Ziqaq Al Yasmin dying to see her sweetheart Waleed, and more determined that ever to declare her love for him. But when she got to the house, her mother shouted at her gloatingly, "Have you heard? Zain, the one you say is your inspiration because she fell in love and married the person she'd chosen herself, has come running home to her father's house and is asking for a divorce!"

The news descended like a bolt of lightning. She had always drawn strength from Zain's example. Zain was the one who'd given her the courage to stand up to the people around her and tell them straight up, "I'm in love, and I'm going to marry the person I'm in love with!" At least that's what she'd been intending to do.

Now she felt chilled to the bone, and with a horrified shiver she wondered: Might the same thing happen to Waleed and me? She dialed the number to Zain's house. No answer. Then she tried calling Zain at her father's house. Her grandmother Hayat answered. Without the usual niceties, Nawal asked to speak to Zain. The minute she heard Zain's voice, she shouted furiously in her ear, "So, is it true this news I'm hearing? Are you asking for a divorce from the guy you raised hell to be able to marry?!"

"Why don't we get together and talk about it?" Zain suggested, maintaining her composure. Even more enraged now because Zain hadn't denied the report the way she'd hoped she should, Nawal snapped, "There'll be no need for that." And she hung up.

* * *

Fadila heaved a sigh of distress. A neighbor woman had seen Mutaa trying to kiss her in the courtyard, and the whole thing had come down on Fadila's head. *I can't believe the way my family reacted when they heard about it. They're all against me. If it weren't for something I'd done wrong, what happened wouldn't have happened, they say! Working a job the way I do now is sinful. The fact that I wear a short headscarf instead of the longer, traditional kind is sinful. And what happened is all my fault. As for Mutaa, he's the perfect gentleman, since he still wants to marry me even though I didn't slap him when he tried to kiss me, but just moved politely away! My God! I don't understand anything anymore. Najm's found a job in Kuwait, and I'd give anything to go there with him. The situation here was hellish enough already, and then Zain went and made it even worse by getting a divorce.*

* * *

Grandma Hayat was planning a visit to her ailing centegenarian sister, and Zain was going along. *Am I really going in honor of my great-aunt? Or am I just going because I'm nostalgic for Hayy Al Maydan, the neighborhood where she lives? My dear Damascus has become so hostile toward me that I may have to leave her.*

The room was empty of visitors when they arrived, and her great-aunt's daughter-in-law had seized the opportunity afforded by Hayat's and Zain's presence to escape briefly from Lord Death's gloomy presence.

Casting her sister a look of non-recognition, the dying woman emitted a feeble scream. "Look at him! Look at him!" she cried pitifully. "For God's sake, look at him!" I saw her point in the direction of the window. Zain didn't know whether she was referring to the light coming in through it, or to the leafless tree outside it. She was so alarmed, at first Zain thought she must be seeing a burglar. Then she realized she was talking about Lord Death. Taking her hand, Zain asked her what she was afraid of.

Staring back at Zain in sheer terror, she shrieked faintly at Grandma Hayat, "Why did you bring this scrawny owl with you? And you brought death along, too! Look at him! He's splitting open a watermelon beside the pond. Now he's coming after me. Look!"

Like a guilty little girl, Grandma Hayat said, "I swear, I left her at home with the kids in the courtyard. I have no idea how she managed to follow me all the way here!"

"Look! Look!" her dying sister screamed, and pointed at Zain. Now Zain was afraid.

"Close your eyes," Grandma Hayat said to her, "so that you can't see him."

The dying woman whispered feebly, her eyes shut, "I still see him clear as day, even with my eyes closed. I don't want to close my eyes. He's… he's…"

Grandma Hayat broke in, saying, "Start reciting from the Qur'an. Say: 'God is One.' He'll be easier on you that way."

As I listened to the two women, I thought of my mother. She was laid out in a coffin, and I lay down beside her to wake her up. I wanted to meet Death and ask him to send her back to me.

The dying woman's voice grew softer. "Look... Look... What is it? Please... What is it?" She didn't say any of the traditional things that Zain had read about people saying when they're passing away.

* * *

Waseem's mother arranged the sitting room, placing the finishing touches on it in preparation for her guests. *Today's the monthly reception at my house, and I'm expecting all the women of the family and all the neighbor ladies to come. It's the first time we've met since the news got out about Zain and Waseem.*

She knew the women coming to visit would outdo themselves saying nasty things about Zain, thinking this would make her happy. It would never have occurred to them that she loved the girl! *She had the guts to do what I always wanted to do myself, but never dared. I wanted to finish my education, but instead I was married off to my cousin, and for that they pulled me out of school when I was just fifteen years old. I didn't know whether I loved him or not. At that age, I didn't even know what love was. I had lots of children, but never once did anybody ask me how I felt about anything. I was just a paddle in a water wheel that kept taking me around and around. When Zain came along and was so in love with my son, it reminded me of the way I'd felt about a neighbor boy back in the day. I buried those feelings, of course, and forgot about him. Then, when Zain had her change of heart toward Waseem, it scared me, because I was reminded of resentments I've struggled with myself. I mean, I'm no saint. In fact, I'm full of regrets. For one thing, I regret not finishing my education. So when I sent food every day to my son's house, I didn't*

*do it just for his sake. I did it for Zain's sake, too, since I wanted her
to be able to go on with her studies. Touching my children's school
books sends an electrical charge through me to this day, because
it makes me think about the chances I was deprived of. I dislike
my poor son-in-law for the simple reason that he married my fair-
skinned, pleasantly plump daughter and bought her a fancy condo
on Abu Rummana Street, which is in an upscale part of town.
Buying her a nice place to live was all right as far as it went, of
course. But then he isolated her from people and took her away
from her studies so that all she does now is have kids and cook big
meals. I liked Zain because she made me think of the way I was
before I was "tamed." How can I hate her for wanting to divorce
her husband, even if he happens to be my son? That's exactly what
I would have liked to do once upon a time, but I didn't have the
courage to go through with it.*

* * *

When Zain came home from the university, she headed
straight for the kitchen, which was where she usually found her
grandmother. As she approached the door, she heard Grandma
Hayat's lovely voice wafting in her direction. As usual, she'd
changed some of the words in the song the way she'd always done
with the stories she told.

My hometown, O my hometown,
I want to go to my hometown,
O my dear, I want to go to my hometown.
It's worth six hometowns put together,
And I've got six kids there.

O Lord, take me back where I belong,
And bring my children home!

Then she said in a plaintive voice, "Everybody lives in a different country now!" Zain laughed affectionately. As far as her grandmother was concerned, leaving Ziqaq Al Yasmin for another neighborhood was the equivalent of going abroad!

Grandma Hayat turned to look at Zain and found her holding a small cat in her arms.

"So," she said happily, "you've brought me a kitty-cat! You know how much I loved the ones that used to make friends with our pet snake[4] back at the house in Ziqaq Al Yasmin."

But after taking a closer look at the little creature, she objected, "What's this sickly, ugly, scabby thing you've dragged in, girl?"

Zain put the cat down on the floor, and as she walked toward the grandmother, she limped from a defect or wound in one of her front legs. She looked so miserable and worn-out, you would have thought she'd been run over by all the cars in Damascus, and her fur looked as though it had been singed by lightning. She kept heading toward Grandma Hayat, doing her best to walk normally.

"All right," the grandmother relented, softening at the sight of the little animal's valiant efforts. "She doesn't hold a candle to your aunt's cat Fulla. But she'll do. Where did you find her?"

"Oh, she was wandering around in the street," Zain replied. "Her owners must have abandoned her. We can't neglect a kitty that's had such lousy luck. We love cats!"

---

[4]   Every house in old Damascus had a small, harmless snake that the people of the household took care of. They would leave food for it in the kitchen, as it was believed to wardoff evil.

"Cats, you say?" the grandmother rejoined with a laugh. "Or do you mean owls? No owls, please!"

Giggling and giving her grandmother a hug, Zain said, "You've already got an owl in the house." She ringed her eyes with her fingers and called out, "Hoo! Hoo! Hoooo!"

Grandma Hayat wrapped her arms around her and drew her close, and Zain found the safe haven she needed.

* * *

One day as Zain walked in exhausted from her shift at work, she nearly bumped into the maid, who was carrying a tray of fancy coffee cups reserved for guests.

Her curiosity aflame, Zain stepped into the sitting room. The guest turned out to be none other than Dr. Manahili. She was gripped with terror. Might he have told her father about her abortion? She stole a fearful glance at her father's face, but saw a happy twinkle in his eyes.

He said to her, "You may not remember Dr. Manahili. You were just a little girl when we used to meet. He was at your wedding, but I'm sure you weren't paying any attention to the guests that night!" Then, his voice tinged with pride, he added, "Dr. Manahili came to congratulate me on the things you've been writing."

"You're really good with words, Zain," the doctor interjected. "I've started buying the newspapers just so I can read what you've published there."

Then, in a meaningful tone he added, "I'm happy to see you looking so well!"

Zain sat down with them happily, and to her infinite relief, not a word was said about her upcoming divorce.

* * *

Fadila paced around the courtyard pond. *My dad is determined to marry me off to Mutaa, since he's rich and comes from a "respectable family." The first time he saw me, my sisters and I were working in our brocade shop because Baba was sick. He said he'd come to buy gifts for some clients of his in the import-export business, and asked to talk to one of my brothers or my father. In other words, he wanted to speak with a man of the family who'd have the smarts to understand business matters. As far as he was concerned, I couldn't possibly have been anything more than a "helper" and wouldn't have been fit to make any decisions! He talked down to me as if I were some pea-brain who didn't know the first thing about Damascene brocade. On top of that, he said something about a plan to market the brocade all over the world, which led me to suspect that he wasn't really there to buy presents but, rather, to find a way to take over my dad's business now that it was being run by his daughters.*

So he turned me off from the start. But now I really don't like him. I'll bet the only reason he wants to marry me is so that he can get his hands on our Damascene brocade, which was "woven from a love story between the sun and the moon, between the silver strands of its fabric and golden threads of sunlight between the blueness of the sea, the darkness of night on Mt. Qasioun, and the red spring flowers of the Ghouta." That's how Zain described our brocade—the material we've spun with our sweat and tears—to a delegation of Westernized Arabs, some of whom had been born in Syria and some of whom had been born abroad, and had come to visit their homeland. As Zain switched back and forth between Arabic and other languages, I heard her giving voice to things I felt but didn't know how to express. I envied her for the chance she'd had to learn so much. Unlike my dad, who's wanted ever since his daughters were born to pawn us off on a respectable suitor, Uncle Amjad made sure Zain got a good education.

I think Mutaa is disgusting. He's nothing but a greedy opportunist. He doesn't love me. Far from it. He wants to get back at me for not liking him by invading me and taking me over. I pulled away when he pretended to touch my hand by accident while I was showing him a piece of brocade. By that time, I'd caught onto the fact that he didn't want to buy some brocade as a gift for some clients. He wanted to buy our whole shop as a gift to himself!

Today we had the ceremony where he put a ring on my finger. As he slipped it on, I closed my eyes and imagined that it was my dear, not-so-well-to-do Najm putting the ring on my hand. If Mutaa kisses me or violates my body some day, I'll pretend he's Najm so that I won't go crazy. Mutaa's hand on my fingers felt so cold, it sent a shiver up my spine. Our families applauded, thinking I was trembling with joy. If only I could be like Zain. If only I could just say, "This is the man I love, and he's the one I'm marrying!" Zain had a steely determination about her that was made even steelier by her passion. Well, I'm just as passionate about Najm as she ever was about Waseem. When Zain was living here in Ziqaq Al Yasmin she was a rebel. According to my mother, her mother Hind's spirit had taken up residence in her body (imagine that!). Still, I don't dare do what she did now that she's let me down. Both families are talking up my engagement to Mutaa. We're scheduled to sign the marriage contract a week from today, and my mother-in-law says the groom's furnished a house for us, which means we won't be living with her. That, as far as my mother is concerned, is the best wedding gift any bride could hope for. On top of that, the house is on Abu Rummana Street, which is in a posh part of town. So what more could I ask? As Mutaa was leaving, he said in a sickening voice, "Whatever you want, just ask!" I nearly said, "All right, then, I want you to take that filthy smooth talk of yours and get out of my life. I don't even like you, much less love you! But I do love school-teacher Najm and I want to spend my life with him whether he's inherited a fortune from his rich uncle abroad, or not!"

I hope I can get up the courage to do what Zain did even though she's gone back on it now with her divorce. She heard Waseem was the black sheep of his family, and people said all sorts of terrible things about him, but she didn't give a damn. She told everybody how things were going to be, and married him. In fact, they had a huge bash of a wedding. Her dad bought her a trousseau fit for a queen, including top-of-the-line fashions, traditional hand-embroidered gowns and modern, machine-made items from Al Hayek's Department Store. Then she spent her wedding night with the man she was in love with, and she said it had been the night of a lifetime.

In any case, after our awful engagement party, where everybody but me had a good time, I mustered the courage to tell my mother how I really felt. As she helped me unbutton my corset, I said, "Mama, I don't love Mutaa. The person I really want to marry is Najm, the school teacher."

My mother looked as if I'd just slapped her in the face. Once she'd collected herself a bit, she said gloatingly, "Oh, haven't you *heard? Zain wants to divorce her husband—the one she was head-over-heels in love with—and she's come back to live with her dad. That's what I heard from your grandma Hayat."*

I didn't tell her I'd gone to see Zain and that I knew everything. I felt so confused and demoralized, I just kept my mouth shut. How was I going to get myself out of the situation I was in?

Chapter Four

*T*omorrow morning's the divorce hearing at the Palace of Justice. That's all I know. I haven't dared ask my dad about the details. I know he wasn't happy about this marriage, and deep down I'll bet he's glad I'm getting divorced. At the same time, I know I've embarrassed him before society and his associates in the national companies they've fought so proudly to incorporate since being liberated from the French mandate. He's bound to these people not only by ties of friendship, but also by the interests of fledgling corporations allied with the Quartet Company, most of which is owned by Waseem's family. Basically everybody in both his family and mine was sure the marriage would fall apart once the flame of teenage romance had died down and the magic carpet had brought us down to earth again.

To my chagrin, I've discovered that society's verdicts aren't always stupid after all. When I fell in love, I was sure the whole world was wrong, and that I alone knew what reality and love were. But now, all I know is that I want to be unshackled from this marriage. There's no harm in my admitting that I made a mistake and that I want to correct it. All that matters now is to let go of my pride and make a new start.

Zain paced the balcony. *Why is Najati so late? He promised to come by so that we could talk about tomorrow. It's the day I've*

dreamed of for so long, yet now that it's almost here, my knees are
wobbly, I'm so scared.

She knew her father hated talking about the issue, and she
didn't blame him, which was why she'd hired Najati, an old friend
of the family's and her father's one-time partner. She called
Najati's house to find out what had kept him. No answer. *I know*
this is the first divorce in the Khayyal family. No woman in the
clan has ever had the nerve to insist on marrying a man because
she was in love with him and then, as if that wasn't bad enough, to
insist on divorcing him a year later because she couldn't stand him
anymore. No woman in all Ziqaq Al Yasmin has ever dared say,
"I'm in love." When a neighbor girl did that some time back, her
mother put a hot coal on her tongue. Well, I committed the same
sin that girl did, and now I'm committing a second one: getting
divorced. I feel so sorry for Fadila, who gave in and let Mutaa put
that ring on her finger!

In need of moral support and wanting to know what awaited
her the following day, Zain tried calling Najati again. When his
wife answered the telephone, she told Zain that he'd been invited
to a book-signing event by a well-known author. "Everybody's
who's anybody in the literary world will be there. Aren't you
going, too?" *That author is so inundated by admirers, he won't*
even notice if Najati didn't show up. As for me, I'm lonely, I'm
worried to death, and I need him, damn it!

Crestfallen, Zain hung up and went back to pacing the
balcony. She decided she would have to face the next day on her
own, unarmed outside and inside.

Her father came out and asked, "Would you like me to go
with you tomorrow?"

There was nothing she would have liked more. But a voice inside said, *Let him be. You've put him through enough as it is.*

"No, dad," she told him. "Najati will be there, and we'll be just fine!"

She could feel her father heaving a silent sigh of relief.

"All right, then," he said. "I'll be turning in early, since I've got briefs to file in several different courts tomorrow."

What she hadn't said was: *I really do want you to go with me tomorrow, and I know you're afraid I'll change my mind. You're going to bed to escape your worries, but you might not sleep a wink. You'll just turn off the light and try not to think about how rash I can be!*

At that moment a flame was ignited in Zain's heart. *I'm going to take hold of my life without anybody's help. I'm not going to let anybody interfere in my decisions or even listen to anybody's opinion unless I've asked for advice.*

When Zain went to bed, she slept fitfully, dreaming off and on. When she couldn't sleep, she journaled. The strong woman that lived inside her wrote about how happy she was that her father had decided not to go with her to the courtroom. Zain told herself that if she'd known how to go through the divorce procedures on her own, she wouldn't even have let Najati come with her. Several times on the same page she wrote, "I want to take hold of my life. I want to own my own destiny. I don't want to depend on anybody but myself. I want the right to make mistakes the way men in Ziqaq Al Yasmin do, and the right to correct them without everybody else getting all bent out of shape over it." She wrote herself to sleep, her owl cooing in her ear.

The morning of the big day finally arrived. A hard-hearted winter had wounded Damascus with its snows, and in through the window wafted the fragrances of a warm, long-awaited spring.

Despite her restless sleep the night before, Zain was alert and ready to go, like a slave on the day of her release.

One night I was staying late at the library getting ready for final exams. The winter winds were blowing wildly outside, making a sound somewhere between a howl and a scream. I sat down in the only vacant seat at a large table next to the window. As I was studying, a car pulled up outside with its radio blasting. An exquisite, captivating voice crooned, "We'll come back some day to our neighborhood and walk down memory lane! However long we're apart, no matter the distance, we'll be back, the nightingale told me on the morning when we met at the bend." Then all of a sudden, I saw Waseem's face peering in through the window. He was spying on me even though I'd announced that I was leaving him.

He gestured for me to come outside. I was about to turn my back to him and just go on with my work. But then I remembered that my intention wasn't to defy him or provoke him. All I wanted was to divorce him and never see him again as long as I lived. So I got up and left the library for fear that if I didn't, he might come in. I didn't want a repeat of the scandalous, violent behavior he'd exhibited one day when he came to my dad's house shouting, "She's coming back home with me right this minute. Otherwise, I'll force her back, and I'll take a second wife!"

He was waiting for me at the campus gate with a bundle of thunderbolts in his hand. I was relieved, since loud ruckuses don't scare me. What scares me is the sound of silence, and luckily for me, silence was a language he didn't know anything about. He opened the door to a fancy new car. "Get in," he barked. As I got into what felt like my coffin, I didn't say a word, and neither did he. He just got in after me and took off like a madman. He drove us to some dark suburb of Damascus and pulled over in front of a cemetery wall.

"Get out," he commanded. I got out of the car and asked him calmly, "What are we doing here?" Aiming a revolver at me, he pushed me over to the wall as though it were an execution platform and said, "This is the Husni Al Za`im Cemetery. And if you refuse to come back to me, you'll be buried here, too."

I don't know what crazy place it came from, but I heard a voice burst out laughing. "What makes you think you can bring a dead love back to life?" I asked him. "What's past is past, and that's that."

Then he shot at me. I don't know whether he aimed and missed, or whether he'd just meant to scare me into submission. I suspect it was the latter. In any case, his plan failed. I took off running but he didn't try to catch me. And when I flagged down a passing car, he just stood there in a daze—confused and half-terrorized by a woman who was so determined to be rid of him that she'd rather die a real death than endure the figurative death of a marriage devoid of love and respect.

The car stopped.

"What's going on?" asked the driver.

"Sorry," I said. "My car's broken down. Could you take me to the Qasr Al Dhiyafa Hotel, Abu Rummana, Parliament Street, or Baghdad Street?"

"Get in," he said. The woman in the passenger's seat, who appeared to be his wife, looked at me suspiciously.

"What brings you here?" she asked coarsely.

"Well, whatever brought you here!" I retorted.

Her husband laughed, and she shot me a nasty look. I didn't say anything the rest of the way even though the husband probed me for details about my situation. I remembered the guy who had given me a ride to the clinic in the village of Rayhaniya the day my cousin shot me. My cousin had pretended to be shooting at a sparrow. Luckily his hand was shaky, but he did manage to wound me. This was after he killed my owl and left it on my bed as a warning. All this had been his way of punishing me for publishing something I'd written in the Readers' Mail column with my picture beside it. What scandalous behavior!

For a minute there I was afraid the couple might try to kidnap me. So, why not tell them what I'd been doing outside a cemetery in the pitch dark? I mean, people are usually kidnapped because they're rich or influential. But what was there to prevent them from kidnapping me out of curiosity—just to get me to tell them my life story, which was a pretty long one? I was old enough to drive myself by this time, but all that really mattered to me was to drive the car of my life. And that was exactly what I intended to do once we finally had our divorce hearing. It was just that my husband had been trying all the stubborn antics he could think of to keep it from happening.

Realizing she probably hadn't slept well, Zain's father came knocking on her door. When she was ready to leave the house, he said solicitously, "I'll go with you."

"I told you I didn't want you to," she assured him earnestly. "I want to depend on myself and correct my mistakes on my own. Besides, Najati will be waiting for me at the door."

I stood before the judge as my husband stood next to the exit. I approached the bench without feeling or acting the least bit intimidated. My wings were flapping and about to carry me away. The judge, who looked at me with visible hostility, wore the turban of a religious cleric, which took me by surprise. Maybe that's the way judges dress in Islamic courts, and I just hadn't known it. He eyed me with as much appreciation and respect as if I'd been a mosquito on his robe. It reminded me of the fact that when Najati came to pick me up, he'd seemed a bit taken aback to see me leaving the house without a headscarf. Actually, it hadn't even occurred to me to put one on. He seemed equally surprised at my stylish white dress, which looked like a miniature wedding gown of sorts. Although he didn't say anything, I got the feeling he was pleased, maybe because, as my aunt had mentioned once, he was "a Communist." Gee whiz!

"Where is your legal guardian?" the judge asked me.

Najati had instructed me to keep my mmouth shut and let him answer. But the question riled me up so much that I blurted out, "I'm my own legal guardian, and I want a divorce."

"I didn't hear what you said," the judge replied, his voice as frigid as a surgeon's scalpel.

"Your Honor," Najati interjected, "Her father, who is her legal guardian, has given me power of attorney."

As if speaking to me directly would have sullied his tongue, the judge instructed Najati to tell me that I would have to waive all financial demands of my husband should he agree to divorce me.

Turning to look behind me, I looked daggers at my husband as if to say: If you don't, I'll spread secrets about you that you aren't going to like one bit!

"I agree," he declared with the laconic good manners of a gentleman. With a nod to my husband, the judge concluded the matter with a speed that astounded me.

I made no objection when the judge had Najati sign the document before I did, and as I exited the courtroom, I didn't look back. All I wanted was to get out of the building and leave it behind. I'd gone by the Palace of Justice countless times as a girl when my father would take me to visit my aunt in the Halabouni neighborhood behind the Hejaz Station. But now it was associated with a different kind of memory, the kind I didn't care to hold onto.

At the door Najati said to me affectionately, "Congratulations on your divorce. You fought for it with everything you had. Would you like me to take you home?"

"No, thanks," I replied. "I'd like to walk. But thanks again."

I came up to him and was about to plant a kiss on his forehead the way I'd always done when I was a little girl. But he pulled away in embarrassment. Looking uneasily this way and that, he said, "God be with you," and got hurriedly into his car. Then he drove away as though he were fleeing from a woman headed for perdition.

As I crossed the street, I glimpsed the man who'd just divorced me—or, rather, the man I'd just divorced—coming in my direction. It was over. I had a lump in my throat, and an ache in my heart. I was going to miss his uncle the wonderful poet, his parents, his brothers and sisters, his aunts, and his nieces and nephews. But I had to put all that behind me now.

I clicked down the sidewalk in my spiky white high heels. With every step I took, I dug them into the pavement in a declaration of resolve. I kept walking without a glance in his direction. It was over. I passed the Hejaz Station, whose big nonfunctional clock was a telling reminder of the way time in my city had come to a standstill.

After turning a corner and heading down another street, I paused on the bridge that spanned the Barada River, kissed the water with my spirit, and continued toward Uncle Abu Umar's Sweets Shop, which sold hard candies, chocolates and pastries. Whenever my dad and I visited the store when I was little, the shop owner would pick me up and stuff my mouth with candy. When he saw me this time, though, he looked the other way. Had I grown up so much that he didn't recognize me? Or was he angry with me because I'd had the cheek to marry somebody my father didn't approve of?

She passed the Brazil Café on the other side of the street. When she came to The Havana, the aroma of coffee accosted her from a table on the sidewalk. She was in the mood for a cup of coffee, and she had enough money with her to buy one. She quietly took a seat at an unoccupied table. As she sat down, she could have sworn she saw a man at the next table sewing his mouth shut with a needle and thread. Meanwhile, the wall next to her table seemed to be sprouting huge red ears that resembled flesh-eating plants, and that gave off the same fetid odor.

She couldn't help but notice that she was the only woman in the cafe. The waiter came up with a bewildered look on his face. The whole place went quiet. Some of the customers who'd been playing backgammon dropped what they were doing to stare, and Zain held her breath. *They're probably thinking: Who does she think she is? How dare a girl come and sit down in here?*

A few minutes later, who should she see walking toward her table but Ghazwan, who'd been hanging out with some friends there that day. *Oh, God, he's coming this way, and he's looking straight at me!* Hailing her enthusiastically, he said, "Well, hello there! If it isn't the Subki Park girl! It's so good to see you again! I must have missed you when you came back out of the pharmacy that day. Or did you run away from me?"

Zain couldn't help but feel happy to see him standing there with his cheerful face and that gorgeous dimpled chin of his, so deep she was sure she could drown in it. She wished she could tell him everything that had happened to her since the day she'd seen him in Subki Park. But she'd been learning the language of silence. The sight of him put a smile of genuine contentment on her face.

"May I?" he asked with his accustomed gentility as he pulled out a chair.

"Be my guest," she replied.

Without further ado, he asked, "Who are you? What's your name? You look like the budding author Zain Khayyal, whose picture I've been seeing in the newspapers. Is that you?"

"And what difference does it make what my name is?" she asked. "Either way, I'm somebody who wants to take hold of her life and find her wings. And I didn't get those words from some textbook, or from a story you published in *The Critic* magazine!"

He gave her a look that bathed her in affection, but she decided not to believe it, especially when she remembered that she'd gotten divorced less than an hour before.

It's weird. I seem to bump into him whenever I'm at a crossroads in my life. The first time was after my abortion, and now I see him again after my divorce. What's going on? Is he fate in the flesh? Well, whatever he is, I'm not going to fall for him! I'm not going to go plunging to my death in those amorous glances, or lose my head over that sweet, handsome face or those mysterious, grotto-deep eyes. No way. I'm running back to the safety of my papers and pens.

"Would you like another cup of coffee?" he asked. To her consternation, she heard herself say, "Yes, I would!" She didn't approve of this new rebelliousness in her senses, and she was determined to suppress it with the lance of her pen, which could numb her like opium compliments of the poet Coleridge.[5] *Never again am I going to let romantic love debase me or rob me of my sense of direction.*

So, the moment the second cup of coffee arrived, she shot out of her seat.

"Goodbye," she said, and headed for the door without waiting for a reply.

He ran after her while the other customers at The Havana sat transfixed by the peculiar scene.

"What do you say we start over by me inviting you for a cup of coffee at The Brazilia across the street?" Ghazwan suggested.

She wanted desperately to say yes, but didn't dare let herself. *I could easily fall in love with this guy, and I've got to get away from him.* But why should she fall in love with him? All she knew about him was that he was a good-looking Palestinian who'd written wonderful lines that she'd read in a newspaper somewhere. He

---

[5]   The English poet Samuel Coleridge (1772-1834) wrote frankly about taking opium in his poem, "The Lotus Eaters."

was also the super-sensitive type and a bit of a crazy, and they were on the same wavelength. *You crazy woman. You thought the very same things about somebody else once, and today you're secretly celebrating your divorce! Are you looking for more misery? Have you already forgotten how much you went through?*

"No, thank you," she said with all the strength she could muster. "I have to go now." It was as if the voice she spoke with came from somewhere deep inside her, but wasn't really hers. Either that, or she'd turned into a rational, level-headed woman who contemplated both herself and everything around her fairly and impartially, unmoved by the logic of tears or sentimental chatter. *Supposing he is the right man, then he's the right man at the wrong time.*

She felt a headache coming on, and decided to take refuge in an aspirin pill.

"I need to go to the Kaddurah Pharmacy," she said faintly.

"Okay," he agreed. "I'll take you there, even though I know you'll disappear on me again! But I'm going to repeat my request: Will you marry me, little girl whose name I don't know?" *When does he ask me to marry me? Right after I've had an abortion, or right after I've gotten divorced. He really is the master of bad timing!*

Zain burst out laughing. Then, as he and the waiter were settling the tab, she ran out and jumped into the first taxi she could find.

When she got to the house, she didn't find her father. In fact, nobody seemed to be home. Maybe he wanted to avoid a confrontation. The empty house came as a happy relief, since what she needed most right then was a tryst with a blank sheet of paper where she could scribble down mysterious symbols that only she could decipher.

She made her way to her father's pistachio-green library, the room where she had once fused passionately with her then-beloved while everyone else in the house was asleep. This then-beloved was the person she had divorced today with the passion of a bright spring morning, washing her hands of all that was past. Seated at her father's desk with a sweetheart who had never betrayed her—her pen—she fused anew with a blank sheet of paper.

She sat writing reflections that had nothing to do with the details of the day's events or the painful loss of her ex-husband. She wrote instead about the pain of having lost herself, about her human weakness and her mistakes. It was as if she were writing herself back into existence. She whispered to the paper, "Other people are me, too."

Suddenly she heard her father saying, "Where have you been?! I looked for you at the Palace of Justice and all the way back to the house. And I called you after I got back."

"Sorry, Baba!" she said in earnest apology. "My mind was somewhere else."

"Najati told me how you defied the judge."

"Well," she said truthfully, "I didn't mean to. Anyway, that's all in the past now, and I'm trying to make a new start. A chapter of my life has ended, and I don't want to talk about it anymore."

Her father heaved a sigh of relief. He didn't want to reopen old wounds any more than she did.

When Zain went to bed that night and escaped through a hole in her pillow into her secret little world, she was greeted by

Ghazwan's extraordinary face. His eyes radiated affection, sorrow and determination. She thought back on how he had been about to drive her for the second time to the Kaddura Pharmacy to see whether she would run away from him again, and how she'd made her getaway even before he'd expected her to.

***

If it weren't for my poor health, there's no way I'd let my daughters leave the house to work at the brocade shop. People say I've lost my mind, and maybe I have, since I don't remember anything from those years when God punished me for what I did to Hind.

Abdulfattah didn't like the idea of his daughters working in his big Damascene brocade store. There'd been a change in Hamida and Fadila, and it bothered him. They weren't tame anymore the way women are supposed to be. There was something about them now that reminded him of his brother's late wife Hind, who had left behind a demon by the name of Zain. Yet despite his misgivings about his daughters' new role, he'd started to enjoy staying home, a fact he blamed on the medicines his doctor had prescribed. He liked spending his days in the big house in Ziqaq Al Yasmin. He sat cross-legged on a stone bench beneath a dome covered with inscriptions and cornices. The bench was spread with a rug, and his back was supported by cushions along the wall behind him. He loved listening to the murmur of the water as it flowed down from the courtyard's elevated fountain inlaid with marble mosaic. Ensconced there holding his prayer beads, he bathed in the fragrances that wafted from planters filled with white jasmine, honeysuckle and basil. From the time he'd been accused of causing Hind's death, his condition had gone from bad to worse. He'd refused to call a doctor to examine her because that would have meant letting a strange man see her body. As a result, she'd bled to death under the midwife's inadequate care. *I regret that. No, I don't. Yes, I do. No, I don't. Yes, I do. No...*

He hated the sound of the phone ringing, and Fadila wasn't answering it. She was busy getting ready to go to work. So Buran answered instead. Fadila could hear her mother giving some caller an extraordinary welcome, and she knew that slimy Mutaa must be on the line. The conversation went on longer than usual. The mother called Fadila. Then, covering the receiver with her hand she crooned happily, "The signing of the marriage contract is scheduled for Friday, and the wedding will be a week after that at the Orient Palace Hotel. So put on your dancing shoes! It's going to be an amazing wedding, and they're covering the whole thing, even though it's usually the bride's family that pays. Anyway, you talk to him. His mother wants to see you at her house. She's been sick, and Mutaa says she has something she wants to talk to you about."

The mother shoved the receiver into her daughter's hand. As she took it, Fadila felt as though she were holding an adder that was about to bite her. The voice she detested (and which her family adored) came over the line saying, "My mom's sick, so she can't come visit you. But she'd like to talk to you and bless our marriage. I'll pass by your workplace this afternoon and the driver will take us to the house. My mother has something important she wants to tell you about. It concerns me, of course, and I think it has to do with my habits, what foods I like and don't like, that sort of thing. I'm sure you won't mind spending some time with a mother who's been sick, but who's happy to be marrying her son off."

Fadila chafed at the phrase, "marrying her son off." After all, she was a person in her own right, with her own plans, who might not marry him after all. In fact, she'd told Mutaa more than once that she didn't love him and wasn't going to marry him. The first time she'd said it was the day when the families had recited the Fatihah.[6] *As far as she was concerned, they might as well have been reciting it over her grave!* When, later on the same day, she'd told him she was in love with somebody else, it seemed to inflame his love for her like never before. When she told Zain about this, Zain warned her that what had been inflamed wasn't love, but the desire to possess. Zain had gone on to add that women rarely know how to distinguish between these two, and that they pay dearly for it.

After hearing Fadila's declaration, Mutaa had asked her with a mixture of sarcasm and apprehension, "So who is this gentleman you've set your heart on?"

"He's a school teacher, and a poet."

"Ah!" he replied mockingly, "So let him try paying the rent and the water and electricity bills with those marvelous poems of his!" Then, looking at the diamond ring he'd given her, he added, "And let him give you a ring made from the jewels of meter and rhyme!"

---

6   The recitation of the Fatihah, the first sura or chapter of the Qur'an, is done when two families agree that their daughter and son will become engaged to be married. Another occasion on which the Fatihah is recited is when people go to visit the grave of a relative or loved one.

She hadn't answered. She was too overwhelmed. She was stuck between a rock and a hard place—the rock of her family, and the hard place of this allegedly ideal groom.

No sooner had Fadila reached the shop than Mutaa started barraging her with telephone calls. He told her his mother was so sick she might not even live long enough to attend the marriage contract signing ceremony. Fadila didn't remind him that she didn't intend to go through with the ceremony anyway, and that the only reason she was coming was to honor an ailing woman who was hoping to see her son get married.

He showed up in his luxury car and the driver got out to open the door for her, but Mutaa, wanting to make a show of "honoring" her, beat him to it. Climbing into the car like somebody getting into her own coffin, Fadila felt alternately curious and reluctant. In the elderly driver's eyes, she detected a look she didn't know how to interpret. It seemed to convey a mixture of guarded warning, fear, and pity. It was the first time she had ever been inside Mutaa's ornate villa on Qusur Street. With its opulent Western-style décor—from the elevator, to the posh European furniture, to the glistening crystal chandeliers with their dazzling moonlike glow—the place was in stark contrast to the large but modest dwelling in Ziqaq Al Yasmin. He took her coat, and she secured her headscarf around her face and neck. Then, in the monotone of a tourist guide, he launched into a bland description of their surroundings: "This chandelier is from Venice, the wall hanging is a French Aubusson tapestry, the lamps are made from Sèvres and Galéa porcelain, and all of them are from Parisian flea markets. The vase had been stolen from the Schönbrunn Palace in Vienna, but it was so beautiful, my dad couldn't resist buying it. The chairs are Louis XV from *Rue du Faubourg Saint-Honoré*, my dad bought the paintings at an auction, and ..."

Weary of his braggadocio, Fadila broke in petulantly, "But your walls are made of cement, while ours were built from stone like the Umayyad Mosque and the Church of St. Paul. Besides, the pond in your courtyard doesn't have any goldfish in it, and you don't have any jasmine trellises. You also don't have a wall fountain in your bay room ..."

Interrupting her with a raucous laugh, he said, "Don't worry! You'll learn to love my things, and me, too!"

"Maybe," she conceded, her tone still defiant, "but I'll still go on loving the things I love." Then she added curtly, "So, why don't you take me to see your mother. Didn't you say she wanted to speak with me?"

"Oh, of course. I'll even carry you to her!"

With that, he came over to her, his nostrils flaring, his breathing loud and accelerated. Before she knew it, he had picked her up, only to slam her down on the floor. Dazed, she had no idea what was happening. He'd turned into a crazed rhinoceros. He butted her red dress, ripping off its buttons and tearing her underwear. Then he proceeded to bite her and thrust his horn between her breasts. He butted her here, there and everywhere. Then, his horn longer than ever, he rammed her in her feminine part. She cried out in pain. He dug his horn in deeper, as if her cry had sent him into the throes of ecstasy. She tried to resist, but the rhino crouched over her with his tremendous weight, leaving her paralyzed. He pumped his horn in and out, in and out like someone stabbing a body with a knife over and over in the same spot. She screamed in agony, but no sound came out, as he held her mouth shut with his foreleg until she could hardly breathe. As the rhino kept stabbing harder and harder in a frenzy of fiendish pleasure, she suddenly realized she had nothing on but her headscarf.

She heard the excited animal letting out a sound that made her pain all the worse: "Ah… ah… ah!" A few seconds, or minutes, later, she heard Mutaa snarl, "Instead of enjoying my body, you fainted, you bitch. Well, at least I know now that you were a virgin! Don't worry. We'll sign the marriage contract the day after tomorrow. But this is what you get for having the nerve to say you don't want to marry me! I own you now, and I give the orders. After all, nobody else would want you anymore. You've spent the last few months being a spoiled smart-ass and insulting my manhood. So now it's time for you to kiss my feet and beg me to take care of you. And if anybody finds out you're not a virgin, I'll say I don't know anything about this. Maybe it was that worthless sweetheart of yours, the poet and school teacher Najm, who took advantage of you."

"So where's your mother?" Fadila asked, trembling from head to toe. "Didn't you say she wanted to see me?"

"Oh, that!" he sneered. "My mother's in Bloudan getting the house ready! Did you really believe she wanted to talk to you?!"

His words dug deep into her flesh, but even then she didn't comprehend their implications. Her only concern now was to tell Najm what had happened, then go home and take a long, long bath.

Shattered, she went out to the car alone. Mutaa didn't even do her the courtesy of escorting her to the car, much less open the door for her and accompany her back to her house. The driver's face registered no surprise. He seemed to be accustomed to the sight of wretched, weeping women. As for her, she didn't shed a tear. She decided she'd have to stand on her own two feet the way Zain had advised her to do after getting the divorce she was so proud of. She headed home prepared to face her fate alone.

"Could you stop in front of a shop somewhere?" she asked the driver in a tremulous voice. "I need to make a phone call."

"As you wish, Miss," he replied, his solicitous tone betraying a hint of disdain.

The shopkeeper asked her to pay for the phone call beforehand and insisted on dialing the number himself to make sure it wasn't long-distance.

The telephone rang in Najm's house. "Please answer!" she thought desperately. "Please!" Then the miracle happened. She heard his voice over the receiver.

"Hello?" That one word was the lifeline she needed.

"Could you meet me in front of Bakdash Ice Cream Parlor in ten minutes?" she asked hurriedly. "It's urgent."

"I'll be there," he replied.

Fadila asked Mutaa's driver to take her to the entrance of Souq Al Hamidiya. Since the car wouldn't be able to make its way down the crowded, winding roofed-in street, she got out and walked the rest of the way to their meeting place. She could hardly believe how much pain she was in. She felt a warm liquid, which she realized was probably blood, running down her thighs, and that scared her. As she approached the ice cream parlor she could hear the clip-clap, clip-clap of the giant wooden paddles in the vats of ice cream. It was a familiar, nostalgic sound that brought tears to her eyes. *Or am I crying about something else?* When she arrived, Najm stood waiting for her. Without wasting a moment, she proceeded to tell him her story, her face drenched in tears. "Mutaa raped me so that I'd have to go through with the wedding. He said now I'd kiss his feet and beg him to marry me!"

She nearly rested her head on Najm's shoulder. But like him, she knew they were surrounded by prying eyes. Doing his best to calm her, he said simply, "I'll marry you. I love you. I really do. In my eyes you're still pure as pure can be, and he's a filthy whore. The monster." She was amazed to hear him call Mutaa a monster, since that's exactly what he had acted like.

She wished she could give him a big hug, but they were right in the middle of the crowded marketplace, so she contented herself with a look that told him how she felt.

"Our love isn't just a physical thing. What matters most to me is your spirit, your determination, your courage."

Fadila felt a sudden pang of hesitation. She remembered that Najm belonged to a certain political party. So, might he turn her into a martyr for some ideological cause as a way of spiting others? Or did he really love her? For the first time she felt sure that the phrase "happy ending" didn't necessarily apply to real life, and that she might be jumping out of one trap and straight into another.

As she stood miserably under the spray of water in their ancient bathroom, whose shower consisted of an unsightly pipe installed on the wall, she thought to herself. *For all I know, Najm will turn out to be a "monster" too. I've got to be careful about everything. I've got to stand on my own two feet, and not go crying on somebody's shoulder about what somebody else did to me when the person whose shoulder I'm crying on might be even worse that the person who hurt me in the first place. As a girl who's only semi-pretty and semi-successful, I've got to learn to depend on myself. At the same time, I don't want to judge Najm unfairly. I want to give him a chance.*

***

Zain was getting ready for work when the telephone rang. Her grandmother answered. It was one of Zain's maternal aunts in Latakia.

"Did he really divorce you?" she wanted to know.

"I'm the one who divorced him!" Zain corrected her.

"Why?" asked the aunt. "Weren't you madly in love with him? What happened?"

Not knowing where to start, Zain stammered, "Well, because…"

Grandma Hayat snatched the receiver and, covering it with her hand, whispered with an unaccustomed imperiousness, "Just say, 'It wasn't meant to be!'"

Zain, who adored her grandmother, repeated parrot-like, "It wasn't meant to be, Auntie."

After hanging up, Zain asked, "Why do I have to keep saying that even now that the divorce is over? Why don't I just tell people the truth and be done with it?"

Grandma Hayat, whom Zain viewed as a repository of the most ancient and revered wisdom, said, "Listen, sweetie. Nobody's interested in hearing the truth, or what really happened to you. They're not even interested in knowing whether you were right or wrong. All they want is some juicy gossip for next month's reception. If you want everybody in town to know your secrets, just make your aunts or your girlfriends promise not to tell anybody what you've told them. You don't know what people are like, Zain. So don't get mad at me for saying this. Just remember how in love you were with your husband, and how you discovered later that he wasn't what you thought he was."

Zain couldn't object to what her grandmother had said. *All right then, nobody's ever going to know why I divorced him—not even Grandma!*

Once again the telephone started howling for attention. Her grandmother answered while Zain sidled up to her to listen in. This time it was a maternal uncle of Zain's in Latakia. When he asked for Zain, Grandma Hayat fibbed, "She's not home. She's got an exam at the university."

Zain was amazed to see what an accomplished liar her pious grandmother was! But she made no objection.

The uncle shouted over the phone, "Tell Zain her mother Hind was a rose that left a thorn behind!" Then he slammed down the receiver.

Zain was equally amazed to hear her uncle describe her mother as a "rose." She knew how furious he'd been with her when she left her aristocratic father's estate in Latakia, hopped on a bus and took off for Damascus to teach French in the National School, where she lived in a residence hall. According to Zain's father, her mother Hind had left the estate on a white horse, though in her dreams it was always a reddish color. She also dreamed about an owl escorting her mother gently away.

"Oh," Zain said suddenly to her grandmother, "I forgot to tell you: Juhaina's coming for a visit this evening after I get home from work." *Juhaina Asiri! The little girl Hind brought with her from Latakia to help her with the housework when she got married. She and Zain grew up together, and I used to take care of both of them. I do love her, but...*

Grandma Hayat hadn't liked the Asiri family, whose venerable old house in Ziqaq Al Yasmin had been fancier than the Khayyal home. Some people even said it was nicer than Azm Palace. In Hayat's opinion, though, none of the houses around the Umayyad Mosque was anything compared to the mosque itself. She felt guilty about it, but she disliked the Asiri family because one of its members had married the daughter of a Turkish pasha. *He thought he was a big shot after that, and his wife acted as if none of the neighbor ladies was good enough for her.* The women of the neighborhood were in general agreement that when Ido Asiri, the pasha's daughter's only son, fell in love with the Khayyal family's servant girl Juhaina, this was God's way of punishing the Asiri family for being such highfalutin snobs.

When Juhaina told Grandma Hayat that her father-in-law was going to give her and her son ownership of the Asiri family dwelling, Hayat had already heard the news. Wanting to make sure it was true, she cautioned Juhaina, saying, "He can't put more than a third of the property in your name, since he's a Sunni Muslim. Besides, your husband Ido is also an heir to the house, and he's taken another wife."

"That's true," Juhaina admitted. "But since he's making me and my son owners of the house while he's still alive, the Islamic inheritance laws won't apply."

After a brief pause, she added, "Please don't tell the other neighbor ladies. I want to keep it a secret."

"Well," Zain said, laughing, "good luck with that! The news is already out. There's no such thing as a well-kept secret in Ziqaq Al Yasmin."

Zain silently gloated to hear people say with obvious envy, "The Khayyal family's servant girl Juhaina (the 'cow girl,' as her mother-in-law referred to her disparagingly) owns the Asiri mansion now!"

All sorts of explanations were put forward for this bizarre turn of events. Some people said the girl's father-in-law was in love with her. Others concluded that Juhaina must have slipped some sort of amulet inside her father-in-law's pillow, since otherwise, how could he have gone from hating her to being putty in her hands?

After being sold by her father to Zain's mother Hind when she was just nine years old, Juhaina had developed into a woman of strength and stunning beauty. The neighborhood boys who hovered around her said she looked just like Sophia Loren, except that Juhaina was prettier.

One of the lessons Grandma Hayat had drilled into Juhaina after Hind died was, "A secret heard is a secret kept." Unfortunately, there was no such thing as keeping a secret in Ziqaq Al Yasmin.

And of course, she wasn't trying to keep any secrets when she scandalized her husband by doing a lurid dance at his wedding to his second wife! That same night, Juhaina found her father-in-law lying half-buried in a rare crop of snow that had blanketed the entire courtyard. She was stunned at the sight. Here, sprawled helpless before her—alone and at her mercy—was the man who, with his wife "the pasha's daughter," had never once treated her

with the respect she deserved as his daughter-in-law and the
mother of his grandchild.

This was the night when Ido would take his second wife,
the daughter of an influential merchant. Her mother-in-law, the
pasha's daughter, had gone to the wedding out of sheer spite. As
a matter of fact, Juhaina herself had been about to leave for the
wedding, where she planned to perform her special dance of
revenge. She could dance better than Tahiya Kariouka and Samia
Jamal, as all the women in the neighborhood could attest.

But just as she was on her way to crash the wedding party
with her little boy in tow, what should she find but the man who
had made her life hell lying on the courtyard floor and struggling
like a cockroach on its back. She could easily have pretended not
to have seen him and left him for dead. And the thought did
occur to her. It also occurred to her father-in-law as he gazed up
at her in terror. But she didn't have the heart. So she picked him
up and carried him to his bed. She saved his life even though she
expected nothing from him but more insults and abuse the next
morning.

The suffering Zain and Juhaina had been through together
as little girls after Hind's death had forged an unbreakable bond
between them. *I'm proud of having taught her to read and write,
although I did it without really trying. I would just come home
from school and share with her whatever I'd learned that day!*

After Juhaina's visit, Grandma Hayat remarked, "Even the
sweetest cowife is a bitter pill to swallow."

Zain mused, "I remember the night when Juhaina crashed
her husband's wedding party and danced that wild, half-naked
dance of hers—which she could get away with since all the guests

were women, and the groom was her own husband! And after that women in the neighborhood started rebelling against any husband who had the nerve to take a second wife. Have you noticed that?"

"You're right," the grandmother agreed. "They've got a deterrent now, don't they!"

"Juhaina's managed to change a lot of things around here," Zain added.

The little cat slipped onto the old woman's lap. It looked worlds better than it had on the day Zain brought it in from the street. In fact, it was almost beautiful. It was walking better, too. Grandma Hayat began stroking it affectionately, and the cat seemed happy with the pampering it had missed as a kitten.

"By the way," said the old woman, giggling, "He's a he, not a she. I've named him Haroun!"

***

From the time Zain and Waseem were divorced, the phone had been ringing off the hook at her house. People seem to get high off scandals.

Another ring of the phone. Zain jumped up to answer it. *I'm not going to use my grandmother as a shield anymore!* To her pleasant surprise, the voice she heard was that of Dr. Manahili, who had called to congratulate her on a short story of hers that he'd just read in a Lebanese newspaper. Dr. Manahili had given her a second chance at life, and he knew it. And the fact that he knew this made her happy. He was also the only person who had never said a word about her divorce. So now they were friends who shared a secret. He invited her to have coffee with him in the outdoor café at the foot of Mt. Qasioun. "It's to the right of the square where you look out over the orchards."

"Have you invited my dad to come?" she asked.

"Your father hates sitting in coffee shops, even the beautiful ones in Dummar, Hameh, and Al Ayn Al Khadra. When I invite him to spend time with friends in places like that, he always turns me down."

"Okay," Zain replied. "I'll be there after I get off work at five."

As little Haroun rubbed up against Zain's legs, Grandma Hayat picked him up and gave him a kiss. *My goodness, this little guy has gotten better fast! He walks as well as any other cat now, and now that his coat is nice and clean, you can see what a beautiful face he has. He's a real character, and he's developed little rituals of flirtation and playful ways of getting our attention. But he can be fierce, too. When the neighbor lady Fitna tried to pet him the day she'd come to gossip about Zain's divorce, he pulled away from her. If fact, he scratched her and hissed in her face. And I'm sure Zain feels exactly the same. She doesn't want to hear another word about her divorce.*

***

Fadila took another bath the next morning, and this time she nearly scrubbed her skin off. She was desperate to wipe those hoof prints not only off her skin, but out of her memory. The very thought of the bastard made her blood boil, and she wanted the whole world to know how despicable he was. *I'm going to tell my family what that son of a bitch did to me. It may be a heavy price to pay to get rid of him and make my family leave me alone, but they'll hate his guts now. Then they'll have*

to open their eyes to what kind of a "groom" he is. My dad will
be so mad, he'll never let him set foot in this house again. No
more rolling out the red carpet for him as if he were this one-in-
a-million son-in-law that's going to lay him golden eggs! My dad
says things to Mutaa like, "If the ground knew who was walking
on it, it would kiss your feet!" My God! It makes me want to
puke! And my mother fawns all over him, too. But now they'll
despise him the way I do, and they'll kick him out. They're sure to
stop pushing me into marrying a man I don't love. I know I was
right to stand up to that horned monster. When he slapped me
with his foreleg, that hurt even more than when he slammed his
horn into me and stabbed me with it every way he could think
of. I resisted, I screamed, I writhed in pain, and he didn't give a
damn. His slaps left visible marks on my cheeks, and pretty soon
they'll start turning black, blue and all shades of hate. I can hide
the bruises on my body, but not the ones on my face, or on my
soul!

As her parents sat drinking their morning coffee with
cardamom pods and rose water, Fadila came in to join them and,
in as few words as possible, told them about the incident. "After
conning me with a story about how his mom was sick at home
and wanted to talk to me, he raped me."

She expected her father to fly into an indignant rage and call
down curses on Mutaa, his father, and all his ancestors. But in
a surprise that stung as cruelly as her father's slaps, he growled,
"You should thank your lucky stars, girl. He spoke to me just a
little while ago and said he wanted to move up the marriage-
contract signing ceremony to tomorrow. So you'd better keep
your mouth shut and quit acting like a spoiled brat. Be grateful

he's still willing to marry you! Who else do you suppose would want you now, huh?"

Her mouth gaping in shock, Fadila sputtered, "But he's the criminal, and I'm the vict…!"

Before she could finish her sentence, her father started calling her names.

For the first time in her life, Fadila interrupted her father: "Najm's prepared to marry me!" she shouted. "I told him what happened, and he told me to take a bath the way a bride does before her wedding and wash off Mutaa's filth. He really loves me, and I love him, too!"

This time the father blew his top. "Love, love, love!" he shrieked mockingly. "What's this stupid nonsense? Ever since Zain got married against the wishes of her father, who got her the poshest trousseau a girl could wish for, all you girls and women in Ziqaq Al Yasmin can talk about is this idiocy. It's the latest fad. And now Zain's divorced, trashed like a stray dog, and her picture's in newspapers and magazines like some nightclub entertainer. For shame!"

"Love isn't some new fad, Baba. And it isn't shameful, either! Zain gave me an Arabic translation of Shakespeare's *Romeo and Juliet*, but I can tell you for a fact that it wasn't Shakespeare who invented romantic love!"

"What would you know? It's just a new-fangled idea that we've got no need for! And I don't want you seeing that perverted cousin of yours ever again!"

"But no, Baba, you're wrong. What about Qays and Layla? Kuthair and Azzah? They were all Arabs…"

"And infidels! All of them were dirty infidels! Have some shame and be grateful he still wants to marry you! Now, I don't

want to see you again until the night of the ceremony, you hear?
Get out of my face, you filthy good-for-nothing!"

"But I didn't do anything. He raped *me!*"

"You're a dirty slut!"

So she left. It was obvious that trying to talk to her father
was a useless proposition. She would never get any support from
him for the simple reason that she was a female. When a cat had
given birth to a litter of kittens once, he'd thrown the females
against the Damascus wall and killed them, but left the males
alone.

Agitated, Fadila's mother came running after her. She'd
expected her mother to say something in her defence, or at least
to sympathize with her. But before she could say a word, her
mother lit into her, crying, "What happened is all your fault!"
Then, her voice rising, she went on, "You're the one who insists
on wearing tight clothes and short headscarves instead of putting
on the traditional headscarf like the one your grandmother
wears, or a three-layered one like mine! You made him rape you,
since you got him all stirred up! Girls like you should stay in line
so men won't go wild and do the things they do."

As if she hadn't gone on long enough already, the mother
added, "Like your father said: Thank your lucky stars he's going
to cover your shame! So cut out this nonsense about wanting to
marry some poor wretch named Najm that you say you're in love
with. We've had enough of this silly talk about love, sweetheart.
Come on now. Pull yourself together. So Mutaa did what he did
to you. Even so, he's an honorable man, and he's prepared to sign
the marriage contract tomorrow. Luckily for you, he's going to
keep you from being scandalized."

"I don't love him, and I don't want to marry him. He's despicable. And I don't care what you think! I want to marry the person I'm in love with the way Zain did. You can't put a hot coal on my tongue the way mothers used to be able to, and neither can any other mother, even in Ziqaq Al Yasmin. Those days are over."

Fadila looked up and saw the neighbor ladies lining the surrounding rooftops like TV antennas. She knew now that the upcoming reception would be devoted not to gossip about Zain's divorce but, rather, to the story of how Mutaa had moved the wedding date up by a day and a night. *I refuse to go through with this marriage. And if they manage to force me into it, I'll commit suicide.*

"Who can tolerate rebellious women? They should be burned as witches. No woman has been allowed to swerve from the path set out for her by males since ancient times." Fadila reread these lines from an article Zain had written and given her a copy of. She decided to try to see Zain and tell her what had happened. Then again, she didn't want advice. All she wanted was a sympathetic ear.

One cloudy morning, Fadila's sister Hamida announced to her mother, "I'll be late getting back this evening. I've joined the Baath party and they're having a meeting."

Buran wouldn't have dared object to her daughter's involvement in the Baath Party. It was the ruling party, after all, and she didn't want to bring trouble on the residents of Ziqaq Al Yasmin. After their mother left the room, Fadila whispered, "Did you mean what you said, or is that just an excuse for coming back late?"

"I don't know," Hamida replied truthfully. "All I know is that I want to be free like my brother and his friends. And I really am a Baathist, so just let my brother try beating me again! I might join some other party later on, but until then, I'm going to find a way to command enough respect not to get knocked around anymore, at least."

* * *

It upset Juhaina that when she visited the Khayyal home, she hadn't had a chance to be alone with Zain. She wanted to vent to her about the torment she'd been going through every night since her husband took another wife. *For weeks now I've lain in bed every night trembling with rage. Gone are the nights when I tremble with pleasure the way I used to when he was in love with me. He would whisper louder and louder, "Juhaina, Juju, my life… aah!" Now I have to listen to him pounding his new wife in the next room. I hear the same whispers and moans of ecstasy that used to take me so high I'd nearly pass out on my pillow. Well, all that's moved to the pillow in my cowife's room, which is right next to mine. It pains me to think that she actually has a face and a name and that she's a human being like me, but even though it's a big house, I can't avoid passing her in the hallway since our rooms are right next to each other. It's as if he gets double the pleasure if there's a woman in the next room who's hurt by what he's doing and who knows every little touch she's missing. For all I know, he'd invite me into their room to watch if he could, since that would take him even higher! Then, if I pounced on him crazed with lust and jealousy, he'd come again, with two women begging for what his body has to give.*

This situation had changed around a month earlier, when the despised cowife began showing signs of being pregnant. The moans of ecstasy coming through the bedroom wall began giving way to angry shouts. So delighted was she at their misfortune, Juhaina nearly reached orgasm just listening to them have it out in the next room. The louder they yelled, the higher she went. She launched out alone on dark waters in the vessel of pleasure until, reaching the end of the churning rapids, she came tumbling down a waterfall of warm, delicious froth. Then she drifted off as the sound of their bickering rocked her to sleep. She knew her husband hated pregnant women, since she'd experienced it firsthand herself, and he couldn't have cared less about a woman after she'd given birth.

This time the argument was about something really trivial, just like the ones she and he had had before. Specifically, it was about an issue that the unemployed Ido, son of the Ottoman pasha's daughter, deemed of life-and-death importance: the matter of the salt in his food! He started blustering furiously at his new wife for daring to cook rice with just a little salt. She told him she'd done this based on orders from his father and his doctor. His shouts even louder now, he started making fun of the elegant way she had of arranging the dishes on the table.

"Do you think putting the rice in a stupid heart-shaped mold is going to make it taste better?" he asked contemptuously.

When Najwa suggested that he sprinkle more salt on his own plate if he wanted to, he launched into a tirade about how salting food after it's cooked isn't the same as salting it while it's still in the pot. *This was the first time I'd ever called my cowife by her name, even in my thoughts.*

The next morning as each of the two wives was making her own coffee in the kitchen, the same stupid argument broke out again. Hearing it being repeated all over again made Juhaina sick to her stomach. She was fed up with the spoiled brat who kept a steady stream of idiotic complaints going into Najwa's ear.

"You lazy bitch, you should cook in two separate pots, one with salt in it for me, and the other without salt for my dad!"

"I can't," she told him, maintaining her composure. "I'm tired and I'm having cravings."

Lighting into her like a crazed bull, he struck her suddenly on the face, sending her reeling to the floor. When she tried to get up, she lost her balance and fell again. Setting aside the food she was preparing for her little boy and the coffee she was making for herself, Juhaina went over to Najwa, held out her hand to her, and lifted her off the floor. Even though short-statured Najwa had taken cover behind Juhaina, Ido managed to hit her a second time. When he moved in for a third blow, Juhaina—both taller and stronger than he was—grabbed him by the arm and hissed, "If you touch her one more time, I'll break your hand. And you know I'll do what I say. Aren't you ashamed of yourself, you pitiful little monster?!"

And he knew she meant business. Once he'd hit Juhaina in the face the way he had Najwa, and like Najwa, she'd been sent sprawling to the floor. But Juhaina had gotten up and hit him back as hard as he'd hit her, and then *he* ended up on the floor. That was when he realized for the first time that her body didn't exist solely for his enjoyment. She'd dealt him an excruciating blow, and from that day on he hated and feared her. Maybe that was why, when he took another wife, he made sure she was shorter than Juhaina and less capable of defending herself. Striking a woman was, after all, part of the fun. He liked feeling he was stronger than she was and that, unlike his henpecked father, he was the one in control. He'd been confident when Juhaina first came along that he could lord it over her to his heart's content. But then she'd stood up to him! Not only that, but she'd started coming to her cowife's defense, and become the owner of the house. God, he hated women!

"Have you lost your mind?" he hissed back. "Have you forgotten the agonized dance you did at her wedding? How can you defend your enemy?"

"It seems my enemy isn't Najwa, or your father, or even your mother," replied Juhaina evenly. "It's you! So why don't you go find yourself a job and leave us alone? Then go marry a third wife, but don't bring her to this house. I've got your number now, and so does poor Najwa."

And with that, Juhaina carried her weeping cowife to the bathroom and washed her face for her, saying, "If he hits you again, I'll break his arm off and make him pick it up himself! If you need anything, I'm right in the next room."

* * *

After Grandma Hayat had updated Zain on Juhaina's and Najwa's news, she remarked, "As I've said before, there's no such thing as a secret around here! The women in the neighborhood are having the time of their lives gossiping about how both Ido Asiri's wives have stopped sleeping with him. Rumor has it that they're lovers now."

Thus far the hearsay hadn't drawn any connection between Ido and the new maid, who looked to be around sixty years old, and who'd been hired by his mother so she wouldn't have to see her two daughters-in-law as they drank coffee together and spent their evenings talking. She couldn't force them out now that her scoundrel of a husband had given the house to the "country bumpkin servant girl," as she referred to Juhaina whenever she was forced to mention her.

* * *

Mutaa actually had the nerve to call me. As if I were his servant now that he'd raped me, he announced, "We've moved the marriage-contract signing ceremony up to tomorrow."

He admitted what he'd done, but instead of being remorseful, he said nonchalantly, "Sorry, the devil must have gotten into me. But I haven't changed my mind about wanting to marry you!" *The arrogant bastard!*

Before Fadila could open her mouth to object, he added, "Your family supports my decision. In fact, they're really happy about it."

In other words, my family's rewarding him for his crime. No way will I ever marry somebody who stoops to such crooked means of getting what he wants, much less a man who's capable of rape!

An aunt of Fadila's passed by the brocade shop, ostensibly to buy a gift. But the minute other people were out of ear range, she said viciously, "What happened is all your fault, you know! No girl with an ounce of self-respect would go to her fiancé's house before they've signed the marriage contract!"

"But he told me his mother was sick at home and wanted to talk to me about something in private!" Fadila shot back. "How was I supposed to say no to a request from somebody he claimed was on her death bed? Besides, my mother had agreed to it!"

"Well, then," the aunt retorted primly, "you should have taken your mother, grandmother or me along. Most of the neighbors agree with me, by the way. Besides, the way you dress is provocative. Do you see now why we're always telling you to wear the traditional veil or a three-layered scarf?"

"But I do wear a headscarf, and nothing shows but my face!"

"That's the bare minimum, my dear, and it shows how weak your faith is. If you don't want to be a source of temptation, you've got to cover yourself up completely."

Temptation! Oh, yeah, that! Her aunt's sermon faded out as Fadila thought back on the temptation she'd experienced one day with Najm. She'd told her parents she was going somewhere with Zain, but went instead with Najm to an orchard belonging to a friend of his in Hameh on the Barada River. She watched him swim at a spot where the river broadens as it runs through a lush valley. When he got out of the water, his luscious body glistening in the sunlight, a rush of desire shot through her pores, and she would have done anything to kiss him all over, then fuse with him—in the water, in the grass, it didn't matter. As she dried him with a towel, she ran her fingers over his shoulders, and nearly gave in to her to her urges. A shudder went through him that awakened even more of her suppressed innocent desires. Then suddenly he said, "Will you marry me? I love you, and I want you!"

So no, there was no way she would ever marry that rhino Mutaa. But she was prepared to take her chances with Najm.

***

The day the marriage contract was to be signed, Abdulfattah woke up counting the hours till his damaged honor could be repaired, however partially. He'd decided that unless Mutaa did what he had promised, he would kill his daughter.

"Get her up," he instructed his wife. "It's ten-thirty in the morning."

Buran went to Fadila's room, but didn't find her. It occurred to her that Fadila might have gone to work early to get away from the house. Even so, she felt a pang of motherly concern. *Where could she be? Virgin or not, she's still my daughter!* She called the shop. Fadila hadn't come in. Then she put in calls to family, friends, and acquaintances, with Zain at the top of the list. Nobody had seen her, and she'd said nothing to anybody about where she'd gone. When Mutaa arrived that evening with the sheikh who'd be officiating at the ceremony, they told him Fadila had disappeared, and said they'd been too embarrassed to notify the police. Mutaa called a man he addressed as "Lieutenant Naji," asking him to issue instructions not to allow so-and-so out of the country by land, sea or air.

"Oh, and regarding our appointment this evening," he added, "can we postpone it till tomorrow?"

By this time Fadila and Najm had reached Beirut with the help of an official in the border town of Jdaidet Yabous. They'd decided to get married there and send a copy of the marriage certificate to her family. She telephoned Zain, who cried, "Where are you, girl?! The whole neighborhood's been looking for you! And maybe the police, too."

"I'm in Beirut with Najm," Fadila assured her. "We'll make our marriage official tomorrow morning, and I'll send my family a copy of the papers with a driver who works for 'Taxi Al Alamayn.'"

"I can't call them, Fadila. You'll have to do that yourself. They hate me enough around here already as it is. In any case, don't call them till after you're officially married. Let them worry about you for a while. Maybe that way they'll remember that you're a human being, and that they might have loved you once upon a time, at least when you were little."

"Najm would like to speak with you."

"Hi, Najm, and congratulations to the two of you. Don't forget that Fadila might have gotten pregnant from what happened the other day. It wasn't her fault, of course. But I didn't want to remind her of it."

"Any child she carries will be mine. All that matters to me is for us to be together."

After they hung up, Zain sat motionless for a while, as if some sorcery had turned her to stone.

For some reason I feel guilty toward Fadila. But why should I? I've never asked anybody to follow my example. We should all do what we think is right and then take responsibility for it. Love is a trek over a tightrope stretched between two stars, and without a safety net. Some people are prepared to take the risk, and some aren't. I personally thought it was worth it. So I tried, and I fell off the rope. I'm only human. But I'm not going to let anyone rob me of my freedom or my right to make mistakes. Love is a gamble, and you can't buy an insurance policy against failure. I'm wounded and let down, but I'm working myself out of it.

On the other hand, Fadila and I have been friends ever since we were little, and I don't want her to go through what I did. I have this feeling of foreboding hanging over me. I'd better do some writing. I see the lives of people I've known—Fadila, Juhaina,

Najwa, Hamida, Fayha—flowing out through the ink in my pen, and I create a world of my own.

As if he picked up on Zain's sadness and confusion, little Haroun jumped into her lap and tried to console her.

I get discombobulated when Juhaina consults me about things and pours her tears onto my writing table. I get the same way when my cousin wants me to tell her which "love lottery" ticket to buy. In fact, I'm discombobulated by everybody who asks for my advice. They don't realize I'm confused myself. On the other hand, their coming to me this way makes my pen happy, and I take refuge in blank sheets of paper. I have to, since I encounter so much hatred in people around me. I struggle with their rejection of me and my passion for freedom. But more than anything else, I struggle with my own mistakes.

Her grandmother's voice jarred her out of her reverie.

"I heard the phone ring," she said, "but I was stirring the yoghurt sauce for the stuffed squash, and I didn't dare leave it for fear it would curdle. Who was it?"

"Oh," Zain replied quickly, "It was a wrong number." Then she whispered to herself, "Your secret is safe with me."

***

Zain opened her eyes one morning with a dream still fresh in her mind, and it got her to wondering. *Why do men cheat? Or, more to the point: Why would a man cheat on a woman he was once so madly in love with that he fought for the chance to marry her? Why is it that once the honeymoon's over, a man goes looking for honey in some other tree? And further, why does he do it knowing full well that his wife will find him out no matter how hard he*

*tries to hide it? There was a time when he couldn't keep his eyes
and hands off her, when a mere brush of her finger would catapult
him to the heights of arousal. Yet despite this, a man might even
betray the woman he loves with a stranger that Fate happens to
throw in his path. So, is there some extraordinary pleasure like
what I experienced in my dream last night, and which I never had
in my marriage? I mean, the kind of pleasure you might have with
somebody you don't even know? If so, then why don't I, or other
women who've written before me, have the guts to give it a try,
whether we do it just so that we can write about it, or whether for
the sheer enjoyment of it—the way men do—without apology, and
without hiding behind the excuse of art or literature?*

Her thoughts were interrupted by the importunate cries of
the telephone. It was her journalist friend Mazen, who wanted to
do a full-page interview with her for his newspaper. She couldn't
really say no, since he had supported her in the past without
flirting with her a single time! Out of politeness, she promised to
come see him once she'd finished her work at the library. Some
people claimed that she had only succeeded because her father
was a well-known lawyer who could pull the right strings for her.
*I don't give a damn about gossip anymore. I'm just going to be
what I am, and that's that.* Looking at herself in the mirror, she
whispered, "Good morning, little owl that doesn't hurt anybody
unless they hurt you!"

Zain's lovely companion sat perched in the window, her
image reflected in Zain's mirror. Every day the bird would appear
in a new incarnation. One day her feathers would be pure white,
other days adorned with brown stripes or forest-green spots.
Zain knew her owl didn't wear masks. She was just moody,

and every mood came with its own color scheme. Sometimes she would alight on the window sill bleeding and moaning, and Zain would let her carry on with her rituals of mourning. Zain understood that like her, there was nothing anybody could do for her little owl, and she needed the freedom to carry on alone. Zain talked to her owl looking straight into the mirror, knowing that if she turned to look back, she would disappear.

After the interview Mazen escorted Zain outside. When they got to the sidewalk, they ran into a towering, extremely good-looking young man. He and Mazen exchanged a hug, and Mazen said to him, "Let me introduce you to Zain, a well-known writer." Turning to Zain, he added, "Zain, meet Amer the poet. He looks like a wrestler, but he's actually quite a gentle soul!"

As she shook Amer's hand, she shuddered as if she'd just wrapped him in a passionate embrace.

"Where's your car?" Mazen asked her.

"I haven't bought one yet!" she said.

Hearing this, Amer offered her a ride. Mazen was about to object when, to his amazement, Zain replied lightly, "Thanks! I'd appreciate that!"

She and Amer got into his car and drove off. Mazen's jaw dropped in amazement. As he stood on the sidewalk watching them disappear into the distance, he thought: Damn it all! I'd been dying to offer her a ride. So why didn't I have the guts to do it?

His voice dripping with desire as he took her in from head to toe, his eyes lingering on certain curves along the way, Amer said, "You're invited for a cup of green tea in my humble basement apartment in Al Rawda. I got a bag of it this morning from a Chinese friend of mine."

From a Chinese friend? Or from the corner grocery store? What difference does it make? She declined at first, even though she was dying for an adventure. *That dream is still tugging at me. Are there situations of raw attraction—the way things were in the wild before language was invented—where the body is entitled to pleasures all its own? Can the prey really be the hunter sometimes? If so, then the trick is to give the hunter the illusion that he's the one doing the catching. Then, while he's enjoying his catch, the prey gets a double enjoyment: the pleasure of the encounter, and the pleasure of the game. Am I writing in my head now, or is this really happening? And will I be able to tell the two apart from now on?*

Zain felt herself setting foot on an unknown continent, led on by her craving for experimentation and discovery. But she figured she must just be writing in her head.

"Come on," he urged. "You've got to try some green tea at my house!"

So, instead of insisting that he take her straight home, Zain relented and accepted his invitation. After he'd pulled up outside his apartment building, he reached for her hand. She didn't resist, or even hesitate. On the contrary, no sooner had he closed the door behind them than she surprised him by planting a feverish kiss on his lips. He picked her up the way one picks up a tiny doll. She wrapped her legs around his massive body and squeezed with all her might as though she wanted to merge with him. Then, without a word of introduction, chatter, or promise, they fell together onto the entranceway floor. Lightning struck with its magic wand, and before she knew it, they were both naked. She nudged him away from her slightly so that she could contemplate his body, which was reminiscent of a statue of a beautiful Greek god that had suddenly come to life. As she did so, he fell upon her with kisses, embraces, and sniffs, and she returned the favor in utter, earnest, mad surrender. Slowly but insistently, his boat entered the coral grotto, the waters alternately frothing up about it and gushing out of the mouth of the cave. She heard what sounded like sighs, moans and gasps coming out of her. Only then did she realize that she'd never really known ecstasy before. As the boat reached the grotto's inner sanctum amid flashes of lightning and peals of thunder coming in rapid succession, she saw Ghazwan's face, and her soundless whispering of his name sent the cave walls crashing down.

With his name still on her lips, she went soaring through space astride a star. She wished she could hear Ghazwan's voice whispering her name in turn. But what she heard instead was the voice of her father calling, "Lunch time! The food's going to get cold while you sit in there scribbling!"

She heard the flip of a light switch, and the green-hued library was bathed in the bright glow of the chandelier.

"You always write under the patch of light from the little desk lamp," her father remarked with concern. "That can't be good for your eyes!"

Zain couldn't tell her dad, "Don't talk to me when you see me busy writing! Don't even come near me!" *When I write, I turn into a crazy owl flying through a dark enchanted forest. My talons tear at the blank page, reopening the wounds of what was and was not.*

Just then Grandma Hayat followed her father into the library saying, "The gas canister ran out before I'd finished frying the bread for the fattat al-makdus. Could you hook a new one up for me?"

Bless you, Grandma!

"Sure," he said to his mother. "So, then," he said to Zain apologetically, "we'll be eating in another ten minutes. Sorry about that!"

"No problem, dad," she replied affectionately, "I'll be right there!"

However, she couldn't tear herself away from the desk, as there were several voices coming simultaneously out of her heart and her pen.

A voice said accusingly, "Ghazwan proposed to you without even knowing your name, and even though you were weak, sick, wounded and helpless, but you ran away and left him stranded in front of the Kaddura Pharmacy, whereas all Amer offered you was a cup of green tea, and you ravished him like a sex-starved maniac! What's wrong with you, anyway?"

Then came a terrified voice from somewhere inside her: "I did no such thing! I woke up this morning, went to the library, did an interview with my friend Mazen, and came home again. A friend of his gave me a ride home, and then I sat down to write. So what's this trial all about?"

"Liar," countered the accusing voice. "Before you sat down here to write, you were setting fire to Amer's cold tile floor."

"I did no such thing. I'm just writing something out of my head! But now I can forgive men for their infidelities, provided that they acknowledge women's right to cheat on them too."

"Yeah, right!" came the accuser's mocking riposte. "Everything you just wrote about, you'd already done. First you went to Amer's cave, and then you came running back to purge yourself at this desk. You think you can exonerate yourself on the pretext that you're a writer, and that you make no distinction between your actions and those of your characters."

"Hurry up, girl. The food's gotten cold!"

And Zain sprinted to the kitchen.

***

A few days later Zain passed by Mazen's office to look over his transcript of their interview before it went to press. As she was about to leave, she noticed that he was wearing a black necktie. When she asked him about it, he said, "You remember Amer, the poet that gave you a ride home after our interview the other day?"

"Of course."

"Well, I'm going to his funeral. He died in a terrible accident on the Aleppo highway. He was a reckless poet. Anyway, do you need a ride home?"

"No, but thank you," Zain replied, wincing at the painful news. *Do you suppose Amer told him what happened between us that day?*

Instead of walking straight home, she took a long detour. *So, it's Lord Death again. He's been my arch enemy ever since I lost my mother. I lay down next to her in her coffin and tried to wake her up, but it didn't work. Now here I am immersed in life, drinking it in with a vengeance without thinking about the fact that I'm really just heading for my own death. When people we know die, we grieve not just because we've lost them, but because we're afraid of losing our own lives.*

When Zain arrived at the house, dark clouds were gathering in her heart.

To her delight, however, she found Juhaina visiting her grandmother. She concluded from the way the two women went quiet when she walked in that they'd been discussing matters of an intimate nature. Might Juhaina have admitted to her relationship with Najwa now that the whole neighborhood was abuzz with the story? It was obvious that she hadn't, since her grandmother appeared relaxed, with Haroun in her lap. Zain greeted Juhaina with a kiss and sat down to join them.

I really don't care what Juhaina's done. Who am I to judge her? The earliest image I have of her goes back to our summer vacation at my dad's farm in Rayhaniya. I was a little girl at the time, and I poked at a beehive with a stick. All I'd really wanted to do was find out what was inside it. In any case, I was attacked by a swarm of bees and went running for cover to Juhaina, who hid me under her long skirt and took the bees' stings for me. That's the kind of person I've always thought of Juhaina as being. I suspect there really is some sort of romantic connection between her and her cowife, but that's her business. Besides, I'll never forget how she saved the life of a man who had never shown her a whit of appreciation or respect. He'd never called her anything but "that country bumpkin servant girl that used to tend the cows." But in spite of it all, she picked him up and carried him to his bed instead of leaving him to die of the cold. Whatever she's doing and whatever people say about her, that's the Juhaina I've always held in my heart.

Picking up on Zain's positive, endearing vibes, Haroun jumped into her lap.

Chapter Five

Zain stood on the porch of her father's house in Sahat Al Midfaa, gazing out at Abu Rummana Street and the trees in the yard. *The voice inside leads me to write about freedom, but what kind of sense does that make if I don't even support myself? I preach freedom, I demand equality, and I claim in newspaper columns to be the spokesperson for liberated girls, yet the whole time I'm being supported financially either by my father or my husband. Oh, and I think of myself as "famous," too. Well, as long as I'm dependent on a man for my support, I'm a pitiful mess!*

The voice of the woman who'd taken up residence in Zain's mind, and who wielded a pen as though it were a rifle, had started to become part of her now. The voice had grown louder and louder since Zain had gone alone to get an abortion, alone to her divorce hearing, and alone to sit for the university exams that she'd barely had time to study for. She adored the books she was reading for her English and World Literature classes, and she adored her professors too—Dr. Varma from India, Dr. Mayan, also from India but less literarily radical than his Indian colleague, Dr. Gilders from the US, and Dr. Musa from Palestine. But her personal life had been wearing her down.

One morning she took out the raincoat her father had given her. It was reversible—black if you wore it one way, and pink if you wore it the other way. Turning the coat pink-side-out, Zain announced to the woman who lived inside her, "I'm going to look for a second job, and I'm going to help my dad pay the household expenses!"

***

She started her search at the school where her mother had taught, and which was bound to her family by ties of friendship. The people who ran the school had an uncle who had volunteered in the Rescue Army that had fought for Palestine in 1948 under the command of Fawzi Al Qawuqji. He had died in the arms of Zain's maternal uncle, who, as she learned from her father when she told him she wanted to apply for a job at the school, had worked as a volunteer physician for the Rescue Army.

She was received at the school by Irfan, the young new principal who had returned from France with a Ph.D. in Engineering. She remembered Irfan's father who, when she had walked one day with her father from Bloudan to Zabadani, had scolded her for wanting to marry somebody she was in love with. He had said to her, "If you go on trying things that haven't worked for other people, you're not thinking right!" He'd been right, as had her father. But that was in the past now. It was over and done with. Besides, she'd been a hard-headed teenager at the time, and as far as she was concerned, she was right and the whole world was wrong! The things some of her girlfriends were saying about her were completely off the mark, so she figured everybody else who criticized her must be wrong, too. She realized now, of course, that what people say can be right sometimes.

Dr. Irfan, who had heard a lot of things about Zain that would have gone against the grain of a traditionally-minded Damascene, said to her, "I see that you'll be getting your Bachelors Degree in English and World Literature, and that you're applying to teach English to elementary students. So actually, this job would be beneath your level. You're overqualified for it."

The woman inside her, who didn't take well to people who say one thing and mean another, whispered, *He's blowing you off politely, the old-fashioned Damascus way. But he's still blowing you off! He used to play with me when I was a little girl. I was five and he was ten, and he'd push me around in a pretty little red car my mother had brought me from Paris since they didn't have that sort of thing in Damascus. I'm sure he hasn't forgotten any of that. Yet he's rejecting me. I've got to quit being stupid and naïve and learn the law of life: everything changes. The friend of the past might be the enemy of the future. Feelings slip and slide like mercury, and worldly interests rule the day. So I need to be careful. I learned a lesson in being careful when I was ten years old. My aunt had slipped a thermometer into my mouth, and I sneaked it into the bathroom and broke it open to get at the mercury inside. I tried to get hold of it, but it kept eluding my grasp. Little did I know at the time that it was poisonous! Stupid kid that I was, I wanted to see what it tasted like! So it was to my benefit that I couldn't get hold of it! Likewise, it might be to my benefit today that Dr. Irfan doesn't want me to teach in his school. The woman inside me added, **The things you write shake people up, scare them. It isn't that they hate you. In fact, what you say arouses their curiosity, and they may even admire you for it. But they don't want you in their lives! Don't give up, though. Remember that**

*women are more likely to sympathize with what some people
around here refer to as your "craziness." So why don't you apply
at the Dawhat Al Fikr School?*

* * *

One morning Zain caught sight of a rainbow. She walked toward
it, and it led her to the Dawhat Al Fikr School. The school's
founder and principal was a dignified woman by the name of
Adela whose eyes were ringed by dark halos like the moon on
a cloudy night. To Zain's amazement, Madame Adela welcomed
her warmly. Her voice tinged with enthusiasm, she told Zain she'd
been a friend of her mother Hind, and that she was proud of the
things Zain was publishing in the newspapers. That night Zain
announced to her father that she had found a job as a twelfth-
grade English teacher.

Zain was still a university student, and high school girls often
had to repeat a grade or two, since they figured there was no use
wasting their time studying if they'd just end up spending their
days in a kitchen once they were married. Consequently, most of
her students were either her age or older.

When Zain gave her first lesson, she discovered that a girl
in the class had been one of her ex-husband's mistresses. To
her surprise, Zain found herself able to relate to the girl, whose
name was Amal, with complete neutrality. She knew then that
she was over her husband once and for all. This discovery came
as a happy relief to her, and she helped and encouraged Amal
just as she did all the other girls in her class. Amal for her part
adored Zain, perhaps even more than she'd adored Zain's ex
at one time. Zain would never have dreamed of such a thing,

of course. What she didn't know was that Amal had suffered badly on account of the man who had once been her teacher's husband although, being Zain's student, she never dared talk to her about him.

***

Zain happily bought a used car from a neighbor, who said he was only selling it so that he could buy one big enough to hold his growing family. It wasn't long, though, before Zain realized that the car was a lemon. She also discovered that the neighbor who had sold it to her didn't have any kids, and that he wasn't even married! She'd been excited at the thought of being able to drive herself places, and of going all alone to Sahat Al Muhajirin to watch the sun set in a golden glow over the domes of her city's mosques and churches.

By the time she realized that her newly acquired vehicle was nothing but a rattle-trap, she'd already made a hefty down-payment with an agreement to pay the rest out of her salary in monthly installments. She was even told it needed an operation people referred to as *khart al-mutur*, which she'd never heard of. After inquiring of people who knew more about cars than she did, she found out from her neighbor Ammo Marwan that it meant replacing the engine! According to Ammo Marwan, she would have to send the car with her father's driver to a place called Ziqaq Al Jinn, or "Goblins' Alley," the neighborhood behind the fire station where all the car repair shops were. Goblins' Alley? She liked the name. As far as she was concerned, Damascus itself was nothing but a goblins' alley with a refined veneer.

When Zain told her father what had happened, he whispered to her, "I knew you'd been taken for a ride when you bought that piece of junk! But I wanted you to learn from the experience." He tactfully refrained from adding "the way you had to learn from your failed marriage!"

Chuckling, he continued, "From now on be careful not to buy things you don't know anything about! And now, go ahead and correct your mistake."

Zain loved the saying, "correct your mistake." She'd grown up on it, and it was what she'd been acting on when she went through with her divorce, whose repercussions had been felt throughout their social circles. "Correct your mistake." She'd decided to make it her personal motto.

Her father went on, "The neighbor's son got rid of his old clunker at your expense, and now you're putting your own time and money into a repair operation that might work, and might not. Anyway, you're an expert now on *khart al-mutur*!" *Okay. So I made another mistake, but it's minor compared to the earlier one, and I'll correct this one, too.*

"But don't worry," her father added, "I'll have my driver take care of it."

Without a word, Zain made up her mind to take care of it herself. To do that, she'd have to find her way to Ziqaq Al Jinn. The first thing she wanted to do was learn how to change a flat tire. Her father thought to himself: If I know Zain, she won't be intimidated by a name like Ziqaq Al Jinn. In fact, she's probably all pumped up now over the idea of going to some part of Damascus she's never seen before. That girl's so determined to assert her autonomy, she'd be prepared to do it even in hell—or especially in hell! She's the new, revised edition of her mother, written in boldface type that nearly punctures the paper and sets it on fire!

***

The minute I got to Goblins' Alley in my little blue car, I knew where it had gotten its name. It's a place where the clanging of hammers against the bare bodies of weary, dilapidated automobiles mingles with the hissing of blow torches and gruff voices, where most faces are blackened with car grease, and where the brawny arms on display weren't chiseled by playing golf, swinging a tennis racket, or swimming laps at some upscale sports club, but by grueling labor day in and day out.

Zain didn't feel the slightest bit awkward or intimidated in this so-called Goblins' Alley. On the contrary, she felt right at home. Unlike the mercurial Jasmine Alley, where people's lips dripped honey one day and poison the next, this was a place where the facts were bare and out in the open. Zain had heard that Abu Kaoud lived in the poorer section of Ziqaq Al Jinn, or, as her Aunt Buran termed it, "the butt-end of the neighborhood," so she headed in that direction. Walking up to a mechanic whose face was smeared with grime, she asked, "Where can I find Abu Kaoud? Ammo Marwan, a neighbor of ours, told me he was the person to fix my car."

Once he'd recovered from the shock of seeing a young woman who'd dared bring her car to Ziqaq Al Yasmin without a legal guardian or even a little brother, Zain went on to explain that she wanted to get her engine replaced. But before that, she wanted to learn how to change a flat tire. *I'm grateful to my ex-husband for at least teaching me to drive. Thanks to his lessons, I passed the road test without any problem.*

It wasn't long before Zain noticed she was the only woman in the entire neighborhood, which wasn't actually a neighborhood so much as a series of open spaces dotted with tired-looking cars, every one of which was the source of a huge racket. *Maybe it's the sound of all that old, worn-out iron moaning and groaning.* Before long, more workers had gathered around her with curious stares. But she didn't feel afraid. On the contrary, they gave her a feeling of camaraderie. *After getting married I worked my tail off just the way they're doing, whether it was studying, doing my job at the library, doing housework, or keeping up appearances at bourgeois social gatherings. I'd have to go to fancy parties wearing a shoulderless, low-cut brocade dress with a gold filigree shawl over it to hide how thin I'd become, stud my hair with diamonds and have it done in a Farah Diba hairstyle,[7] and put on pointed high heels I could hardly stand up in, much less walk in. On top of that, I'd have to lie to anybody who asked how old I was, adding a few years to my age so that they wouldn't say, "Who's that little girl playing dress-up?" But here in Ziqaq Al Jinn, people don't wear masks.*

Zain got a lesson in how to loosen the nuts on the hubcap of the flat tire, jack up the car, take off the flat and put on the spare. She also learned how to change the oil and the sparkplugs. The scene was a source of amusement to the men who managed to slip away from their work stations to come see this high-society girl who was silly enough to want to learn her driver's profession.

---

[7]   A hairstyle modeled on that of Farah Diba Pahlavi, Empress of Iran and wife of Shah Reza Pahlavi, became widely popular in the early 1960's.

When Zain was ready to leave, Abu Kaoud insisted on giving her a ride home. Thinking that she still lived in Ziqaq Al Yasmin, he drove her to the entrance of Souq Al Hamidiya. Zain didn't say anything. She welcomed the chance to go walking down the streets of Damascus, the city she loved and that had given her so much strength. Before dropping her off, Abu Kaoud admonished, "Don't come to get the car, child. I'll deliver it to the door of your father's office."

"But why?" she asked him, surprised.

He didn't reply at first, but just smiled. "Let's put it this way," he said after a pause. "Ziqaq Al Jinn is no place for you!"

"Thanks, Abu Kaoud," she said in farewell. She'd been about to say, "That's not true. It's just the place for me, and for any other citizen!" but thought better of it.

"By the way," he added, "You were planning to drive it to Beirut, right? Well, you shouldn't try that, Miss Zain. After you put a new engine in a car, it needs some time to recuperate, just like people do after they've been sick. So you'll have to go easy on it for a while."

"I see," she said. "So for how many kilometers do I need to 'spoil' it?"

But he drove off without answering. Her question had been drowned out by the honking of the driver behind him.

Once I've gotten the engine replaced, I'll sell the car and buy another one. "There's plenty more fish in the sea!" as my favorite aunt in Homs always used to tell me.

Zain walked from the entrance of Souq Al Hamidiya to the Hejaz Station, and from there to the Barada River, where she paused on the bridge. Next to Sahat Al Muhajirin, it was her favorite spot. It surprised her that Abu Kaoud hadn't heard the news of her moving from Ziqaq Al Yasmin to Sahat Al Midfaa. *I guess working-class folks aren't that interested in other people's gossip.*

No sooner had she taken a few steps than she glimpsed the face of a young man who seemed to have emerged from the land of legend and myth. He was getting out of a dilapidated, antique-looking car that looked as though it had come straight from Ziqaq Al Jinn. She recognized it as the face of Ghazwan— Ghazwan, whose name she had repeated soundlessly over and over to herself during her adventure with the late Amer!

"Oh!" he exclaimed brightly when he saw her, "You're the Subki Park and Havana girl! Do you remember me?"

She couldn't have forgotten him if she'd tried! Nor would she have wanted to forget that most endearing Palestinian face of all time.

"The first time I met you was in Subki Park. Do you remember?"

"No."

"Man, are you a bad liar! You were like a little sparrow with a broken wing. Then I saw you again at the Havana Café, where women never go! You were sitting there relishing your coffee and spreading your wings like nobody's business. I saw them sprouting with my own two eyes. And then today I saw you in Ziqaq Al Jinn—another place where women never go! I watched you from a distance, and you were surrounded by male goblins. You gave Abu Sitam a warm handshake, and when I saw you leaving with Abu Kaoud, I followed you. So who are you, you little pixie!?"

With a calmness that belied the intoxication she felt when she was near him, she said, "I'm a Syrian citizen. And now, would you be so kind as to take me to Kaddura Pharmacy?"

"So that you can disappear again? Well, I'll do whatever you ask. I know now, by the way, that Kaddura Pharmacy has a back door that opens onto the alley, and that you'll make your getaway through there. The second time we met I asked you if you had a sweetheart. And you said, 'Yes, and its name is freedom.' So who is your sweetheart now? Is it money? Do you want stylish, expensive clothes? Or is it madness? It might be, judging from the fact that you went driving alone through Ziqaq Al Jinn!"

"My one and only sweetheart is called Freedom. Everything else is a luxury, and I can do without it!"

As she got into the car with him, he said, "What do you say we take a quick tour of the 'Green Grass and Fresh Air Pharmacy,' AKA, the Ghouta? I can take you to Kaddura Pharmacy after that."

She looked at him, fully intending to say no. But she started drowning in the dimple on his chin, his luminous, captivating eyes, and his overwhelming good looks. From there she got to thinking about how ingenious, smart, and funny he was, and she was a goner.

"Okay," she said at last. "Why not?"

"You do your best to say no even when you say yes!"

The conversation flowed as smoothly between them as the water in her grandfather's wall fountain. And since she had read the short story collection he'd published a month earlier, she gave him an entertaining description of the things she had liked about it. *Like, what author would pass up a chance to hear from an admiring reader? Besides, if I distract him with conversation about his writing, he won't be able to ask me questions about myself.*

There's nothing half as wonderful as the Ghouta in springtime. The newly budding trees had produced a riot of white, pink, and crimson that was complemented by red anemones and other wild flowers on the ground beneath. It was springtime written in Mother Nature's brightly colored inks, and scented with the perfumes exhaled by blossoms of every shape and kind. *It's springtime in Ghazwan's face, too. I'm soaking up bliss in a momentary escape from my difficult existence. But what's happening to me? I used to think the failure of my first love meant any love after that would fail just as miserably. But I'm higher now than I was the day I stood in Sahat Qasioun with my fiancé, sure that nothing like it would ever happen again. Even my owl seems happy as she flies proudly alongside Ghazwan's old jalopy with flowers on her head.*

***

When Zain walked into the dirt-floored café at the foot of Mt. Qasioun, she found Dr. Manahili waiting for her as usual. He greeted her warmly, and then launched into an animated monologue on his impressions of what she was writing. He was so enthused about his topic, she couldn't get a word in edgewise! *A few days after my abortion I was walking down Salihiyah Street when I saw him coming in my direction. I nearly panicked. It was like coming face to face with a ghost from the past. I imagined him surrounded by scissors, tubes, needles and anesthetic gas masks— and I hate masks no matter what kind they are. Terrified that he might see me too, I ducked into a shop. And now here I am thoroughly enjoying a conversation with him with nary a mention of my abortion! It's as if he senses that I don't want to talk about it.*

"Does your father read what you've written before it goes to press?" he asked.

"Yes. He's afraid I'll make some grammar mistake! But he doesn't comment on the content no matter how radical it gets. He's never objected to a single word. I guess deep down, he's a rebel like me!"

"Do you plan to collect your stories into a book?"

"Yes, I've already done that, actually. I put them all together and sent them to a publishing house in Beirut, and I'm waiting to hear back."

"And what's the news on that lemon-of-a-car you bought from your neighbor?"

"Well," she said mischievously, "I'm jealous of my freedom even when it comes to the mistakes I make! But my dad felt sorry for me after what happened, so he's decided to buy me another little car and give the lemon to somebody he doesn't like."

The two of them burst out laughing. Then they fell silent as they sat looking out over ancient yet modern Damascus, which lay before them gentle as a kitten, and ferocious as a lion.

"In the Fall, Baba and I used to go walking down a dirt path that leads through these orchards. I loved the sound of the leaves crunching when we stepped on them. It was as though they were welcoming us and kissing the bottoms of our feet… By the way, will you be coming to the seminar at the University of Damascus?"

"You bet I will."

"Another story writer and two poets will be reading pieces, too."

"I'll listen to yours, and then run!"

"Actually, I'm the last one on the program anyway!"

They left the café and lingered for a while in Sahat Al Muhajirin.

"Look at that ugly cement building in the middle of the orchards!" Zain remarked. "I hope they don't build any more monstrosities like that around here!"

***

"Rosanna, Rosanna, the good she's done who can tell? Rosanna, Rosanna, may God reward her well!" When Zain got home she found her grandmother singing in the kitchen, and Haroun and the new household helper making circles around her. *I've never figured out those odd songs Grandma Hayat sings. They were passed down by her grandmother, and by her grandmother's grandmother, and her grandmother's grandmother's grandmother! Anyway, if nobody can tell what good Rosanna did, then why does the song go on to say, "may God reward her well?" Which reminds me: There's that lullaby that says, "Sleep, little boy, sleep, I'll slaughter you a sheep!" Was it the sheep's fault that the little boy couldn't go to sleep? And why should the green bird strut around singing sadly, "My mama slaughtered me, my father ate my flesh, and my loving sister gathers my bones"? What a world! Why would we eat each other? What is this violence that lurks inside us?*

Grandma Hayat welcomed Zain home, and then hurried over and sat down in front of the television as she peeled some garlic. *When I started appearing on television, the new-fangled gadget that's invaded our homes lately, some people liked me better than before, and others hated me. I'll never forget how happy my grandmother was to see me when I got home from the station after my first TV appearance. Certain neighbor ladies, and even some family members, only welcome me because my face has appeared on a lit-up screen a few times, while others hold secret grudges against me. But I still adore Ziqaq Al Yasmin. I can't get enough of Damascus's old traditional neighborhoods, and I don't take pride in the fact that I live in Abu Rummana or some other part of town where new high rises have replaced the gardens and parks I love so much.*

***

Now that Zain wasn't banished from Ziqaq Al Yasmin anymore the way she had been right after her divorce, she volunteered to take her grandmother to Fadila's house to check on her family and see how they were handling Fadila's elopement. They arrived in the middle of an argument between Zain's uncle Abdulfattah and his sister.

"Now quit being such a doggone worry wart, will you, woman?!" he shouted. "My health is just fine, and I'm not going to the doctor!"

Turning and noticing the two visitors, he asked suspiciously, "Who are you? Have you come to beg? Get out of my house, damn it!"

Saddened by her son's condition, Grandma Hayat replied in a feeble voice, "No, sweetheart, we aren't here to beg. I'm your mother."

"Poor thing," she whispered to Zain. "Fadila's made him lose his mind all over again."

After an abbreviated visit, they got up to leave on the pretext
that they needed to see Juhaina, and returned to the house with
heavy hearts.

***

I went to mom's hometown of Latakia to participate in a literary
seminar with a couple of poets and another story writer at a local
cultural center. As in Damascus, I'd been scheduled to do my
reading last, since I'm just a beginner that nobody's heard of, and
they were afraid that if I read first, people would get up and walk
out before the seminar was over!

When my turn came, I was shaking all over. But I was
determined not to let my voice quaver. So I decided to pretend I
was reading my story to my mother at her graveside. I wanted her
to realize that she was still alive in a sense, and that through me
she was reading her own poems and stories and being applauded
by the people who had silenced her during her lifetime.

When I went up to the podium and began to read, an old lady
at the tender age of twenty years, the room fell completely silent. I
wasn't reading only with my physical voice, but with the voice of
my spirit, the voice of my heart. And I wasn't afraid the way I'd
thought I would be. Instead, I felt myself melting into the audience,
sharing their sorrows, hopes, illusions, and disappointments.
I read as though I knew each of them personally. My maternal
uncle, a poet himself, wasn't in the audience. After all, he was the
one who had insisted that my mother publish under a pseudonym
for fear that she might besmirch the family's honor. I'd wanted him
to attend, since I thought that if he saw me that night, he might
also see my mother, her face stained with tears of grief and anger

over being robbed of the chance to reveal her creativity for what it was.

On that planet of sorrows past, I read my short story not to avenge my mother, but to do her justice, and to my amazement, no one got up and walked out! In fact, when I finished I heard loud applause, and some people even gave me a standing ovation. It didn't make me feel proud or conceited. All I felt was the satisfaction of having helped repay a debt to my mother, who hadn't been given the chance she deserved. My little owl, who sat perched on the podium, started flapping her wings in applause, and I think I saw my mother's ghost smiling at me.

After the seminar was over, who should Zain see but her long-lost poet uncle. He'd apparently been sitting in the back row, positioned for a quick escape in the event that her performance was a disaster. In spite of his demeaning attitude toward her, she was happy to see him again.

"You can spend the night at my house—your grandfather's house," he offered unexpectedly.

She explained that she'd been invited for dinner at the sports club across from her hotel.

"But," she hastened to add, "after the dinner's over I'd love to come spend the night there."

Surprising Zain for a second time, her uncle pulled something out of his pocket, saying, "Here's the house key. Feel free to come over after your outing, and I'll see you in the morning. You'll also get to see your cousins."

After being honored at the dinner with her fellow litterateurs, Zain realized what power words can have. *All through childhood and adolescence I was the butt of jokes and insults, and I spent*

most of my life having to justify my existence because I'd been born
"Zain" and not "Zain Al Abidin." Yet here I am being showered
with rose petals at a dinner hosted in my honor. No wonder so
many people want to be writers! I've never been so pampered in
my whole life.

I've never written as an act of either vengeance or defense. Even
so, writing has put me through plenty of trials. As a teenager I used
to write out my secret sorrows, disappointments, and distresses in
a journal I kept hidden under my mattress. Wednesdays always
made me nervous, because Wednesday was the day when linens
were washed, so I'd move the journal to the bottom of my section of
the closet—this was before I had my own room. If I forgot to move
it, Wednesday would turn into a day from hell. I'd sit in school
worrying that my mean aunt might find it and, worse still, read
it, since if she did, I'd be in for a tanning when I got home. I didn't
realize at the time that this aunt would never have read anything
anybody had written no matter how curious she got. She was
illiterate, and happily so, since, as far she was concerned, writing
was a tool of the devil.

I stayed out late that night with my fellow writers in Latakia. I
even allowed myself to enjoy some of the flattery coming my way. I
didn't believe most of the nice things people were saying about me,
but after the cruel blows life had dealt my self-esteem in my earlier
years, I let myself bask in the positive attention.

After the celebration I headed back to my grandfather's house, let
myself in, and headed straight for what had once been my mother's
room. I sniffed the pillow, hoping to pick up her scent. Unfortunately,
my uncle's wife, clean freak that she is, hadn't forgotten to change the
linens. When I stretched out on the bed, I heard my uncle stirring in

the bathroom one door down. He was doing his ritual ablution for the dawn prayer. I had an overwhelming urge to get up and pray with him, but my overwhelming fatigue won out. When I woke up, sunlight was streaming in through the window and onto my face. I headed for the bathroom, and on my way there, I heard people arguing in another room. My uncle was angry because the man his daughter wanted to marry, although he was Latakian and rich to boot, wasn't from a high-heeled family like theirs. The would-be groom's father was from a small village. "But don't forget," my aunt piped up in defence, "he managed to start up Latakia's first bus transport company. So the man deserves some respect in my opinion!"

I almost barged in on them with my nightgown on to give my uncle a piece of my mind. But before I could make a move, I heard my maternal grandmother chime in sarcastically, saying, "Well, you've got a lot of room to talk! You're still the new kid on the block yourself when it comes to material success!"

I sympathized with my cousin, but didn't say anything. I'd finally been learning a lesson Grandma Hayat had mastered long before me: not to butt into other people's business. Actually, I feel as though everything that happens on Earth is my business in one way or another. Even so, I went back to my room and got dressed without making a peep. Before leaving, I went in and kissed my uncle's hand (as much as I hate this tradition). As I did so, I sensed that it might be our final farewell, and that the next time I made it to Latakia, he might not be alive. I hugged my aunt and my cousin, wishing I could have taken up for her, and headed back to my own concerns in Damascus crowned with the success of my literary evening in Latakia.

***

How do I dare tell my wife and my half-brother Farah that I turned down a chance to sell my share of the old house in Ziqaq Al Yasmin today? Somebody wants to build a restaurant there, one that serves traditional dishes and that will attract tourists. Farah, a merchant in Souq Al Bazzuriya, has been staying in Damascus for my sake.

How can I tell Brigitte I'm not going back to Paris with her, and that I want to spend the rest of my life in my beloved Damascus? If I were younger, I'd climb the stairs to the top of the minaret and sound the dawn call to prayer the way I used to do before going to school some mornings.

As Rahif Manahili stood at the window with his back to the black-and-white television set, he heard a lovely voice singing, "Djamela, proud, brave and strong…" He turned and saw the Algerian singer Warda, fresh as a rose, as she went on singing in her captivating voice, "They thought there was only one Djamela. But all of us are Djamela! All of us would give our lives for our motherland."

His heart was suddenly aflame with a zeal that had nearly been extinguished. He had been so disillusioned with his country that he'd once nearly settled in Paris with a friend of his, Sharif Al Khurma, who had married a French woman and joined the Socialist Party. It was said that Sharif's French mother had had something to do with his decision. *But my mother is Damascene through and through from a neighborhood near Qabratkeh. My uncles on both sides have businesses in the Souq Al Sarouja, Al Hariqah, and Al Marjah, and my father is a full-blooded Damascene, too. As much as I love Brigitte, I wasn't really being honest with her when I told her I only wanted to come back to Damascus in order to liquidate my properties so that I'd have*

enough money to buy a clinic near the Eiffel Tower or on Fosh
Avenue. At the time I didn't realize how hard it would be to cut
the umbilical cord between me and my mother city Damascus...
It's raining outside. I've always loved the warm, gentle rain in
Damascus. It refreshes my weary heart like a sprinkle of water on a
feverish brow. I feel like taking a stroll down toward the Parliament
Building and Hejaz Square. Then I'll turn left and head in the
direction of Souq Al Hamidiyah and the Umayyad Mosque and
then...

His daydreaming was cut short as Brigitte cried excitedly in
French, "Come look! Isn't the girl on the screen the same one we
performed an abortion on that day?"

He turned and glanced at the television screen. It came as
no surprise, of course, to see Zain engaged in a spirited defense
of her first book. What did surprise him, however, was the type
of program she was appearing on. *How on earth did she end up*
on a show devoted to the concerns of wives and mothers? It looks
as though those fiery, subversive writings of hers have catapulted
her to notoriety. Audiences like excitement, and the program host
wants to grow her audience. So...!

"No, that isn't her," he said to his wife. "She does look a lot like
her, though. I'm going out for a walk."

"Are you sure it isn't the same girl?" she asked.

Not wanting to lie any more than he had to, Dr. Manahili
changed the subject, saying, "Would you like to come with me?"

"Sure," she said enthusiastically. "I'll change my clothes and
be right out."

He was glad his wife had left the room, since it gave him the
chance to drink in Zain's intoxicating words one at a time, in all

their ferocity and insubordination. *Her writings are upsetting to people who aren't rational, and who don't question inherited ideas and beliefs. People like that don't want to be forced out of their blissful hibernation. But that's exactly what Zain does through the things she writes.*

He gazed at her on the screen, enchanted. Was he in love with her? Did he wish she were the daughter he'd never had? Or was he happy she wasn't his daughter? Then again, maybe he just saw his orphaned self reflected in her. He honestly didn't know. *Zain's presence in my life makes me positive and optimistic. Ever since the first time she came to the clinic, I've had a hard time defining my feelings toward her. But one thing is certain: I'm delighted to see her taking life by the horns rather than playing the miserable, helpless divorcee.*

He listened to Zain with rapt attention as she spoke truth to power, and as the moderator tried in vain to shut her up.

"I'm ready to go, my luny Damascene!" he heard Brigitte announce brightly. He drew her close to him. Mingled with a rush of tenderness, he felt a pang of guilt toward this noble woman, who had agreed to marry not only him, but his city as well. And as if that hadn't been enough, she had agreed not to have any children as long he didn't want to have any himself. He held her tight, as though Zain's feisty but vivacious television appearance had infected him with a vitality he couldn't suppress.

Then suddenly he asked, "Would you be willing to have my child?"

Fireworks went off in her eyes, which were soon moist with tears. "Isn't it too late?" she asked. "I'm thirty-five now, and you're forty-five."

"No, not at all," he assured her. "Don't forget what a good doctor I am! I promise we'll have a little girl and we'll call her Zain."

"You call her whatever you like!" she replied with a laugh. "What matters is for her to be born."

"And…," he continued with some difficulty, "would you be willing to stay here in Damascus with me instead of moving to France?"

After some hesitation she replied, "I'd be willing to stay with you even in hell. Isn't that what I've been doing ever since we met?"

A rush of affection for her swept through his heart. He knew he couldn't rely on his feelings, which came and went in waves. So, digging his fingers into his chest, he made the motion of taking his heart out and offering it to her. *I'm amazed I didn't see any blood!* As he did so, he expected her to say, "What's that? A prickly pear?"

And for the first time he noticed that this was exactly what his heart had been: a big cactus plant.

He imagined himself saying, "Like a coconut, a cactus is tender on the inside, which is why it protects itself with a hard exterior!"

As for Brigitte, she was too happy to hear his self-denigration. All she could think about was the fact that for the first time ever, her husband had invited her along on his nightly jaunt around Damascus, and for the first time ever, he'd broached the subject of their becoming parents.

* * *

Amjad Khayyal had started coming home from work early, drawn to the daughter whose company he so enjoyed. He was proud of the success of her first book, which had been received well in the Beirut press, and irritated at the attacks it had been subjected to in some Damascus press outlets.

When he arrived, he found her, as usual, working at the table in his study. He wanted to support her with all the influence and prestige he had at his disposal. Rather than telling her this directly, however, he went all out praising her work instead. A certain enraged religious cleric had issued a statement declaring open season on Zain and had signed it "the girls of Hamah," although news of it had been hushed up temporarily thanks to Amjad Khayyal's intervention. Similarly, he had stood by Zain when certain newspapers had incited attacks on her in the name of religion.

Zain had won the enthusiastic support of Mr. Wadee, owner of a newspaper known as *Jaridat Al Intisar*, together with his wife and son. Their son Raja'i, a student at the American University in Beirut, regularly brought her encouraging, positive articles being written about her in the Beirut press.

He tiptoed into the library so as not to disturb her. Of course, she was so engrossed in what she was doing, he could probably have exploded a hand grenade next to her without her noticing. From over her shoulder he read aloud the last line she'd written: "My eyes should give away everything but my age." Laughing in spite of himself, he exclaimed, "What's this? You're still young, but you're writing as if you were an old woman!"

Looking up at him wearily as though she'd just trekked thousands of miles across time zones and cultures, she said,

"That isn't me, Baba. I'm a sixty year old woman talking to herself in a story I'm writing. When I create characters, I become them. I live their lives."

Kissing her on her forehead, her father said, "Sorry to interrupt you, but the owner of *Al Jara'id* newspaper called from Beirut while you were out. He said he'd like to come to Damascus to interview you. Editors from *Al Deek* and *Kull Al Ashya'* newspapers want to do interviews with you, too, and the man who called said he could bring a delegation to the house if you'd like."

He left their telephone numbers at the edge of the table and withdrew.

As he slipped out of the study now taken over by his daughter, he felt proud and gratified. *I'm repaying a debt to Zain's mother. I didn't appreciate her writing the way I should have. In fact, I was almost hostile toward it. Even though she'd barely survived her labor with Zain, all I cared about was for her to give me a son. If they hadn't done a C-section, she wouldn't have made it. No judge could pronounce sentence on me, but I murdered her. If it weren't for that damned young guy Nizar Qabbani and the poem he read at her memorial service, nobody would have realized that she died a victim of my determination to have another child.*

I feel guilty as hell toward Hind, and I'm trying to make it up to her by taking the best care I can of "Hind No. 2." Through Zain, Fate's given me a chance to atone for leaving her mother when she needed me most. Just when her due date was approaching, I went traipsing off to some medical conferences even though I knew that if she went into labor, my brother Abdulfattah wouldn't take her to the hospital for fear of her being examined by a male doctor! So she

died, and I mourned her, and so did everyone at the old house in
Ziqaq Al Yasmin.

* * *

Zain finished recording her radio program, "Poetry, Music and
Zain." which aired at midnight after everybody had gone to bed
(!). Trying to flirt with her from behind his shades, a certain
Salah Muharib said to her one day, "When I hear that lilting
voice of yours reciting your translations of Shakespeare, Herrick,
Wordsworth, Byron, Keats and Shelley, I imagine how beautiful
you'd look dressed for a samah dance performance!"

"Well, let me tell you this," she replied, not pulling any
punches. "First of all, I don't like the samah dance. I like some
parts of our tradition, but not the ones that reflect subservience.
I wouldn't want to dress up as a slave girl, and I wouldn't want
to dance like one, either. I'd rather move to the beat of a bongo
drum, or dance Isadora Duncan style. Women who perform
the samah dance might know how to move to a slow, erotic
rhythm, but they're spoiled and lazy as far as I'm concerned."

Salah looked uncomfortable, and she didn't blame him.
He'd begun to realize she was something of a "bad ass"—as
everyone else had started calling her. She was ready to go
to war, and he was already worn out from his own personal
battles. So he decided to cut his losses and get away from
her before the bliss she'd appeared to promise turned to
misery.

When she got home that day, Zain said to her father, "I'm
thinking of finishing my studies in Beirut and applying for a job
there."

"Whatever you decide, I'll do my best to help you," he assured her.

"I'll have to apply to the American University in Beirut."

"No worries there. Two of the deans at AUB are friends of mine—Dr. Qastantin and Dr. Fouad. They've known you ever since you were a little girl."

***

"Hello, may I speak with Ms. Zain Khayyal?"

"This is Zain. Who's speaking?"

"My name is Sadduqi Ibrahim. I'm a writer, and…"

"Oh! Of course I've heard of you! What can I do for you?"

Getting straight to the point, Dr. Sadduqi explained in his usual matter-of-fact, serious manner, "We've been invited by the Writers' Union in West Germany to send a delegation to their country for a month-long visit. It's a kind of goodwill and cultural exchange program. The delegation will be made up of four writers of literature and two journalists. So I thought of you."

"Oh, that's fantastic. I'd love to come!"

"Wouldn't you like to know who the other delegates will be?"

"Oh, that's all right. I'm sure you'll make all the right choices. Besides, I wouldn't be going on account of the other delegation members. I'd be going to represent my country. But why did you choose me, if I might ask?"

"Well, I'll be straight with you. The other delegation members all speak Arabic and French, but none of them has good English. Some of us speak English, of course, but not that fluently."

"So," Zain said with a laugh, "You just want me to be your interpreter?'"

"No, Miss Zain. It isn't as simple as that. I've been reading your stories since the time they started appearing in the newspapers, and I hear they were released recently in book form by a reputable publishing house in Beirut. You're not just a lover of freedom. You're a gifted writer, too, and that's why you've been invited to join us on this visit. What do you think?"

"As I said before, I'd love to. I never pass up a chance to learn new things or go new places."

"Don't you want to consult with your father about it?"

"No need. I make my own decisions."

***

Zain made a point of arriving early for her usual coffee rendezvous with Dr. Manahili. She ascended the staircase carved into the foothill of Mt. Qasioun and looked out over her beloved city. As she did so, she imagined herself a mother gently caressing her infant lying before her. *The sight of the city stretched out before me this way makes me think of eternity. I'm just passing through Damascus the way others have done for thousands of years. I'm reminded of how miniscule and fragile I am. My life is nothing but a tiny speck in Damascus's vast sky. Thinking this way makes my own troubles seem less scary. Sometimes I feel the weight of the world on my shoulders, but when I take in the sight of this huge city stretching as far as the eye can see, my problems seem like nothing but a grain of sand on a vast shore, and peace floods my heart.*

As my literary circle includes more and more people, some good, some bad, some noble, some despicable, there are moments when I feel like a butterfly caught in the web of some huge deadly spider. But then I think about Damascus, and I see myself in the right perspective again. I'm not a boulder on Mt. Qasioun. I'm just a grain of sand on Damascus's boundless shore.

She was wakened out of her thoughts by the endearing presence of her friend Dr. Manahili.

"Did I keep you waiting?" he asked apologetically.

"Oh, no!" she said. "I just felt like getting here early today. I love this city so much, I never get tired of just looking at it, and especially from this spot. There isn't much traffic, and it's surrounded by an aura of calm. There aren't many buildings up here either. I just wish it were covered with trees instead of cement."

Lingering over coffee flavored with cardamom and rosewater, they shared news of happenings in their lives since their last meeting. Zain was thrilled to hear what had transpired between the doctor and his wife, who'd had surgery just the day before to enable her to have children. It also made her happy to learn of the positive energy she had brought into her friend's life.

When she told him about her upcoming visit to West Germany, he remarked, "You need a trip like this! But I'll really miss you!"

***

"Hello, Miss Zain."

She couldn't help but notice that everybody was addressing her as "Miss" instead of "Mrs." *So, then, I'm not the only one who's left the past behind.*

"Hello, Professor Sadduqi. I received the invitation you sent, and I've got my visa to West Germany. After picking it up from the consulate, I took the consul for a spin in my new car. I took him around to see Mt. Qasioun, Al Ghouta, Sahat Al Marjah, and…"

"I know," Professor Sadduqi broke in, "He tells me you scared him to death with your wild driving! Where are you trying to go in such a hurry?"

"To freedom," she replied simply. "Even if I die getting there. There's only one thing that holds me back: the fear that I might hurt somebody in another car. Otherwise, I'd probably go flying off the road!"

"In any case," he said, laughing, "now we have to go to the Intelligence Division to get travel permits."

"What!" cried Zain, taken aback. "How dare they treat us this way? Syria is our country, and we should be able to leave it and come back to it whenever we want!"

"We have an appointment with the intelligence officer, Lieutenant Nahi, at ten in the morning day after tomorrow. I'll come by so that we can go together, and we'll meet the others there."

Zain was tempted to scrap the whole trip in protest against this indignity. But this was the first chance she'd ever had to go to Europe, which was a dream come true for her.

She told Sadduqi, "You're a Baathist, so you sympathize with any decision the government makes. But frankly, this thing of having to get permission to travel from the Intelligence Division—I don't like it one bit! Isn't the Baathist motto 'Unity, Freedom, Socialism'? Well, then, where's the freedom you're talking about if I have to ask for permission to leave my country and come back to it?"

"These are routine measures to ensure citizens' well-being," Professor Sadduqi retorted stiffly.

Undaunted, Zain insisted, "Well, you ensure people's well-being by giving them their freedom. Freedom may have its drawbacks, but suppressing it has worse drawbacks, and the world's advanced societies understand this fact."

With barely suppressed rage, Sadduqi said coolly, "I'll be at your door day after tomorrow at nine-thirty in the morning, Miss Troublemaker. Don't forget: I work hard for my money, of which I don't make that much, and so does my wife."

"Believe me," Zain replied, "I realize you're honest and broke. I see that. But you don't want to support the people who get rich off government overthrows the way they get rich off wars."

"My God, you really are a rebel, aren't you? Why did I even ask you to come along?!"

"It's because in your heart of hearts, you love freedom more than you love your party affiliations. You're a rebel, too."

***

Once again Zain arrived early for her appointment with Dr. Manahili. She practically flew over the dirt staircase leading up to the rustic coffee shop on Sahat Al Muhajirin. *This is where I regain my sense of calm and clarity. As soon as I see the end of one tunnel, I find myself in another one, and I'm worn out. So my trip to West Germany will be a much-needed break. I've got a growing list of so-called friends who try to impose their points of view on me. Instead of respecting my right to express my own opinions, they want to use me for their own purposes on the pretext that they've supported me and contributed to my rise to fame. "Say good things about so-and-so!" and "Tear so-and-so apart!" they tell me, as though I were some sort of literary slave. But I don't do it. I scream and shout, not just with my voice, but with my actions. As for Sheikh Shafiq, he still has it out for me, and on top of that, he claims to speak in the name of women who've never read what I've written or even heard of me. My father warned me, saying, "Our household is moderately religious. But don't underestimate what he can do with that bamboo rod of his. He's well thought of among certain people who don't know how to read or write, and as far as they're concerned, his word is law."*

I just go from one failure to the next. I keep on trying, at least, but is that success? When I interviewed at a TV station once for a job as a scriptwriter, the interviewer tried to brush me off nicely, saying, "Why don't you go to the United States and study script writing there?"

He might have been right to suggest that I do a degree in the field. But the person he ended up hiring was a semi-illiterate who happened to belong to the ruling party. On the other hand, Baathist poet Alwan Ibn Al Silmiyah offered me the chance to present a radio program even though he knew I wasn't a Baathist myself, and Poetry, Music and Zain has been a real hit.

Here comes Dr. Manahili. I'm always so happy to see him. The times we spend together are a respite from the painful parts of my life, and with him I get a taste of genuine human warmth.

***

At long last Zain met Lieutenant Nahi, whose influence far exceeded his rank. Word had it that given his tyrannical, violent tendencies, Lieutenant Nahi would make a perfect scapegoat if necessity required. It was also said that his superior, Lieutenant Colonel Samir, was the one who pulled the strings backstage. The upshot was that Lieutenant Nahi decided who was granted entrance into the paradise of Beirut or wherever else one hoped to go, and who stayed in the paradise of Dummar, where he had invited Zain and the other delegation members for dinner.

Before Zain went with Professor Sadduqi to the dinner party, her father briefly met with Sadduqi and asked a number of questions about the upcoming trip. As they were about to leave the house, Zain kissed her father on the forehead and whispered in his ear, "You don't need to worry about me. You can worry instead about what I'll do to them!" Her father exploded with laughter.

As Zain and Sadduqi descended the stairs on their way out, he asked, "What did you say to your father that made him laugh so hard?"

"Oh," she replied, "That's our secret!"

Once they were in the car, Sadduqi said, "I'll be honest with you. Even the intellectual community is in shock over the way your father went on supporting you after you insisted on marrying someone he and your family didn't approve of, and then divorced him against everybody's wishes as well. So why did you separate from your husband after wanting so badly to marry him?"

Having learned the age-old Damascene art of the understated response, Zain said simply, "What's past is past."

Lieutenant Nahi made a point of seating Zain next to him during the evening's gathering, and when he started flirting with her, it was obvious to her travel companions that she was the sole reason behind the dinner invitation.

***

Zain arrived early for her session at the radio station and recorded four episodes of Poetry, Music and Zain. She suspected that one reason Alwan had scheduled her program in the middle of the night was that it gave him an excuse to hand her Baathist tracts to read. This way he could either enlist her as a supporter or, if she didn't cooperate, shun her. *A new current is growing, and its motto is: "If you're not for us, you're against us." And being against them comes with a price. Whoever you are, you're under suspicion until you prove your innocence by joining the party. It's either us, or nobody. But I want the freedom either to agree with them, which I do some of the time, or question them or out-and-out reject what they stand for, which I do most of the time.*

To Zain's surprise, Alwan was waiting for her when she came out of the studio. She felt a rush of friendly affection toward him. As usual, he was wearing his shabby sandals and a half-ironed shirt. He represented a world at total odds with that of Lieutenant Nahi, who, on the two occasions when Zain had encountered him—at the Dummar dinner party, and during her visit to his office with other members of the Syrian delegation to West Germany to apply for travel permits—had been clad in top-of-the-line Parisian footwear. On his desk lay a bag of French-made Sulka neckties that he couldn't possibly have afforded on the salary he was making. *A bribe, no doubt. Thanks to my ex's family, I know a thing or two about upscale men's attire.*

Alwan invited Zain for a cup of coffee at Al Rawda Café. Since his antique sandals were his sole means of transportation, they went in her car.

The minute they sat down, he asked her, "So, what's the story with your divorce?"

Kind though he was, she gave Alwan the same answer she'd been giving everybody else: "It wasn't meant to be." *As Grandma Hayat always tells me, "Better a heartache in private than humiliation in public!"*

"Why do you want to spy on my heart?" she asked him in turn. "Does my divorce have anything to do with my radio program?"

"No!" he admitted. "But it does have something to do with a poem I'm writing, since it was inspired by you!"

"My friend," she said, "poetry's all shadow and ambiguity. It bears no connection to the things we go through in our everyday lives. So just write, and don't ask any questions." *Why should I tell him I'm not "a squeezed lemon"—that I'm no different to women who hold out in the face of their sorrowful marriages? What need is there to tell him that a woman isn't finished after a failed love affair, but has the right to put her life back together again? Doesn't he know that being divorced doesn't make a woman free game for men's lusts? I just noticed that I'm the only woman in the coffee shop, and it doesn't bother me. Pretty soon it will be a routine thing to see women in places that were once the sole province of men.*

* * *

After a month in Germany packed with memorable experiences, the delegation of Syrian writers boarded a nighttime flight headed for Damascus. Not in the mood to converse with her fellow travelers, Zain closed her eyes and withdrew into herself to mull over the month's events. In her mind's eye she pried open the cabin window, climbed out and flew alongside the aircraft with her trusty owl. *Never in my life have I been feted as a writer the way I was during this trip. I was constantly worried about making sure my English pronunciation was right and that people could understand me clearly, but I did my best to be a good representative of my home country, especially its women. Some Germans have the odd notion that we Arab women are still living in the age of* The Arabian Nights. *It was as if some people expected me at any moment to get up and perform a striptease, like the "Dance of the Seven Veils"! On the other hand, they were happy to see that I try to learn about other peoples and cultures and to teach people from other places about my heritage.*

And did they ever spoil us! First we went down to Hamburg. From there we headed further south to cities I used to dream of visiting as I poured over a map of the world: Dresden, Cologne, Bonn, Berlin... Then there was that enchanted trip down the River Rhine to Munich and the tour of the amazing province of Bavaria. Oh, and the museums! From the time we toured Beethoven's house-turned-museum, I had his music stuck in my head, so that was the soundtrack for the rest of the trip. And as if they weren't spoiling us enough with everything else, they wined and dined us wherever we went. I'd never tasted alcohol before, and I didn't have any on this trip either. Even when they took us to the oldest pub in Munich, I ordered something non-alcoholic. But they served the other delegates beer with the appetizers, red wine with red meat, and white wine with fish. There were so many dishes I can't remember them all.

As my owl and I soared along next to the airplane, I saw her eyes twinkling in the dark like little stars. She looked happy, as though she were feeling the same things I was. After a while she and I slipped back into the plane, and before I knew it, we were home. "Please fasten your seatbelts and extinguish all smoking materials," I heard an airline stewardess say. We'd begun our descent toward Damascus. I'd returned from my voyage as solid as a boulder on Mt. Qasioun. At the same time, I'd been overwhelmed by the freedom of expression I saw people enjoying in the country we'd visited. I hadn't seen lips or ears sprouting from the walls of any German coffee shops. I hadn't seen any men sewing their mouths shut with needles and black thread like the one I'd seen at the Havana Café the day of my divorce. I'd been equally overwhelmed by the contentment I observed in the villages we stopped in along the Rhine. The villagers seemed to be having the time of their lives as they danced and made music together in preparation for the beer festivals. How I miss seeing joy in my country. But all I see anymore is people struggling to survive from one coup to the next, from one ruler to the next, from one excruciating division to the next.

When I rang the doorbell, I wasn't greeted by the housekeeper the way I usually am, but by my father. He was crying, and his tears dripped onto his hand as I kissed it. Yet whereas as a little girl I'd only kissed his hand out of duty, this time I did it out of sheer love and affection.

* * *

As she often did, Zain went to the outdoor café at the foot of Mt. Qasioun half an hour before her appointment with Dr. Manahili so she could have some time to herself. It was their first coffee rendezvous since her return from Germany. *I have to get ready for my move to Beirut.*

The doctor arrived with a copy of her first book, which he had had beautifully bound. Ignoring the fact that she'd been away, he placed the book before her, saying, "I'd like a dedication and an autograph, please!"

She was starting to give him a rundown of her trip to Germany, complete with details of the honors she had received, when he interrupted her, saying, "I know everything. I saw Professor Sadduqi on television yesterday evening. He went on at length about your role on the trip, and he mentioned that your first book is now being translated into German. He was so proud of you!" *It made me happy to hear that. I admit it—I'm a sucker for compliments.*

Then he added, "I won't give myself a chance to miss you when you move to Beirut, since I'll be visiting you regularly. I'll bring you jasmine-blossom necklaces, since I can tell from your stories that jasmine is one of your favorite flowers."

"I'm leaving for Beirut tomorrow morning," she said. "I need to make some arrangements and take the university entrance exam. I went to see Lieutenant Nahi today, and he gave me a travel permit."

"Watch out for him," Dr. Manahili warned. "You never know when that snake will bite."

"I know. I've heard a lot about how crooked he is. He was about to make a pass at me when one of his aides walked in. Then he invited me to dinner." *I didn't tell him the rest of the story, which is that after he wrote me up a travel permit with his golden pen, he had to leave the room with his assistant. While he was out, I grabbed the paper and hid it in my purse so that the next time I needed to leave the country, I wouldn't have to come back and ask for permission again. When he got back, he stared at the stack of travel permits on his desk as if he suspected what had happened. But then he was distracted by a call from his ex-wife. He told the switchboard operator, "Tell her I don't want to hear her voice, and that she'd better quit calling." He wrote out a second travel permit, after which he got up and came around the desk to hand it to me. Just as he was about to try to kiss me, his aide knocked on the door again. When the aide came in, I made my get-away with the miracle document I'd hidden in my purse, and without which I wouldn't be able to fly away on my magic carpet.*

"Don't go," Dr. Manahil pleaded urgently. "He's obsessed with collecting mistresses from good families. He must be getting revenge for the years when girls didn't pay any attention to him. He's started making radio stations play songs by the half-rate singer Ludjana Hamsir, and I've seen her getting into a new black Mercedes reserved for government officials."

"Please don't worry. I'm being careful. In fact, that's why I'm making this visit to Beirut. I'm arranging to teach at a school in Choueifat not far from Beirut. I'm also planning to board there with some other teachers while I finish my degree at the AUB, since I might not find a room in the dorm. My dad's managed to enroll me tentatively through a couple of friends of his who are deans there, but I still have to sit for the entrance exam."

"What's the name of the school you'll be working for? And how did you get the job?"

"People in Beirut—people in literary and press circles, I mean—like me for the same reasons that some people here hate me! Edward, who praised my first book in the Lebanese press, found out through me in a telephone conversation that I was interested in finding a teaching job, and he told me this school's principal was a friend of his. I'm going there to sign the contract and get to know the place a bit—if they haven't changed their minds by the time I get there, of course!"

"So what was the name of the school?"

When she mentioned the name to him, Dr. Manahili exclaimed, "Oh! The owner of that school is a doctor I've met at medical conferences, and his wife is the director. I'll go to Beirut with you and put in a good word for you."

"Actually, I'd rather drive up there alone. I like to depend on myself!"

"All right, then. I'll give them a call tonight and put in a good word for you that way! Oh, and the next time you need to go see Lieutenant Nahi for a travel permit, don't go alone. Take me with you."

"Do you know him?"

"I met him some time back because he wanted a service from me."

Zain figured the service had been to perform an abortion on one of his mistresses, so she didn't ask any questions.

"He's a bastard," Dr. Manahili commented. "Once when I was with him, his wife—or ex-wife—called him, and he refused to talk to her even when he was told the call had to do with their little boy. He just yelled at the assistant, 'So she wants to capitalize off our son, does she? Before long I'll take him away from her!

Anyway, I don't want to hear you breathe a word about her from now on. I've had enough of her obnoxious calls."

"I hear people have started to get fed up with his pranks. He and his cronies make life hell for people. They waste public money buying influence, fancy cars, and escorts for their wives and mistresses. As for bribes, they've become a duty! Some of these guys import expired medications, change the expiration date on them, and resell them to people under the label, 'God is the Healer'—as if calling it that will justify their filthy crimes! And on top of that, they…"

"Don't write a word about any of that," Dr. Manahili broke in. "Just focus now on getting yourself settled in Beirut. Then you can deal with other things as they come."

Chapter Six

Once in Beirut, Zain had the pleasure of meeting her publisher and his wife. At the publishing house, which had put out her first book, she met a young journalist by the name of Marlene who took her under her wing and offered to show her a few pages of the Beirut book.

Zain's day had begun at the Choueifat School, where she'd been received by the director and Mr. Edward, the literary critic who had been instrumental in her hiring. To her surprise, even the head mistress was in attendance that day thanks to a telephone call she had received from Dr. Manahili. From the school she had gone to the university to sit for the entrance exam, which had been so easy, it appeared to be nothing but a formality. *The only way to fail would have been not to know a word of English!*

After leaving the publishing house, Zain and Marlene passed by the Lords Hotel, where Zain's father had advised her to stay the night, since its owners were friends of his who would make sure to give her a room with a view of the sea. *That alone would have been reason enough to spend the night here. I'm in love with the sea in Latakia, and now I can get acquainted with its Beirut face.*

Marlene took Zain to dinner at Faisal's, a restaurant on Bliss Street across from the AUB's main gate, saying, "A lot of intellectuals, politicians and writers are regulars here." She whispered the names of those present, who included Lebanese and other Arabs whose writing, art or political thought was familiar to Zain. A similar scene repeated itself at a café a few doors down known as Uncle Sam's, where the two young women went for a cup of coffee. From there they headed to The Horseshoe on Hamra Street. Wherever they went, people came up to greet Marlene or introduce themselves to Zain, saying they'd read her book and seen her picture on the cover. Zain didn't feel like a stranger at all. On the contrary, she felt herself among friends. Everyone was relaxed and spontaneous, and around the tables women were planted like succulent roses, clad in fashionable attire that would have been judged immodest by Ziqaq Al Yasmin standards, and engaged in lively discussions and debates.

Thanking her hostess, Zain said, "I'd better get back to the hotel. I'll be driving back in the morning." What she didn't say was that she'd been on the lookout for Ghazwan. Picking up on Zain's preoccupation, Marlene asked, "You're looking for somebody, aren't you? Don't think I haven't noticed! Just tell me who it is—I know everybody's favorite haunt around here."

"Well," Zain replied coyly, "I don't want to lie, so I'm not going to answer your question!"

"And I don't want to lie to you either!" Marlene shot back sassily. "Do you think I invited you to dinner and took you on a tour of the social-intellectual scene out of the sheer goodness of my heart? There's a hidden price tag, and you'll have to pay up now! I want to interview you for my magazine, and we'll do that at the Dolce Vita in Raouché."

Invigorated by all the new names and places, Zain could feel herself spreading her wings. At the Dolce Vita, which

was basically an extension of the sidewalk, they walked up to
a small table where a handsome young man was seated. As
he and Marlene exchanged kisses on the cheek, Marlene said
unapologetically, "This is my sweetheart of the month!" She and
her boyfriend burst out laughing, and Zain joined in, still hoping
to pick Ghazwan's face out of the crowd. Marlene whisked out
pencil and paper, and as Zain sat enchanted by the moonlit
path on the sea visible from the other side of the street, a young
man approached from a neighboring table from which raucous
laughter had been emanating. Addressing himself to Zain, he
said, "Hello! We recognized you from your pictures. Munih Bek
is inviting you to his table."

Sensing Zain's awkward surprise, Marlene replied, "She'll be
there in a minute. Get a seat ready for her."

As the young man made his way back to his group, Marlene
explained, "Munih Bek's a well-known intellectual who prefers
oral exchanges over written ones. Each table has it own
customs, protocol and rituals, and Munih Bek's forum has a
light-heartedness about it no matter how serious the topic of
conversation happens to be. He's brilliant and single, too! Go join
them, and don't worry about a thing. Just be yourself."

"But what about our interview?"

"Get to know Beirut's cultural and intellectual scene first.
Based on what I've read of your writings, I think you're going
to like it. You'll fit in easily around here. You're passionate for
freedom and artistic madness, so our coffee shops are just the
place for you!"

Gathering her courage, Zain went hesitantly over to Munih
Bek's table, saying over and over to herself, "I'm a boulder on Mt.

Qasioun." And before she knew it, she had fallen into a searing spotlight. She knew there were people in the group who would be only too willing to crucify her intellectually right on the table top if she couldn't hold her own against their witty, scathing repartee.

Once Zain had joined the group, Munih Bek said to her, "You're the first girl I've ever invited to my roundtable discussion," to which she replied without missing a beat, "I bet you say that to all the ladies." And they all burst out laughing. She didn't feel the least bit the outsider with Munih Bek and his group, and from then on she referred to him as "the proletariat gentleman."

The conversation flowed wittily and enjoyably, and as Marlene had predicted, she fit right in. *The walls have ears wherever you go, but here, at least, you won't end up in a dungeon as a result! Or is the moonlight jamming my brainwaves?*

Before long another young man came up and said to Zain, "You're invited to the 'conversationalists' table.'"

He pointed to a group that was roaring with laughter.

"Well," Zain said, excusing herself from Munih Bek's gathering, "you don't appreciate the good you've got till you try something different!"

Feeling light as a cloud, she got up and made her way over to the other table, where she was introduced to the "chief conversationalist," an elderly man from the Saadawi clan, and to her amazement, his table was merrier than Munih Bek's. She could hardly feel the time passing as their conversation and laughter went flying through the crisp night air like sparks from a bonfire.

***

As Zain drove through Hameh to Dummar, she noticed a tributary of the Barada River flowing to her left. The sight filled her with nostalgic affection for "the City of the Seven Rivers"[8] that she had come to bid farewell to. To her right loomed a boulder on which someone had written, "Remember me always." Beneath these words someone else had written, "I'll never forget you!" Zain liked to imagine that she was the person who had written those words to Damascus, and that Damascus had written back to her, "I'll never forget you!"

She had no intention of slipping away like a thief in the night or reneging on any of her commitments. First of all, she would give both the Dawhat al-Fikr School and the library notice of her resignation so that they could find replacements for her. All her associates welcomed her desire to study in Beirut. *Or maybe they just welcome getting rid of a trouble maker like me, who arrived with a broken wing, but then started flying from newspaper columns to television screens!* When she went to say goodbye to people at the library, they invited her to a get-together at a farm owned by a poet by the name of Azmi. As she walked around the farm, she discovered an old abandoned well. She didn't know why, but she had a sudden, irresistible urge to explore the inside of the well and find out what sorts of creatures lived in it. Despite everyone's protestations, Zain headed down the iron ladder that led to the well's bottom. As she descended, she could hear her colleagues pleading with her to be careful and warning

---

[8]   Damascus has been referred to as "the City of the Seven Rivers" because, as it flows through the city, the Barada River divides into six additional branches: Yazid, Thawra, Al Mazawi, Al Dirani, Qanawat, and Banyas.

her against the scorpions, snakes and insects that inhabited the place. The light filtering in from above grew fainter with every rung of the ladder. *I'm at the bottom of the well of my life, and I mustn't be afraid, since if I am, I'm sure to fall. And once I've explored the underworld, I must learn to come up again.*

By the time Zain reappeared, everyone else was in a panic, especially Azmi, who was terrified at the thought that harm might come to this daughter of a prominent lawyer, since by all rights he should have had the well covered. As Zain climbed out, there was a black tarantula on her shoulder. She flicked it off, thinking of Lieutenant Nahi!

***

When Zain arrived home, her father was looking glum, so she didn't dare tell him about her well adventure. She was obsessed with getting to the bottom of things, wells included, but this apparently wasn't the time to remind him of that fact.

The library director had informed her father of her exploit even before she got back to the house, but he feigned ignorance.

"I'll miss you when you're gone," he told her, "and I'll come see you. By the way, Najati has your passport. He has friends who can pull some strings for him, and before he gives it back to you, he's going to have Egypt added to the list of countries you're allowed to visit."

"That's good," she said. "Cairo's the cultural capital of the Arab world. If I can't prove myself there, I won't make it anywhere else either. But if I can, I'll have passed through the eye of the needle."

Early the next morning, with Fairouz's beautiful voice singing "Marushka... in the sorrowful forest" in the background, Zain telephoned Lieutenant Nahi's aide about the magical paper that would allow her to go to Beirut, asking him to keep it with him so that she could pick it up the next day.

"Just a minute," he said. "I'll check with Lieutenant Nahi."

A few minutes later he came back on the line, saying, "Lieutenant Nahi wants to talk to you."

"Hello, Zain. This is Lieutenant Nahi."

"Hello."

"I'll be expecting you at ten, and I'll give you the permit myself."

"You mean in an hour and forty-five minutes?"

"No. Ten tonight. After signing the permit, I'll take you to dinner, and then to a party that will probably last a while. Tell your dad you'll be spending the night at a friend's house." Then he hung up before she could protest!

She was trembling with rage. *Should I go get the paper and tell him politely that my father is sick and I have to get straight back home? Should I go by the old Syrian adage: "If you can't beat 'em, kiss their hands and pray down curses on their heads"? There's no way in hell I'm going to join that bastard's team or try to get on his good side. And even though it probably won't work, I'll try to bring the curse down on him myself.*

Zain called her poet acquaintance Alwan and said, "Can you meet me tonight at Al Rawda Café?"

"Is this some kind of joke?"

"No, it's no joke. Let's meet there at 9:30 p.m. for a bowl of kishk al-fuqara, mihlaya, or rice pudding."

"My treat," she added.

Laughing, he said, "I'm sure this isn't about feeding me or listening to my latest poem! So what's up?"

"I'll tell you when I see you."

She spent the rest of the day polishing the story she was reading at the Sukaina Literary Forum. *I'm tempted to forge the date on the travel permit Nahi started to write me that day and use it to get out of here right now. He wants to close in on my mind and snap it shut like a trap. But I can't let Professor Thurayya down. She was a good friend of my mom's, and she's already sent out the invitations. I've got to chill out.*

At nine-twenty that evening, Zain sat waiting for Alwan at Al Rawda Café. *From the time I was a little girl, my dad taught me to be prompt. So what's wrong with this guy? Didn't his parents teach him to be on time? I swear, I always get to places at least half an hour before the other person shows up! And they all have the same excuse: traffic!*

When Alwan finally showed up, they were approached by Kamel, a witty poet who assailed them with a barrage of admiring chatter. He announced that he'd come from his village to celebrate the victory of the ruling party.

"Why don't you join our party?" he asked Zain. "The girl comrades aren't pretty like you!"

"So what are you looking for?" Zain replied acerbically, "A comrade, or a concubine?"

Still in celebration mode, he replied, "This is the age of the 'minor prophets.' That's the name I invented for the party leaders. Don't you think it fits?"

"Well, there are 'minor prophets' and there are the 'minor demons,' too."

"Nothing's good enough for you liberals!" he retorted. "I'm going to go celebrate at another table!" And he walked off.

"Why were you so hostile to Comrade Kamel?" Alwan wanted to know.

"Because I've had it," she said. "I'm fightin' mad. I need to get to Lebanon, and your 'comrade' Nahi wants me to go to his office at ten o'clock tonight—that's right, tonight—so that he can give me 'a travel permit' to Beirut."

"You're kidding."

"People are starting to talk about the way he and others like him act, and how repressive they are. They threw Lieutenant Baher, the poet Amer's brother from a village near Banyas, into jail for being a unionist and for opposing your party's monopoly on power."

"You're kidding."

"He's in Mezzeh Prison now. I found out from a Palestinian cousin of mine, who wants to go to Beirut to put out a new magazine there with a writer by the name of Ghazwan Ayed, and who's under pressure from Nahi's henchmen to write reports for the secret police."

"You're kidding."

"And there's talk around town about his dirty business deals. His partners buy up expired medications, change the date on them and resell them. They've even done it with children's vaccines."

"I don't believe it."

"The party leaders get journalists—and poets, too, of course—to glorify them and the 'one and only party,' which makes them all the more self-righteous and dishonest. They only see one side of things, and they've got delusions of grandeur. Haven't you read the last poem by your friend Kamel about the so-called 'minor prophets'? People who portray the party leadership as though they were mouthpieces for the Almighty aren't helping the revolution—they're hurting it. They encourage people like Nahi to think they're God's gift to humanity. So they turn into petty tyrants who make decisions without listening to anybody but themselves."

"You're kidding."

"All people talk about these days is the way they're gradually clamping down on all our freedoms, squandering public funds, and getting more and more corrupt."

"You're kidding."

"We've got to fight this corruption now, before the worms eat the fruit off the vine."

"..."

Contemplating Alwan's ancient sandals and his threadbare shirt, Zain went on, "I know you're broke, and clean as a whistle, and when I'm with you I never feel there's a trap ready to snap shut on me with every step I take and every word I say. You're not like Lieutenant Nahi…"

After a pause, Zain went on, her tone caustic, "He's just a bastard who tries to exploit his position for sexual favors, bribes, revenge, personal advantage, you name it. Whatever satisfies his ego, no matter how sleazy it is. And that's just part of it! As far as he's concerned, Socialism is just a way of replacing a wealthy class with a bankrupt class that goes on doing the same things with the help of its corrupt elements while ordinary Syrians slave away for every penny they make and dream of having enough to eat and being able to educate their children."

"I don't believe it."

"I've thought of reporting Nahi to his immediate superiors, but I'm afraid they might be in cahoots with him, or at least too scared to speak up, since Nahi's known for being a bully. He wouldn't think twice about following in the footsteps of the Red Sultan[9] and dissolving his enemy in a barrel of acid."

"I don't believe it."

"All right, then. If you don't believe me, come and see for yourself whether I'm lying, or whether Nahi's been waiting for me for the last ten minutes."

"I don't believe it."

"He might talk about revolution, but all he cares about is riches."

"I don't believe it."

"Having people like him in charge is downright dangerous. Instead we need democratic, pluralist institutions."

"I don't believe it."

"Well, then, damn it, come with me and see what happens, and then decide whether you believe it or not!"

Zain got up and, trancelike, Alwan rose and followed her out. As they left, the waiter shot them a bewildered look. They hadn't paid the slightest attention to him from the time they arrived, they hadn't ordered a thing, and they hadn't even engrossed themselves in romantic conversation. *I'm a boulder on Mt. Qasioun. Nahi can't scare me, and I'm not going*

---

9   Abdul Hamid II, who ruled the Ottoman Empire from 1876 until he was deposed shortly after the 1908 Young Turk Revolution, was referred to abroad as "the Red Sultan" because of the widespread pogroms and government-sanctioned massacres of Armenians and Bulgarians over which he presided.

to kiss his... I'll expose him instead. Then whatever happens, happens. Yes, I'm divorced, and that's counted against me in this society. But who doesn't have a skeleton in their closet? At least I show my faults openly. What people see is what they get. Neither of them said a word as she sped down the road. *I'm a stupid idiot! How can I think of doing this when I know how much power this man has? But no. I'm not stupid. I'm a boulder on Mt. Qasioun. Don't be afraid, Zain. No... I'm not afraid.*

Zain parked in front of the Intelligence Bureau. No lights were on. Even so, she got out of the car. Not wanting to believe any of what Zain had told him, Alwan said, "See? The place is closed."

Without a word, she gestured for him to follow her.

They approached the entrance. Zain nudged the door with her finger, and it opened. She headed down the dimly lit corridor toward Lieutenant Nahi's office. Overwhelmed by the magnitude of what appeared to be happening, Alwan was lagging, his legs barely holding him up. When Nahi's assistant saw Zain approaching, he asked her no questions, but simply greeted her with a nod as though he'd been expecting her. No sooner had she entered Lieutenant Nahi's office than he wrapped her in an excited embrace, saying, "I knew you'd come! You'd die to get this travel permit, wouldn't you?"

He laughed as she grabbed the permit out of his hand and struggled to free herself from his grip. Just then an incredulous Alwan appeared in the doorway shouting, "No, comrade! No!" He lunged at Nahi and managed to get him away from Zain, who took off running, permit in hand, fled the building, and

drove off in a panic, leaving the two men engrossed in a debate
on ideology!

***

"What kept you out so late?" her father asked, his tone warm but
anxious.

"Sorry, Baba," she replied. "I should have called you, but I
didn't want to bother you with the details of my day—it was a
rough one."

After escaping the Intelligence Bureau, its corridors
ringing hideously with the agonized moans coming from its
underground cells, Zain had taken off like mad for the square at
the foot of Mt. Qasioun. As she went, she alternately hooted and
breathed in as deeply as she could. She opened her car windows
and screeched at the top of her lungs like an owl whose wings
are being clipped, "I might be bloodied by my sorrows and
drenched in ink, but I'll keep on flying and singing: freedom,
freedom, freedom!"

The phone didn't ring long at the Sukaina Literary Forum
before it was answered by Professor Thurayya, who doubled,
tripled and quadrupled as the Forum's owner, secretary,
switchboard operator, and décor engineer.

The caller, who introduced himself as an assistant to
Lieutenant Nahi at the Intelligence Bureau, said he'd seen an
invitation in a local newspaper to a joint presentation that night
by well-known attorney Amjad Khayyal and his daughter Zain.

"Oh, yes!" Professor Thurayya broke in excitedly. "It's an
open invitation, and we'd be delighted to see you there, as well
as Lieutenant Nahi and anyone else you'd like to bring along!"

As if he hadn't heard what she said, the speaker added stiffly, "I believe you'll have to cancel tonight's event. Zain is a German intelligence agent."

"Now listen here!" Professor Thurayya shouted into the receiver, "I don't put up with these sorts of rude pranks! Don't you have anything better to do than spread ugly lies about people? Or did that sheikh of yours who declared open season on Zain put you up to this?"

Then she slammed the receiver down. Little did she know that the hateful prankster she'd just hung up on was Lieutenant Nahi himself!

***

After the evening's event, which had been extremely well attended, Professor Thurayya relaxed into her chair. *I'm exhausted, but I'll sleep well tonight. The forum was packed just the way I'd suspected it would be. It's the biggest crowd I've ever had! It's a good thing we arranged for extra seating in the two rooms off the lecture hall. It was standing room only! We had journalists, intellectuals, professors from Syrian Universities, colleagues of Dr. Amjad's, trainees from his law office, curious onlookers, some spongers, and even some people who came not because they like the presenters, but because they don't like them! I commented to Zain as she was leaving that her success had started getting a rise out of some people. I told her some prattler had called me this afternoon claiming to represent Lieutenant Nahi at the Intelligence Bureau and telling me he wanted me to cancel the event. I'd expected her to laugh when I told her about it, but instead she got a worried look on her face. Maybe she was just tired from reading that sad story of hers. I must have misinterpreted her reaction...*

* * *

As Zain drove home with her father next to her, it consoled her to see how happy he was over the evening's success. *I was feeling good about the way things had gone this evening when, on my way out, Professor Thurayya jokingly mentioned some troublemaker who'd called her this morning. Claiming to be Nahi's assistant, he'd told her to cancel tonight's event, and she hung up on him, assuming it was a sick joke! She doesn't realize it's no joke at all! Nahi's wasting no time getting his revenge. It's no small thing to be accused of spying for West Germany. Trumping up charges against people is one of his specialties, it seems. We freed ourselves of the French mandate, and I have no intention of letting national rule turn into a mandate for some local tyrant! I'll resist him with all I've got. I'll go on exposing him and others like them for what they really are. I'm a boulder on Mt. Qasioun, and I can't be moved.*

For his part, Zain's father was happily reliving every moment of the wonderful evening. *Imagine. My own daughter has become a recognized author like May Ziade. But instead of them driving her crazy, she'll be the one to drive them crazy![10] I robbed her mother of the chance to meet people even in public forums, and I*

---

10 May Ziade (1886-1941) is remembered as a prominent Lebanese-Palestinian poet, essayist, translator and feminist. During a period of deep depression over the loss of her parents and other loved ones, Ziade was placed by relatives in a mental institution, apparently in hopes of taking over her estate. She was eventually released with a medical report affirming her sound mental state.

feel as though I've finally repaid my debt to her. My main concern now is to protect Zain's future rather than crying over my past.

Breaking the silence at last, Zain said, "I learned something important from you today on the subject of successful lecturing, namely, to start by getting people to laugh. I loved the joke you cracked at the beginning about how you were going to give your lecture before I read my story, since if I'd read my story first, everybody would have left before you got to say anything!"

This compliment from his daughter made him all the happier. What he didn't realize, of course, was that even though her words were sincere, they were also an attempt through light-hearted banter to conceal her deepening anxiety over Nahi's reprehensible, and dangerous, accusation.

***

The telephone rang at *Al Ta'ah* newspaper's office. It was answered by its editor-in-chief, its sole editor-at-large, and the head of its ads section. Of these three positions, it was the third that he took the most seriously.

"Hello," said the caller. "I'm the assistant to Lieutenant Nahi at the Intelligence Bureau."

"Oh, hello! It's always good to hear from you over there!"

"We see you published an illustrated report yesterday on Zain Khayyal, who fancies herself an author."

"That's right. I thought she looked pretty hot in the photos, so I included them to give the report some extrapizzazz."

"Well," the caller went on, "that hot divorcee happens to be spying on our country for West Germany. So you'd better not publish anything complimentary about her from now on."

"Oh, I didn't realize that. Our apologies! So then, would you like us to run an article critical of her?"

"It would serve her right."

"Of course, of course."

"We'll be inviting bids to sell intelligence staff uniforms and winter boots, and we want to run a full-page ad in your newspaper."

"It would be our pleasure, sir."

"I hear you and your brother do business in this area."

"That's right, sir."

"Well, then, consider the bid yours, and start making the necessary preparations."

"Thank you."

"Don't worry. I'll see to the matter myself."

"I'll be most grateful."

"A literary critic I know is studying Miss Khayyal's first book. This girl's nothing but a bourgeois radical, and an ideological critique will expose her for what she really is. She'll accuse us of being Zhdanovists,[11] but nobody will be willing to publish that kind of nonsense for her."

* * *

---

[11] Zhdanovism, also referred to as the Zhdanov Doctrine, was a Soviet cultural doctrine developed in 1946 by Andrei Zhdanov. Zhdanov was expected to be the successor to Joseph Stalin, but he died prematurely in 1948. According to Zhdanovism, the world was divided into two camps: the "imperialistic," headed by the United States; and the "democratic," headed by the Soviet Union. Despite its democratic claims, however, Zhdanovism was used to suppress independent thinking among Soviet artists, writers and thinkers, who were required to conform to the party line or risk persecution. The policy remained in effect until Stalin's death in 1953.

The phone rang for a long time at the *Al Intisar* newspaper. Its owner, Mr. Wadee, didn't answer it. He was engrossed in editing the newspaper's political pages, which he needed to go over word for word before they went to press early the next morning.

Mihyu, editor of the cultural page, came in to Mr. Wadee's office and announced that the assistant to Lieutenant Nahi had called objecting to Zain Khayyal's column and demanding that they pull it because, as he had said, Zain was "a West German intelligence operative." Mr. Wadee was about to burst out laughing at the sheer inanity of the accusation when Mihyu added, "He's still on the line, and he wants to talk to you."

Grudgingly lifting the receiver, Mr. Wadee uttered a gruff-sounding, "Yes?"

Putting on his best show of phony gentility, Nahi began, "Good morning, dear sir! I'm the assistant to Lieutenant Nahi at the Intelligence Bureau. I was just telling your cultural editor that it would be better for you not to publish any more articles by Zain Khayyal."

"And why not?" shot back Wadee, his voice sharp and defiant.

"Because she's been accused of spying for West Germany."

Laughing out loud, Mr. Wadee said, "What is this? Some kind of April Fool's?"

"I'm dead serious," replied the voice darkly. "A travel ban was issued today against Miss Khayyal, with orders to intercept her at the border and bring her in for interrogation."

"Anyone accused of a crime is innocent till proven guilty in a court of law," Wadee objected. "So until she's convicted of some wrongdoing, I'll go on publishing what she writes."

Mr. Wadee didn't realize, of course, that his interlocutor was Nahi himself. As for Nahi, who wasn't accustomed to having his wishes questioned, he barked, "Don't publish anything she writes. And that's that."

His fuse lit now, Wadee shouted, "The name of my newspaper is *Al Intisar*—The Defense—and that's what it's about: defending against repression and people who prey on people's freedom of speech. So I'm going to go on publishing Zain Khayyal's literary column. And if I receive a piece expressing an opposing point of view, I'll publish it alongside hers. Beyond that, there's nothing I can do for you."

The call ended as Nahi slammed the receiver down.

Mr. Wadee called Mihyu into his office and asked, "What's the title of the last article Zain sent in?"

"It's called, 'Women Were Born Free.'"

"Run it on the front page tomorrow."

The following night a reply to Zain's article was deposited in an envelope at the newspaper office door. It was typewritten, and the author's name was masculine and appeared to be a pseudonym. "Run it tomorrow," Mr. Wadee instructed Mihyu.

Zain had a response ready the following day entitled, to Wadee's delight, "Men Should Demand Liberation, Too." Mr. Wadee was gratified to see this duel of ideas and opinions, which was just the thing his newspaper was all about.

The second response article was signed by a group referred to in the article as "the Daughters of Hama," who objected to being given the right to vote!

Zain's response this time was an article entitled, "Pray for the Slave Girl Who Revels in Her Servitude." In it Zain put forth the view that these women had been robbed of their will and that the article that purported to represent their views had been authored and signed by a male religious cleric who considered it his duty to ensure their chastity, as though women were lascivious by nature and have to be reined in.

Zain called Mr. Wadee to thank him, but without mentioning her travel plans. However, he learned from his son Raja'i that Zain was on her way to Beirut to continue her studies at the AUB and to write for newspapers in the "Seaside Capital of Freedom" as the city was known among Arab intellectuals.

"So we're losing her," Wadee remarked sadly, "and most people won't even notice. They're trying to destroy her writing career. They're even launching legal and political attacks against her the way they did to her mother."

* * *

The only way Zain's Grandma Hayat knew to pamper her granddaughter was to give her big hugs and feed her her favorite dishes. With Haroun rubbing up against her legs, she said, "I can feel a trip in the air. I gather from things you and your father have been saying that you're going away to study. Well, good for you, girl! You're not like your old granny, who only knows the A-B-C song!"

Zain giggled and threw her arms around her grandmother, who added, "I made fattat makdus and imam bayaldi today, and before you go, I'll make you sitt zabaqi, basmashkat, zunud al-banat, tabbakh rouhou, shaykh al-mahshi, baba ghannoush, and harraq isba`u!"

When Zain's father got home, he delivered a perfunctory greeting and said to Zain, "I need a word with you in the study."

Wriggling out of her grandmother's arms, Zain followed her father out of the room.

"You're not going to be able to go anywhere, Zain," he said, getting straight to the point.

"Why not?"

"When Najati went to the Passports Department to add Egypt to the list of countries you can visit, the employee—the son of a friend of his—showed him a circular forbidding you to leave the country. If you're caught at the border, you'll be arrested." *My father doesn't know anything about Lieutenant Nahi and what happened—or rather, what didn't happen— between us, or how I exposed him in front of Comrade Alwan and left the two of them on the verge of a fist fight. If I don't want him to worry, I'm going to have to lie to him. I never want to make him unhappy again.*

"Oh!" she said with a feigned giggle. "I heard about that, too. It seems there's been a mix-up between me and somebody else with the same name. Early next week I'll go get a paper that clears up the confusion, and then I'll be able to leave. Don't worry, Baba."

Sighing with relief, her father said, "Najati and I nearly flipped when we heard about it! While we were talking it over, Dr. Manahili happened to walk in with a relative of his who's a client of ours, and we told him what we were worried about. Dr. Manahili told us he was friends with Lieutenant—I can't remember his name now—and that he'd look into it and report back to us."

"Forget about it, Baba. I'll call him right now and tell him about the name mix-up."

* * *

The next time Zain and Dr. Manahili had an appointment to meet at the outdoor cafe, they both arrived half an hour early!

"I hear you found out from my dad about the travel ban I'm under."

"And that they're accusing you of spying for West Germany!"

"That's right. I'm the Matahari of the Arab world. So I suppose I've got no choice but to escape to Beirut without Lieutenant Nahi's knowledge."

"He wants a favor from me, and I was planning to say I couldn't do it, but now I've decided to agree to it so that I can help get you out. Are you sure that's what you want to do?"

"Well, it beats being convicted in a kangaroo court presided over by a judge on the take, and then rotting in prison!"

"All right, then. I'll help you make your get-away."

"Please… I don't want to mix you up in this. I've got the travel permit he signed for me earlier. So I'll use that, and try to distract the border official from opening the register that contains the list of people wanted by the authorities. I'll offer to autograph my book for him, and I'll ask him for the names of his family members so that I can include them in my dedication."

"I've got a better plan. I'll give you a ride there and claim you're my cousin."

"No…," Zain hesitated. "I don't want to implicate you in this, since I might be discovered."

"Are you worried about me?"

"Maybe."

"Don't you think it was a mistake to expose him in front of your friend Alwan?"

"Maybe. I don't know what's right and what's wrong, or by what criteria. All I know is that if I'm an agent or a spy, I'm not doing it for West Germany. I'm doing it for the truth."

"Anyway, don't worry. We'll go by your plan. Then, if you see the border official starting to open the big black notebook that lists the people who've incurred the wrath of the powers that be—which includes you now—tell him your cousin's waiting for you in Lieutenant Nasser's office. Nasser heads the Jdaidet Yabous checkpoint on the Syrian-Lebanese border. So don't forget that name. Lieutenant Nahi's going to tell him to give me special treatment. I'll be with him if your plan doesn't work. So now let's agree on the day and the time."

* * *

As she descended the dirt staircase, Zain soaked up the sight of Damascus's orchards and domes with love and longing. The thought that her weekly visits here would soon be a thing of the past made her ache inside. She almost started to cry, she was so overcome with nostalgia and affection. She gazed up at barren Mt. Qasioun and thought: In Bavaria I saw mountains covered with lush green forests, their peaks haloed by mists that came rolling magically down their slopes like a lover bathing his beloved's neck and arms with impassioned kisses. But to me this will always be the most beautiful mountain in the world!

The minute she walked in the house, she said to Grandma Hayat, "What do you say we go to Grandpa's house in Ziqaq Al Yasmin? I miss it!"

"All right," her grandmother replied agreeably. "I'll get dressed and cover my head real quick."

Zain didn't tell her grandmother she wanted to go there to say goodbye. And her grandmother, for her part, didn't tell her that the old ladies in Ziqaq Al Yasmin didn't want to see her anymore. As far as they were concerned, Zain had corrupted the other girls in the neighborhood by saying that when any of them got married, she should have her right to initiate a divorce written into the marriage contract so that if things didn't go well, her husband couldn't demean her or force her to stay with him against her will and best interests. The neighbor ladies had even gone so far as to call down God's mercy on her late mother who, as they put it, "was so meek and mild she would have let the cat eat her dinner without saying a thing!"

With Zain supporting her grandmother on her arm, they made their way to the center of Souq Al Hamidiya.

"Let's stop for some ice cream at Bakdash," the grandmother suggested. It was clear she needed to rest a bit. Cars couldn't drive through the market's narrow, pedestrian-packed passageways, so Zain had parked at the market entrance, which was a fair distance from their destination. Zain ordered hers with an extra dollop of cream on top, and devoured it in no time at all. As she gobbled down her delicious treat, she got a lump in her throat thinking about the fact that it might be for the last time.

Zain had expected to receive a warm welcome when they got to her grandfather's house, but she'd been mistaken. She rapped the knocker on the beautiful old door, and then walked in with the reverence of someone entering a sacred space. It made her happy to see that Ziqaq Al Yasmin was the same as it always had been.

She wanted to check on the goldfish in the pond at the center of the courtyard and to breathe in the scents of jasmine, honeysuckle, basil, roses, narcissus, and bitter orange. She wanted to hear the call to the mid-afternoon prayer coming from the nearby Umayyad Mosque and the other sounds she remembered from Ziqaq Al Yasmin—orange sounds, green sounds, lavender sounds, the sounds that had been imprinted in her memory from childhood: from the trills that rang out at weddings and other happy occasions, to the wails that pierced the air at funeral processions, to the gurgling of hookas, the purling of the wall fountain, and everything else she knew she'd pine for once she was far from her beloved Damascus.

To her sorrow and amazement, Zain encountered very little of what she'd imagined she would. With no one around to pamper them and whisper sweet nothings in their ears, the plants had dried up and withered, and she heard cousins, neighbors, and friends engaged in one shouting match after another.

"You infidel Communist!" shrieked a voice.

"You reactionary!"

"You Marxist!"

"You're one of Michel Aflaq's yes-men."

"You're a rabble rouser."

"You're a Palestinian, an Arab nationalist, so you'll never get where I'm coming from."

"You're a Syrian nationalist."

"You're a foreign agent."

"You're a bourgeois traitor."

"You're just like everybody else in your family!"

Accusations hurled back and forth across the aisle. Shouting. Wailing. There wasn't anything remotely resembling a dialogue. If one of them had been holding a revolver, he'd have been sure to fire.

Her aunt Buran came and gave them a grudging welcome. The atmosphere wasn't to Grandma Hayat's liking, and it saddened her to see her son Abdulfattah sitting on the stone bench with a blank stare on his face. His illness was upon him again, and he didn't recognize either her or Zain. *If only he were well enough to remember me, even if that had meant lashing out at me and calling me names!* Lifting her gaze, Zain saw a huge procession of the living and the dead. Her mother smiled down at her from the balcony as her owl flapped her wings in welcome. She even caught a glimpse of her uncle Sufyan, who had died before she was born and who had fought in the Great Syrian Revolt on Jabal al-Druze and in the Ghouta between 1925 and 1927. She saw women and men present and absent. Before her eyes leapt images of Lu'ay, Hamida, who had left the house a little while earlier, Fadila, now in Kuwait, Fayha, married and living in Aleppo, Muti`a, Buran, Duraid, Qamar, Razan, Mawiya, Hani, and… and…

Against the raucous arguments going on in the background, Grandma Hayat announced with her accustomed diplomacy, "I'm going to the reception at Umm Mazhar's house. Anybody want to come along?"

Before she and Zain left, Zain looked into the courtyard pond to say goodbye to the goldfish, but was shocked to find that they were gone. They'd either died or been taken away, and the pond was nearly dry.

"I'm sorry, Grandma," she said, "but I really don't feel up to attending the reception."

"Don't worry," Grandma Hayat reassured her. "Mazhar can walk me to the end of Souq Al Hamidiya, and then give me a ride home in his car. I used to be his nanny, and I'm closer to him than his own mother."

Zain made herself scarce as fast as she could. Hearing the hostile exchanges between her relatives and their so-called comrades had stabbed her like a knife. Hooting all the way with her trusty owl, she tore through Souq Al Hamidiya like someone fleeing a ghost, or rather, a legion of ghosts. *I try to make my way into the future, but I keep stumbling onto the past! I know I can't forget, but maybe I can forgive myself and others.*

When she reached the house, Haroun lunged at her happily as if to cheer her up. Returning the sentiment, she said, "I won't be seeing you after today, sweet Haroun. I don't know where I'll spend tomorrow night—whether in some prison here, or in Lebanon."

* * *

It was her last night in Damascus, and the next day's journey was full of unknowns.

Zain got in bed, but she couldn't sleep. As she tossed and turned, her owl hopped around the bed as if she were worried too.

I doze off and wake up again. I'm in a tunnel, and I'm running toward the light at the end of it. The sheikh who has it out for me is on my trail. His beard, now braided, has grown into a rope that he wants to hang me with. Nahi runs after me with a Che Guevara-style beard that's down to his feet, and he wants to hang me, too. I'm also being chased by the neighbor lady who put a hot coal on her daughter's tongue for admitting she was in love. She's carrying a brazier filled with burning embers and wants to empty it on my head. Ziqaq Al Yasmin's gossips, smoking hookas that they want to smash into my face, are after me, too.

Another of my pursuers is some self-styled literary critic who's determined to force me into submission either with a carrot of praise or with a blow of his pen on my backside as if I were a little child. As he runs, he reads the book of my body from head to toe: line by line, comma by comma. He's panting, simultaneously ablaze with lust and hatred. After all, as a woman I'm a work of the devil! He unsheathes his pen and tries to stab me in the heart, but I get away from him, and he accuses me of having a man do my writing for me. After all, no woman would be competent enough to write the way I claim to, and divorced women are there for the taking. I keep racing toward the end of the tunnel, my owl right behind me.

Is this just a bad dream? Or is it that, when we go to sleep at night, we jump through windows in our pillows into an alternative reality where we're stripped bare of our masks and pretenses?

My owl swoops down over my pursuers' heads to frighten them away. But then they're joined by my paternal aunt. She's carrying some kind of food I hate and tries to force it down me. Her eyes glint with a malicious determination to repress the girls of the family on the pretext of raising them to be "good." I sob inwardly, knowing that if I didn't have to run for my life, I wouldn't be leaving, and that if I weren't so weary, I would have blown down the streets in a loud, stormy farewell. I would have swept through Sahat Al Muhajirin, Souq Saroujeh, Al Miskiyeh, Al Qubabiyeh, Souq Tafadhdhali Ya Sitt, Al Maydan, and Al Shaghour. I would have gone wailing like an ambulance down every Damascus road I'd ever fallen in love with. I would have visited every school I'd ever gone to and cried in every one of their courtyards. My spirit would have gone wandering through the university campus, and hovered wistfully over the shelves of a library that lives in my heart. I would have planted a goodbye kiss on every book I'd ever catalogued before depositing it lovingly on its shelf. I would have bidden farewell with caresses of longing to the books I kept on the shelves in my dad's study. I would have burst into sobs over every tome that had taught me so much in whatever language. I would have thrown my arms around the ancestors I'd come to know through the books that hold my literary heritage—the ones I read at first because my father made me read them, only to fall in love with them on my own, the way a girl might fall serendipitously in love with the man she's been forced to marry.

I haven't said goodbye to anyone. I haven't even told anybody of my plans for fear that I might weaken and change my mind. When I keep things to myself, I hold myself together better.

It's three-thirty in the morning, and everybody else in the house is asleep. I get out of bed. I pick up my little suitcase and a briefcase that holds drafts of some stories and other things. Then I sneak out to my car, put them in the trunk, and come back inside without waking anybody up. I don't want my dad to see me leaving with my luggage. I don't want to tell him goodbye or cause him any more worry than I have to. I'll call him from Beirut—if I get there!

Zain got back in bed and tried once again to sleep, but without success. The myriad faces of repression went parading again before her mind's eye. Her limbs and organs lay scattered on and around the bed, and her head had fallen on the carpet.

At length she was rescued from her troubled thoughts by Haroun, who had slipped into bed beside her. She got up to get dressed. The time for her to leap into the political boxing ring had come.

***

As Zain drove to the ominous Jdaidet Yabous checkpoint where she might well be arrested, she was trembling with fright. To calm herself she began reciting some prayers she had memorized as her owl flew alongside her with anxious sounding hoots. When she passed the burial site of Yousef Al Azmah in Maysaloun,[12] she didn't stop to pay her respects the way her father had always taught her to do. *I admit it: I'm terrified. I don't regret anything I've done or said. At the same time, I don't want to join the people whose screams I heard coming from Nahi's underground cells the night I went with Alwan to his office at the Intelligence Bureau.*

But when she pulled up in front of the border crossing, she didn't feel frightened the way she'd expected to. Instead she felt exhilarated, as if she knew this was part of the process of taking hold of who she really was. *I seem to enjoy the kind of adventure that sends the blood rushing through my veins with the speed of a waterfall. Instead of being scared, I'm excited. I can almost hear my heart beating. I'm high on the thrill of dangerous adventure. Like a gambler, I want to win the round. And it's a hell of a gamble. I might win my life, or I might lose it. I feel as though I have an enchanted glow about me that could make people do my bidding. Or am I just imagining things?*

---

[12]   Yousef Al Azmah (1883-1920) was the Minister of War under King Faisal, and is remembered with reverence for leading the Syrian forces into battle against a French invasion at the Battle of Maysaloun, in which he was killed.

Putting on her prettiest smile, Zain strode coolly into the office where passengers' travel documents were checked and handed the border official the semi-forged travel permit she had filched from Lieutenant Nahi. As she did so, her owl perched on his shoulder without his noticing a thing. Then, to keep him from opening his large black notebook and finding her name on the wanted list, she placed a copy of her book in front of him and said innocuously, "I'd like to write you something in the front flap of this book (she didn't tell him she was its author). So can you tell me your name, and the names of your wife and children? That way I can include them in the dedication." *Man, what an idiot I am! What ever gave me the idea I could get past border officials this way? Of course I've seen movies where the lead character makes his getaway like this, but real life isn't like that. This is what I get for watching so many action flicks.*

She prayed he'd remember having seen her on television and decide to let her write something in her book for him. But he ignored her, picking up his massive black notebook without a word, and without even a glance in her direction despite the fact that her invisible owl had started beating him on the head with her wing. *It looks like I've got no choice but to let Dr. Manahili step in.*

She added, "Lieutenant Nasser is waiting for me with my cousin, Dr. Rahif Manahili."

Here the official looked at her with new-found respect and, hurriedly handing her papers back to her along with her passport, jumped out of his seat, saying, "Why didn't you say so from the start? You need to be on your way, then!"

*My book? Who gives a damn about that? But name-dropping—
that's a language people understand!*

The minute Zain walked into Lieutenant Nasser's office, Dr.
Manahili jumped to his feet, saying earnestly, "Oh, there you are!
What kept you? Did you get so busy with your fiancé that you
forgot I have to leave for a medical conference at the Continental
Hotel in Beirut? Why don't you ride with me and let my driver
take your car? No offense, but you're a slow poke, like all the
women I know!"

Lieutenant Nasser, who smirked admiringly at the doctor's
sexist comment, was under instructions from Nahi to do
whatever Dr. Manahili asked. He figured Zain must be the
doctor's mistress, which was none of his business, of course,
as long as "Comrade" Nahi approved. Zain disappeared into
Dr. Manahili's car with record speed, and they took off in the
direction of the Masnaa checkpoint.

From here on out there was no need to worry. Lebanon
welcomed everyone, and Zain was received with particular
warmth when she flashed her acceptance letter from the
American University in Beirut.

Now on Lebanese soil, she heaved a huge sigh of relief.

When they arrived in Chtaura, Dr. Manahili said, "I'm taking
you to lunch at the Akl Restaurant."

Before she'd had a chance to reply, he'd parked the car.

"I'll call my dad from the restaurant to let him know
I got here safely and that I'm on my way to the school in
Choueifat."

* * *

After a delicious lunch in the course of which Dr. Manahili treated himself to some arak, he said to her. "I'll ask my driver to escort you there so that I can make sure you get there all right."

Her voice full of earnestness, Zain said, "This is the second time you've saved my life. I'll never forget you!"

"I wouldn't let you forget me anyway!" he replied jovially. "I'll come visit you every week, with or without my wife." *So, is this the daughter I wish I'd had? Or the one I hoped not to have?*

Zain's thoughts went to Dr. Manahili's wife Brigitte. *What a brave, loyal lady she is! She volunteers her time to teach French to little children in spite of all the hostility she faces as a foreigner.*

"I would love for Brigitte to come with you," Zain offered. "A wife like her would be hard to find."

***

Zain had never envied Cinderella for having to leave that wonderful ball at midnight. And now she had to be back at her dorm by eleven o'clock if she wanted a safe place to sleep. Once the clock struck eleven, the towering iron gate that led into the Choueifat campus was bolted shut till morning. So no matter how pumped up she was from the stimulating conversations going on around her, she had to leave the cinema, or the theatre, or the restaurant, or the Diplomat Café, or the Dolce Vita, or anywhere else she happened to be by ten-thirty in the evening, hopefully without leaving one of her glass slippers behind, and drive like a maniac back to the Choueifat campus. If she'd been in Raouché, she would drive past Ramlet *al-Baida*, the St. Simon swimming pools, St. Michel, al-Awza`i, and Choueifat, then turn at the top of a hill onto a dirt road that led to the school.

Because of her curfew, Zain had to decline an invitation to attend what would have been a thoroughly enjoyable session with her journalist friend Marlene, by now a regular companion of hers at the Dolce Vita and other coffee shops. The nicest thing about these places was the possibility of finding some fugitive Arab dictator having an amicable debate with a dissident that had fled the country before him, and who had been persecuted by the very dictator in question. *Imagine: If they'd sat down and talked like this in their own country, neither of them would be here!*

Zain loved the intellectual-literary-political atmosphere that permeated Beirut's coffee houses, where Nasserites, Marxists, and Arab nationalists mixed freely with spies, artists, conspirators, propagandists and critics, the charming and the tasteless alike. They were a dizzying hodgepodge of folks from other Arab countries, and Beirutis who were willing to put up with pretty much anybody.

Zain drove down the Awza`i Highway, a coastal road from whose narrow shoulder you could step directly onto a beach of fine white sand. *What a magical night that was! I'd never seen the moon so huge in all my life. With its rays it had drawn a highway of light that stretched to the ends of the horizon.*

As she passed the airport on her left, she glanced at her watch and sped up. Then suddenly the car swerved. She gripped the steering wheel, pressing down on it with both arms, and took her foot off the gas pedal. The car started to shimmy and shake, and she knew she had a flat tire. When she got out to see what had happened, she discovered that the culprit was the left front tire. She was grateful for the moonlight, which was a lot more generous than the stingy streetlamps. She calmly got the jack out of the trunk and started loosening the nuts on the offending tire in preparation to change it.

Not a car passed without offers of help from male drivers, and she almost accepted one of them. *What is this? How can I demand equality with men, then let them change my flat tires for me? If the airplane bringing us back from Germany had crashed, would I have rushed with the women to get first place on a lifeboat, or would I have demanded equal opportunity with men to burn to death inside a downed aircraft? I rail against double standards, but don't I apply them myself when it suits me? If not, then why was I just about to make things easy on myself by letting a guy change my flat tire for me?*

By the time Zain finished changing the flat, she was so frustrated she felt like throwing the stupid thing into the sea. If she hadn't been so exhausted, and if the tire hadn't been so heavy, she probably would have. *On the other hand, it cost too much to throw away. I'd better fix it instead. My dad isn't supporting me anymore, and I've got a budget to stick to.*

The luminous path the moon had etched across the water's surface and the charm of Awza`i Beach's pristine sands lured her to lie down for a while and take in the beauty before her. *It's nearly eleven, and there's no way I'll get back in time, so I'll have to find somewhere else to spend the night.* She went walking through the clean white sand. The sound of the waves rose higher as they flirted with the shore, washing in and washing out, in and out. Then suddenly she plopped down on the beach and lay staring into the moonlight. She closed her eyes, conjuring images of Damascus. *Ever since I got to Beirut I've been running all over the place, high on the thrill of discovery. I've accepted every invitation that's come my way: from heads of universities, religious clerics, authors, both Christians and Muslims, journalists, lawyers, and intellectuals from all walks of life. Some of them have hosted me in their homes, where I've met their families, and others have taken me to classy restaurants in Jounieh, Sidon, Triboli, Jbeil, Tyre, and on and on. But sometimes I feel like the hen that belonged to Grandma Hayat back in Ziqaq Al Yasmin. When I was a little girl, they chopped its head off so that they could cook it and eat it. I'll never forget the terror I felt when I saw it running around like crazy without a head. All I could do was cry and scream. Am I the hen that goes running headless from one Beirut intellectual forum to another? Is this what I've turned into now that I know I can never see Damascus again?*

With a sigh of contentment, Zain went imagined herself strolling down the moonlit path on the sea. *Just like I've always dreamed of doing, I'm lying on a beach all by myself, on a planet of my own. And I'm free, free…* She fell fast asleep. Then suddenly she was roused by something crawling over her bare arms. She opened her eyes to find a convoy of tiny newborn crabs making their way across her on their way to the water. Just as she was about to jump up in a fright, she remembered hearing how painful crab bites could be even if the crab was small. So with all the willpower she could muster, she held still until the procession had passed. Then she leapt off the sand like a madwoman and took off running to her car. *Dreams of freedom, when they come true, aren't without their bites and stings!*

It was three-thirty in the morning. Duly humbled and sobered, Zain drove back to the school and parked outside its closed gate. She locked her car doors and tried to get some sleep.

By this time she'd made up her mind to rent herself an apartment
of her own, a freedom flat that she could come home to any hour
of the day or night.

***

It didn't take long for Zain to find a place to live on her own,
a place where she could sleep by herself without a husband
persecuting her, or a father interrogating her, or aunts and uncles
who went around operating traffic signals. *Red: Don't pass this
way. Green: Enter another marriage—that is, if anybody would be
willing to marry a rebellious divorcee like you.* It was easy, in fact.
One day she was reading a newspaper that had run a critique of
her book when she noticed an ad for apartments for rent in a new
building. *That means the walls will be clean and freshly painted,
the tile will still be smooth and shiny and easy to clean, I won't have
rust and ants gushing out of the water faucets, and I won't have to
call a repairman, a carpenter, or a plumber for a long time. It also
means I won't be haunted by former tenants' ghosts. Instead, I can
leave my ghost to haunt the people who move in after me.*

Zain called the number listed in the ad. Then she went to the
bank to apply for a loan to cover the three-month advance she'd
have to pay in order to move into the apartment. When she told
the bank teller her name, he jumped up excitedly, saying, "How
are you, Zain? I'm Abu Jurais's son—Widad and Sara's brother.
Your dad used to rent a summer house from us in Bloudan! I'll
give you the apartment for a month, and you can see if you like
it. If you do, we'll talk about the rest of the details then."

Then he gave her the key and the address, and called the
building's concierge so that he could be expecting her.

As I left the bank, I wondered: How did so many Syrians end up here in Beirut? I seem to run into a Syrian everywhere I go. Then the bank teller turns out to be from Bab Tuma, of all places!

A sparsely furnished tenth-floor efficiency apartment in the Ramal al-Zarif neighborhood, it was hers for a month subject to extension. Even though it was a single room, she was happy with it. *As far as I'm concerned, I wouldn't even need walls. All I want is the sun, open space, and a chance to sleep on a cloud.* She felt free as the wind. Besides the refrigerator, all the furniture she had was a writing table, a chair, and a bed, and with that she was content.

After buying herself some linens, she settled in for her first night. She walked up and down the spacious balcony that ran around the apartment's periphery, pleased with her tiny new abode. She was also pleased that she'd been able to pay the month's rent out of the salaries she made from her job writing a weekly magazine column and articles drawn from her university studies, and from her English-teaching position at the Choueifat School. She was free now. Alone, and free.

Dr. Manahili had offered to lend her some money, but she'd declined, saying, "If I need a loan, I can ask my dad." Then she'd added, "If I borrowed money from you, you'd have a say in my choice of apartment and other decisions. You could also impose your opinions on me. When you owe people money, you lose some of your freedom!"

"You're right," he said

"So if you knew that," Zain inquired curiously, "why did you offer me a loan?'"

"Well," he admitted sheepishly, "I'd like to rob you of some of your freedom! I envy you. I envy you because I've never been free myself."

As she lay in bed on her first night there, she experienced at last the pleasure of sleeping through the night without anybody to wake her up, whether out of love or desire, and without having to take part in Friday morning food rituals of pita bread dipped in tasqiya, foul mudammas, or any other traditional breakfast for that matter.

All she kept in her house was coffee. After drinking her morning cup, she went to teach her class, her senses heightened as they'd never been before. She felt liberated, energized. That night she studied at the library until the doors closed. Then she went back to her penthouse lair on the tenth floor of the night of stars. The thrill she felt over her new-found autonomy drowned out any misgivings that might have darkened the horizon. She had brought a phonograph player with her, and a recording of Charles Aznavour singing, "La Bohème." She felt as though it was her own song, and when she lay down to go to sleep, she was drunk on freedom. *Never again will I cry on a balcony in defeat and humiliation.*

Zain went to sleep dreaming she could fly. It was a dream that had stayed with her ever since she was a teenager. Before long, however, she wakened to the sound of a thud on her balcony. She was such a light sleeper that a feather dropping nearby could have roused her. *I must be imagining things. Or am I?* She turned on the light next to the bed, jumped up and flipped the switch that lit up the balcony. The suspicious-sounding movement stopped, which confirmed to her that there was somebody out there who didn't want to be discovered. Was it a burglar? She didn't have anything a burglar would have been interested in. But after hearing what sounded like men whispering and somebody climbing the wall, she crept outside for a peek, but didn't see anyone.

The following night she awoke to the same sounds, and this time she was terrified. When the scene repeated itself on the third night, she was convinced that somebody was jumping from the roof onto her balcony. But who? And why? That was when she realized that living in a lair of her own, however free that made her feel, was tantamount to baiting a fisherman's hook. Freedom, she now saw, comes with a price, and the price in her case was to give up the protection that had been provided for her by all the people she'd run away from. So now she would have to either retreat into a safe place, or face the dangers of freedom without anybody else's help.

It had become apparent that even if they were only a figment of her imagination or the pitter-patter of some Shakespearian phantom, the footsteps retreated when she switched on the light at her bedside.

She described what had happened to Rajih, a member of the group she hung out with at the Dabibu Café, a coffee shop that sat perched on the cliff opposite the famed Raouché Boulder. In response, he casually pulled a revolver out of his pocket, saying, "Here. You can defend yourself with this. I've cocked it for you and pulled out the safety pin, so all you have to do is pull the trigger. Nobody will charge you with a crime, because if you kill your attacker, it will be in self-defense, and I'll testify for you in court!"

It was the first time she'd seen a gun anywhere but in a movie theatre, still less touched one. Beirut—what a place! She decided to go back to sleeping in the teachers' dormitory at the Choueifat School. Until then, she'd keep the revolver just in case. She figured if anybody tried to attack her, she could shoot it into the air to scare them off.

Early the next morning, she woke to the sound of scuffling and shouting. At first she stayed holed up in her fortress, trembling like a leaf. *So then, freedom isn't quite the bed of roses I'd thought it was. Next time I rent an apartment, I'll look for one that's well-protected, not some bird's nest on a low tree branch. And it might be good to have a roommate or two.*

Zain took the elevator down to the underground parking garage. The elevator door opened to reveal scores of policemen, one of whom prevented her from going to her car.

"Sorry, Ma'am," he said. "This is a crime scene."

"But I live here," she protested, "and I need to get to my car so I can drive to the university and my job."

"You're a resident? If so, then you're a potential witness. Wait over there," he said, pointing to a group of neighbors standing over to their right.

"What happened?" Zain asked him.

"Jeannie, a nightclub dancer who lives in the building, was coming home from work at dawn when, according to her, two doormen tried to assault her in the parking garage. She says she shot at them, and one of them's dead now. We're here to check out her account."

Sure enough, Zain read in the newspapers the next day about what people referred to as "Jeannie's building," where Jeannie had allegedly killed a concierge because he and a coworker had tried to attack her in the basement parking garage. *Boy, a lot I know! I've been running after my dreams of freedom without seeing what's going on right around me: plots to hurt people, and so-called "guards" jumping off roofs to check out their next victims! I may not be as alluring a victim as a voluptuous nightclub dancer who comes home from work drunk in the wee hours of the morning. But I'm still a potential victim. Ironically, the fact that I haven't slept well since my mother died rescued me from what could have been a deadly assault. And imagine: Jeannie—the neighbor I'd never heard of before or even seen in the elevator, although I suppose I might not have recognized her since she was wearing street clothes like me—was carrying a revolver like the one I've been putting under my pillow.*

It was Zain's last night in her freedom flat, as she liked to call it, and she was packing up her things. That night she shot at a cloud where the moon lived on heaven's sixth floor. As she fired, she asked the cloud, "Why do you put all these obstacles in the way of my freedom? Or is this just the price we freedom-lovers have to pay?"

When she fired the shot, the revolver kicked back in her hand. She tightened her grip on it, afraid that it might strike her in the face. Her hand was so sore afterwards that she found it hard to drive or write for days on end. *How could Rajih put a gun in my hand just like that without telling me what to expect? Lebanese people's relationship with weapons scares me. And it scares me to think how easily I got a gun... I can't wait to give it back!*

* * *

When Dr. Manahili and Zain met for lunch at Faysal's, he told
her, "I came from Damascus just to see you." And she believed
him.

"You look bright," he added, "and pretty happy!"

"Well," she replied, "if it weren't for the fact that I can't visit
Damascus, I could say I was completely happy. I'm working on
my second short story collection, and I'm also a teacher and a
journalist!"

Their conversation was interrupted by a politician who came
over from another table to greet Zain, and by an author who
presented her with an invitation to attend a lecture he'd be giving
at a local symposium.

"I've got two pieces of news," Dr. Manahili told her after their
visitors had departed. "One's happy, and the other's sad. Which
one should I start with?"

"With the happy one, of course," she said.

"My wife is pregnant."

Squealing with excitement, Zain jumped spontaneously
out of her chair and planted a kiss on his cheek in plain view of
everyone in the restaurant.

"You're still your old self, Zain!" he said with a chuckle.

"And now for the sad news," she said. "What's up?"

"Well," he said, "Lieutenant Nahi's little boy died."

"Oh no! How?"

"Of a fever. The antibiotic his ex-wife had bought for him
from a local pharmacy turned out to be no good. She tried to
contact Nahi about it but he wouldn't talk to her. Once I was
with him when she tried to phone him and he refused to take the
call. In any case, the antibiotic she'd given their little boy was one

of the expired medications Nahi and his partner had forged the dates on so they could get rich off other people's backs."

"Oh, my God. I wonder if she's heard about the medicine scandal."

"He murdered his own son."

"I feel terrible for the little boy and his mother! But it looks like Lieutenant Nahi's gotten a taste of his own medicine now."

After a pause, Zain went on, "So has he learned to show people a little more compassion now that he knows what it feels like to suffer?"

"I'm afraid not. In fact, he's meaner than ever now. He had a friend of his thrown in jail on false charges just for having the nerve to beat him at a game of chess!"

Just then a waiter came up and said to Zain, "You have a call from a journalist by the name of Mr. Asaad."

Zain got up and followed the waiter to the telephone. "Hello," she began. "How are you, Mr. Asaad?"

Dispensing with the usual niceties, he asked, "Have you read the newspaper?"

"No, not yet," she said. "What is it?"

"They've arrested three saboteurs belonging to the Syrian secret police, and they've confessed that one of the things they were sent to do was to kidnap you and take you back to Syria!"

Wobbly kneed, Zain made her way back to the table and told Dr. Manahili what she'd learned from Mr. Asaad.

"I'd heard about it, actually," Dr. Manahili confessed, "but I didn't want to worry you. I could tell you didn't know about it yet. Nahi's furious that you managed to leave Syria, and he's out to get you. Fortunately, he doesn't know that my 'cousin' was you!"

"But why would he send a network of saboteurs to Beirut when he knows full well that it's the only safe haven he'll have himself once he's deposed from his throne? God help us from people like him."

* * *

Zain was sitting with Marlene one day at the Diplomat Café when they were approached by none other than the poet Alwan, clad in his usual prehistoric sandals and his tattered shirt. Zain jumped up to welcome him and introduce him to Marlene. Marlene told him she'd read most of his poems and that she was a fan of his.

Zain sensed special vibes between Marlene and Alwan of the sort she knew well.

"Are you just here on a short visit, Alwan?" Zain asked. "And how's the radio station?"

Turning to Marlene, Zain added, "Comrade Alwan isn't just a fantastic poet. He's a mainstay of the Syrian Radio Broadcast."

Correcting her, Alwan said, "I'm not a mainstay of anything anymore. I've been on the outs with Nahi ever since our tussle that night, and like you, I had to get out of Syria. He denied everything, of course, and accused me of trying to trump up charges against him. So it looks like I'll be a permanent guest around here."

"You're welcome to stay for as long as you like," Marlene said cheerfully. "I think the newspaper I work for has a job opening. We recently lost our literary editor, who'd been in exile and who recently went back to his home country to serve as Minister of Culture after the regime there was overthrown."

Chapter Seven

Beirut simmered like a hot brew of clashing ideas. But instead of feeling lost and alone, Zain loved the place. She had found her intellectual home. Nor did she see herself as a fugitive or a refugee, but as a citizen in her own country. Oddly, the Lebanese had a way of being more welcoming to people from elsewhere than they were to each other!

There were arguments, of course, over who was the true patriot—the Arab nationalist? The unionist? The isolationist? But the only weapon anybody pulled on his interlocutor was a pen. Accusations would fly, but with a kind of reserve, and via a kind of polite subterfuge. Whenever people met, they exchanged kisses on the cheek, and they were known for doing pendulum swings between the poles of intellectual attraction and its countless, moody variations!

Zain viewed everything with a neutral eye. After all, she had come from a city with a completely different climate, where falsely accusing somebody of being a foreign agent was enough to get the accused locked up and murdered. In Beirut, by contrast, the same accusation would be grounds for nothing more than a pointed debate. There were people who tried to get her to take a stance on issues, but if she had, it wouldn't have made her a candidate for being framed on charges of treason and ending up on the gallows or in prison for life. It would just have led to a heated discussion over a cup of coffee and an attempt to change her mind.

Beirut was a city devoted to intellectual growth and exchange, not to burying people alive. It was a place where people were vibrant with thought, literature, and dialogue from whatever platform was available, be it a magazine, a journal, a newspaper, or a radio station, and where everyone's competing ideas were bared for all to see. It was a place that had captured Zain's heart. One scene reflective of this lively, liberated climate was especially dear to her heart. One day as she sat in the Dolce Vita, she saw a former Arab ruler, now deposed and in exile, sitting at a table with the remnants of his following. And at a neighboring table she spied an enemy of his whose own exile to Beirut (and what a lovely place to be exiled to!) had been caused by that same ruler. Seeing this kind of thing thrilled her heart.

She never turned down an invitation from any party to a debate. She wanted to know, to be informed. She wanted to probe the depths of human nature, then slip out with girlfriends to Café Azar for a cup of Turkish coffee scented with rosewater the way she used to do in Damascus.

As Zain and Marlene sat together at the barny Café Azar, which was located in a major office building, Marlene said, "How would you like to visit the *Muharririn* newspaper office and meet some of the folks there? It's housed right here in this building. Then I could take you to the bookstore in the Capital Building. This neighborhood's full of publishing houses and newspapers. The *Dhaw*' newspaper and the publishing house where you and I met for the first time are both in the El Khandak El Ghamik neighborhood not far from here."

"That'd be nice," Zain said, hesitating. "But actually, I need to study this afternoon, so I think I'll just head to the library."

While she was at the café, a number of editors came up to greet Zain, who had rarely received such acclaim for her work back in her home town. *In Damascus I was surrounded by the canes and whips of suspicion, hostility and prejudice for being a member of the bourgeoisie. Certain people in power in my home country hated me for being a renegade against their doctrines. So they tried to put me in my place, exploiting my being a woman— and divorced—to hurt me double-time. But I even had enemies in the class I supposedly belonged to, like the religious clerics who hated me so much they issued legal rulings saying it was permissible to kill me. And back in Ziqaq Al Yasmin I was a "corrupting influence" because I'd defected from the conservative, rightest class I came from. So I was damned if I did, damned if I didn't!* As these thoughts were running through Zain's mind, she looked up and who should she see but Ghazwan! He was talking to a waiter behind a counter and ordering an espresso to go.

"That's Ghazwan Ayed," Marlene whispered. "You may have heard of him. He works at the newspaper on the third floor."

As she glanced again in Ghazwan's direction, she saw him staring back at her in disbelief. He looked like somebody who had just come across a rare bird he'd been looking for forever in the forests of the night. He came up to their table. Then, ignoring Marlene, he said in a voice charged with earnest emotion, "You're the Subki Park girl, aren't you? You're the girl I proposed to but who turned me down."

Zain nodded in affirmation.

Marlene, bewildered at the serious, romantic turn the conversation had just taken between an editor-in-chief who'd held his post for exactly one week and an author he was supposedly meeting for the first time, sat there without saying a word.

Transported suddenly out of space and time, Zain and Ghazwan forgot where they were and what day it was. They forgot Marlene. Each of them stood there staring at the other like somebody he or she had lost in an earthquake and had never expected to see again. Wanting nothing but to be alone with her, far from prying eyes, he invited her to lunch. Then, acknowledging Marlene's presence at last, he said to her with the light wit that seemed to follow him wherever he went, "You, my dear, aren't invited. See you!"

Then, taking Zain by the hand, he pulled her toward the exit. When the lift was slow to reach their floor, he pulled her onto the stairs.

As they ran down the stairwell like a couple of kids, he said, "I'm not going to let you get away from me again!"

His car was half vintage, half rattletrap. But as she got in, Zain felt as though she were boarding a spaceship about to take off for the moon.

"Where to?" he asked as he pulled out of the basement parking lot.

Feeling relieved to be above ground—ever since the incident in Jeannie's building, as it had come to be referred to, she'd hated underground parking garages, which made her feel she was about to suffocate—she said without hesitation, "To the sea... the sea."

Then suddenly, looking at her with his honey-sweet eyes, he said sadly, "I asked you to marry me and you turned me down. I asked you even before I knew your name or anything about you. From the first time I saw you, I knew you were my woman, my one true love on this planet."

Zain heard herself say calmly, "Turn left here to get out of this traffic jam. Then head for the sea."

"All the places I've found you—Subki Park, the Havana Café, Ziqaq Al Jinn—you've run away from my madness instead of being infected with it. Your madness is the studied kind. You've got it walled in. But I've gotten to know some facets of it through your stories, and they're all linked by an invisible thread of caution. Nothing shakes you or diverts you from the path of cold logic. You've got an incredible mind, but you haven't mastered the art of vertigo."

It started to rain inside her. *If only that really were true!* Her silent weeping closed her off from everything Ghazwan was saying. Then it went and stuffed its sorrows into the recesses of her heart the way an addict stuffs bottles of booze into his coat pockets. She felt the need to run away. *I'm not going to fall in love again, damn it. I can't take another disappointment. My divorce should have inoculated me against love's scourge.* She had paid dearly for her freedom. She had suffered in silence at first, secretly grieving her degradation and humiliation until, at last, she'd rebelled. And once she'd started rebelling, she hadn't stopped.

She thought back on how she used to stand sobbing on the back balcony off the kitchen, and how her elderly neighbor Mrs. Kotalli would try to console her. *For all I know, she was more*

*miserable than I was! As depressed, disillusioned and lost as I felt
back then, I always knew deep down that poor Mrs. Kotalli was
more lost than I was. Otherwise, she wouldn't have been standing
outside on a dark balcony herself!*

Ghazwan reached out and took her hand in his. She drew it
away, resisting the urge to come out from behind her shield and
bare her sorrows to him. Besides, he had sorrows of his own.
So the only way to survive was to stay on her own. She'd once
thrown herself into love's quagmire, and if she hadn't rescued
herself at the last minute, she would have been pulled under by
the quicksand. *I'm never jumping into love's bog again. I'm not
letting it take me down. I swore never to let love debase me again,
and I don't want to forget that.*

Ghazwan took her to the Pigeon's Grotto, a cliff-side café
that overlooks *Raouché Boulder. Looking down at the arched
tunnel that runs through the rock's base,* Zain thought back on
a recent adventure. *When I first came here I started learning to
water ski at the Long Beach swimming pool complex. Just yesterday
I tried skiing under that stone archway, and the slightest mistake
would have dashed me against the rocks. But I made it—I won
the challenge—and I was high as a kite. My whole life has been
a gamble, actually. But I blame myself now for not contacting
Ghazwan earlier. Why didn't I look him up as soon as I got here? I
knew where he was, and what a brilliant writer he is, impassioned
for Palestine.*

After making short shrift of the waiter by ordering for both of
them without consulting her, Ghazwan said half-apologetically,
"You're thin. I know you prefer lean meat and lots of vegetables
and tabbouli! But I also ordered you a big glass of fire water. I

want you to get drunk if possible. When I saw you in Subki Park, there was some secret you were hiding. Then you escaped out the back door of the Kaddura Pharmacy. At the time I didn't know anything about you, not even your name. I remember asking you to marry me, and I meant it."

...

"Then you disappeared. I'd see pictures in the newspapers of a young woman who looked a lot like you. She was a story writer and had published a book in Beirut. I wanted to believe she was the Subki Park girl, that girl who'd been hurting and scared and broken-hearted, but holding herself together. As wounded as she was, she was determined to make it. Or at least, that's how it seemed to me when I put my coat around her shoulders to keep her warm. After that I named her the blasé Havana Café girl, then the defiant Ziqaq Al Jinn girl who also ran away from me. I think that's when I really got attached to her. And now I know she was you, after all."

...

"Actually, I think I got attached to you from the moment I first saw you. Love at first sight is real. I know that now, because it's happened to me, even though I reject it on the level of plain logic. I tried to explain my attraction to you by telling myself that since you were so crushed, so in pain, so defeated for some reason unknown to me but so determined to go on, you must have represented 'the act of resistance' for me. In other words, I'd fallen in love with your spirit."

After a pause, he added with his accustomed drollness, "I've got nothing against your body, of course. In fact, I'm all for it!"

They both burst out laughing.

They ate as if they'd never eaten before, and drank as though they'd never drunk before. (In Zain's case, of course, she really hadn't drunk before!)

As they left the Pigeon's Grotto, Ghazwan announced that he'd be taking her for tea to a seaside café in Jounieh. Once there, Ghazwan ordered the tea, which was duly served by the waiter. Then, as if on a whim, he jumped up and pulled Zain out of her seat. Taking her by the hand, he led her back out of the café as if he were under the spell of beautiful lights emanating from an enchanted cloud. Hand in hand, they headed for the sea, leaving their papers in the café next to their untouched tea.

We sat there in the sand as time committed suicide and the world's clocks went into a collective swoon. Trancelike, we answered the call of the sun as it danced with its beloved the sea, shimmying gracefully in the garb of multihued clouds. We went strolling hand in hand over a rainbow toward the sun, hoping it would never meet the horizon. The atmosphere charged with bliss, we wanted to stop time at that magical moment. We didn't notice that we'd waded out to sea until the salty waves were nearly up to our necks.

With a timid laugh Ghazwan confessed, "I'm not a very good swimmer. How about you?"

"I'm not bad myself," she replied, "but if you start to go under, don't count on me to save you!"

They giggled like a couple of kids. By the time they headed back to shore, they were drenched to the bone. When they walked back into the café, the other patrons were laughing. They'd been watching them from the balcony. As they took their seats with the aplomb of someone who has no idea he's dripping wet, someone sitting nearby started clapping. Then the rest of his table joined in. By this time everybody was in stitches, as though Ghazwan and Zain had done what they'd wished they could do but would never have dared to. It was one of those sweet moments that escape time's grasp.

The entire place was infused with a spirit of merriment now, and as the waiter brought them fresh hot tea, he said jovially, "You deserve it! By the way, I thought the two of you were going to swim to Cyprus so you wouldn't have to pay the tab!"

But when Ghazwan tried to do just that—that is, pay the tab—the waiter made him put his money away, saying, "Come every day! You'll help us attract more customers!"

They were still sopping wet when they got back into his car, dying for a couple of sets of dry clothes.

To Zain, Ghazwan's whole person—his skin, his clothes, his everything—gave off the fragrance of the Acre Sea, Jaffa, and tears of nostalgia. He smelled like Palestine.

"Is there some way I could pick up your scent with a camera?" Zain asked him. "I want to take a picture of your feelings, you loved-racked soul! I want other people to see your passion for your homeland, the love that emanates from every word you write. It isn't Zain you're madly in love with. It's Palestine."

They both fell silent for a long time. Then suddenly he blurted out, "But I *am* in love with you, Zain. I've loved you since the first time we met. I fell in love with the Subki Park teenager who turned down my marriage proposal, and with the Havana Café fruitcake who rejected me for the second time!"

After a pause, he added, "It didn't occur to me when we were in Subki Park that I was falling in love with a time bomb that would turn into a writer who'd compete with me in my profession!"

...

"On second thought," he added, "I won't let you compete with me!"

Her tone earnest, she replied, "Nobody could ever match your love for your country, whether in word or in deed. I ask so many questions because I lack certainty. But you know the answers, so you're stronger than I am."

Zain felt herself tottering on the brink of love. But she'd be damned if she was going to fall into that hole again. She didn't dare give in to this person that she wanted so badly to give in to, since if she did, she might lose him. *Does a man always stop loving a woman when she admits she loves him back? Is that just human nature? Or do only some men do that?*

Ghazwan pulled over to the side of the road, leaned over and stole a kiss which he apparently thought people driving by wouldn't take any notice of. But the kiss lasted a lot longer than he thought it would, and Zain was afraid some self-righteous somebody might come down on them with a bamboo cane. *Actually, people in Beirut show a lot of tolerance toward both politicians and lovers. But a kiss like that on the streets of Damascus might have cost me my life, or my reputation, at least.*

The lips that had just touched hers were strewn with mines. *No! I'll be damned if I'm going to let myself get burned a second time.* She had a powerful, sinking feeling she really might fall for him. *Romantic love might be a mirage, but it's more real than any other fact of life.*

As they drew apart, she thought to herself: All right, I might end up loving Ghazwan. But if I do, I'll also end up hating him.

So if he's a huge love in the making, he's a huge tragedy in the making, too.

***

Beirut amazed her, nay, enchanted her. With every step she took, she came upon a new sidewalk, a new side street, a new path to explore. She was captivated by the city's simultaneous embrace of the modern and contemporary, the ancient and traditional. After lingering in spots she'd visited with her father as a little girl, she continued on her way to the AUB campus. She headed first for Bustani Hall, a girls' dormitory, to visit her classmate Lamis who'd come down with a cold and a cough. From there she headed for Uncle Sam's across from the AUB's Main Gate. On her way there she climbed a staircase leading to the Medical Gate surrounded by lush greenery. She strolled alongside the wall, gazing thoughtfully at the campus's marvelous, aged trees. The nip of Autumn had turned their leaves a rich brown and golden hue, and she thought wistfully back on the goldens of Damascus—the fallen leaves she used to go stomping through gleefully with her father in the orchards around their house in Sahat Al Midfaa. After a hike up the foothill of Mount Qasioun to Sahat Al Umawiyyin, he had once said to her, "They're going to be expanding this square. As you can see, they're constructing a huge building which, I've been told, is going to house a TV and radio station."

It had always been great fun to step on a pile of goldens and hear them crackle under her feet. The crunch-crunching of the dry leaves sounded joyful, as if there was nothing they wanted more than to be crushed, go back into the soil as fertilizer, then spring up again. Her father had always told her, "Nothing dies. Everything comes back to life again, but in another form."

Zain walked along, reminiscing about sweet times spent with her father, walking through the orchards, in the Ghouta, on his farm along the bank of the Barada River in Rayhaniya, climbing up Mt. Qasioun. But across the street she saw the present. A large sign announced that a movie theatre called the Orly would be opening soon. There was Abul Abed's shop, which sold toasted sandwiches featuring tongue and other meats and cheeses, a luggage store, Khayyat's Bookshop, which she'd decided to raid some day, and Faysal's. Faysal's was right next to an alley where, according to a sign at the alley entrance, the Sheikh Hotel was located. When she came to the Main Gate, she crossed the street to Uncle Sam's, which served pizza, hamburgers, and other student fare. As she stepped inside, she inserted a few coins in the jukebox to listen to Edith Piaf sing, "Non, je ne regrette rien."

She asked Abu Zakkour, the elderly waiter, to bring her a hamburger, which she planned to devour on the spot before rushing off to her lecture with Dr. Jewell. She buried herself in her notebook to the sound of Edith Piaf's lovely voice crooning: "No, I don't regret a thing, neither the good nor the bad." She was lifting her papers off the table to make room for her food when she sensed somebody standing in front of her. Assuming it was Abu Zakkour with her order, she looked up. But instead of seeing Abu Zakkour, she saw Ghazwan instead! He seemed to have appeared out of thin air like a genie from a bottle. In the morning newspaper she'd read a newly published story of his that overflowed with his impassioned ache for Palestine, his stolen homeland. He reached out and shook her hand, and she was reminded of how a handshake can feel like an embrace. She invited him to sit down. There was something aristocratic about this handsome, hardworking, inspired freedom fighter. Abu Zakkour brought Zain's order, and as he placed it before her, he shot Ghazwan a look of mild disapproval for his intrusion.

"Would you like anything, sir?" he asked.

"An espresso and a pack of Lucky Strikes, please," Ghazwan replied.

As Zain gulped down her hamburger, she took in Ghazwan's handsome features with no less gusto. She mentally ran her fingertips over his face, which had a tearful look about it, whether from fatigue or infatuation. Her glance traveled from his forehead, to his eyes, to his cheeks and at last to his chin, where they settled in that endearing dimple of his. He was sitting there in silent surrender to her eyes' loving caresses when, suddenly, she said, "I've got to get to class!"

Abu Zakkour brought the coffee and the cigarettes, and as Zain got up abruptly to leave, Ghazwan got up too, taken off guard by the suddenness of her movement and the shift in her psychological wavelength. Zain stuffed a bill into Abu Zakkour's hand to pay for both their orders. He tried to give her the change, but she said, "No, it's yours. Thanks!"

Ghazwan followed her out like somebody being swept away by a flood.

"Can I see you after your class?" he asked.

As they exited the restaurant, somebody put money in the jukebox to listen to another round of, "Non, je ne regrette rien."

"You'll regret it," she said to Ghazwan.

"The only thing I'll ever regret is the time I've spent without you since the day I first met you in Subki Park!"

She laughed, thinking about the psychological eons that had passed since that encounter, and how much she had learned.

As she walked through the AUB's Main Gate on her way to her class in Main Hall, she said, "Well, I'm sure we'll end up meeting again and again by coincidence, the way we always do!"

"Actually," Ghazwan replied, still keeping pace with her, "I didn't just happen to run into you today, and from now on I'm not letting you out of my sight. Like a good detective, I followed you in my car all the way from Choueifat to Bustani Hall. I bribed a guard to let me stay close enough to the building to see when you came out again. Then I stalked you some more you as you went strolling from the Medical Gate to Uncle Sam's. Nothing will be able to keep me away from you, not even you! So…I'll be waiting for you when you get out of class."

Zain grinned skeptically. *Guys are so good at lying when they're after something! Then the minute you give it to them, they forget all about you.*

"I'll never be parted from you again," Ghazwan went on, "and I won't let you run away from me. I love you, and that's that."

She didn't believe him. But to her amazement, when she walked out of her class, he was at the door waiting for her, staring at an upside down book!

You already know a little about what I went through, but don't waste your time digging into my wounds. And don't expect me to fall to pieces like some silly teenager and say, "You're the only guy who's ever understood me! You're the only one I can confide in and depend on!" I know you're as confused and tormented as I am, if

*not more so. You might share some of my hard times, and maybe
even some of my good ones. But you aren't my savior, and I'm not
yours. We're companions on life's road, and that's all. I'm not one of
those girls who press flowers between the pages of their diaries, or
who wear pink velvet and lace gloves drenched in tears.*

Somewhat to her chagrin, that night Zain took a blossom
from a jasmine necklace Ghazwan had bought for her from a
vendor on the Corniche and pressed it between the pages of
her journal. *What a cheesy thing to do! But he ran after me like
a teenager, and was so happy to see me, I felt like his long-lost
homeland!*

* * *

Zain walked into the office of the magazine she wrote a weekly
column for and handed her materials to the editorial secretary,
who invited her to stay for a cup of coffee. The telephone rang.
Zain was about to leave his office out of politeness when he said,
"It's for you!" So he left instead!

"Hello?" Zain answered.

"Don't have any coffee there," she heard Ghazwan's voice say.
"You're having coffee with me at the Horseshoe Café."

"I can't believe this! Is somebody paying you to keep me
under 24-hour surveillance?"

"Well, that's one way of looking at it," he replied. "That
'somebody' is my heart. I've made it my profession to keep you
under surveillance, and my salary is a knot in the stomach! I love
you, you crazy girl. And now you're driving me crazy with your
cool sensibility. As I told you before, I've loved you since the day
I saw you sitting broken-hearted on a bench in Subki Park—a

situation which, by the way, I'm going to interrogate you about you some day. I admit, I hadn't expected you to go from being the tormented to being the tormentor. You torment me by killing my indifference towards the opposite sex. In any case, I'm waiting for us to go to the mountains, or to the sea, or to hell, or to the Horseshoe Café for a cup of coffee if you'd prefer. What matters is for us to be together."

"A colleague of mine needs to use the phone," Zain broke in.

"Come over here, then!" he shouted. "I'm calling from the grocery store across the street!"

* * *

"Hello? Zain? This is Fadila. I'm calling from Kuwait. Good evening!"

"Oh, my goodness!" Zain gasped with surprised delight. "A good evening to you, sweetie!"

Unable to contain her curiosity, Zain added, "So how did you get the school's telephone number?"

"Uncle Amjad gave it to me."

"It's so wonderful to hear your voice! How are you?"

"I'm really good. I'm happy with Najm, and I don't regret a thing. I'm not pregnant, either! I thought you'd like to know!"

And indeed, it came as a huge relief to learn that the rhino's assault on Fadila hadn't brought the added ordeal of pregnancy.

Fadila went on, "I just wanted to thank you for your encouragement."

"Don't worry," Zain reassured her. "The people in Ziqaq Al Yasmin will welcome you with open arms when you go back. And if you show up with a baby and a loving husband at your side, they'll put on a big celebration! You know how people in our old neighborhood are. When they get mad, they froth up like boiled-over milk. But after a while they forgive you, and everything settles down again."

Fadila's telephone call sparked Zain's nostalgia for Damascus and everybody she'd known there—well, almost everybody! She got in her car and went driving aimlessly around. She drove up Beirut's sea front as far as Ayn Al Marisa. Then she drove back up the Damascus Highway as far as Dar Al Sayyad in Al Hazmiyeh. On her way to Choueifat via Aley, she tried to pass a truck, in a hurry to get back to the school before the eleven o'clock curfew. Then she noticed that the truck had a Syrian license plate.

By this time she was so homesick. She stopped trying to pass the truck and instead just kept driving behind it, wishing she could follow it all the way to Syria.

Trance-like, she drove behind the truck, oblivious to the exhaust fumes it was belching and the obnoxious growl of its motor. She was drawn inexorably to this unsightly truck, whose driver could go back to his house in Syria when he got off his shift. Before they got to Bhamdoun, she realized she would have to turn around and go back if she wanted to sleep at the school that night. She was dying to see her father, her grandmother, Ziqaq Al Yasmin and Qubbat Al Sayyar on Mount Qasioun. *I'm not really a boulder on Mt. Qasioun. I'm just a girl crying because she misses home.*

* * *

The network of saboteurs Lieutenant Nahi had sent to abduct Zain and take her back to Syria had been arrested. Yet since the day she heard about them, she'd developed the habit of checking her rearview mirror to make sure nobody was following her with malicious intent whenever she turned at the Choueifat intersection to head for Beirut. And she did the same thing on her way back to Choueifat every night. One evening on her way home from Beirut, she glimpsed a vehicle following her in her rearview mirror. On closer inspection, she realized that the car behind her belonged to none other than Ghazwan, who was trailing her out of love. Before arriving at the school gate, she pulled over, and so did he.

They got out of their cars, walked toward each other, and met halfway.

"Why do you follow me at night?" she wanted to know. "Are you jealous? You realize, don't you, that I've got a school curfew to meet, and that after that time I can't go anywhere?"

"And you realize, do you not, that I read every word printed in my newspaper before it goes to press? You and I both know they could make another attempt at kidnapping you."

...

"I know Lieutenant Nahi has it out for you. I also happen to know from my own sources why he has it out for you. He's backed by Lieutenant Colonel Samir, whose dirty work he does for him. In short, he's one hell of a dangerous guy."

...

"I don't want anything bad to happen to you. That's all. Unlike me, you don't belong to the Arab Nationalist Movement, or to any organization or party that might protect you for that matter."

Zain reached out and placed her hand on Ghazwan's lips. "Please," she said, "don't try to politicize me and recruit me into your organization. Don't claim to love me when all you really want is to spread your views or make me into a 'comrade' who'll make the coffee in your revolutionary kitchen."

"Actually," he quipped, "I'd been thinking of another job for you, like highjacking airplanes, for example!"

Then he added in a whisper, "I love you no matter what you are—unless, of course, you're a spy for Israel!"

"So," she said, "you've heard that I'm the Syrian Mata Hari who spies against her country for West Germany."

"That's bullshit," he scoffed. "Everybody knows that. And everybody knows why he made the accusation."

"Yes, it is bullshit," she replied, her voice quivering. "But he's got the power to ruin my life with it. He could have me thrown in prison just like that. Did you think I'd come to Beirut to run after you? I came here to rescue my freedom."

Trying to direct the conversation away from the minefield it had just veered into, Ghazwan said, "I'll see you tomorrow at Uncle Sam's after your class finishes at noon."

Then he rushed off before she had a chance to refuse!

Chapter Eight

Zain's heart leapt for joy when she heard her father's voice over the phone. He had called her with a happy surprise. "Hello? Zain? I'm at the Continental Hotel with Najati. We're attending an open seminar at the invitation of the Lebanon Bar Association. We got here a little while ago, and I'll be leaving Beirut on Tuesday evening. My lecture is scheduled for Monday, the day after tomorrow. I was hoping you could spend the weekend with me. If you don't have other commitments, we could go to the summer houses in the mountains tomorrow."

As immersed as she was in her new life in Beirut, nothing could have made Zain happier than to hear the voice of her father, the one person in the world she could confide anything to without being afraid he would use her confidence to hurt or exploit her.

"Oh! I'll come over right now!" she exclaimed. The excitement in her voice reminded her father of the squeals of delight she used to give as a little girl when he would push her in the swing on holidays. "We could have lunch somewhere! Then we'll spend Sunday together, and I'll be in the front row clapping for you when you speak at the seminar on Monday. I'm on my way!"

"No, sweetheart," she heard her father say, his voice betraying a hint of fatigue. "Why don't you come this evening? I'm feeling really tired right now, and I need to take a nap. I'm having some stomach pain, and I might ask you to make me a doctor's appointment. There's a well-known gastroenterologist here by the name of Munir Shamma`a. If I can get in to see him, I might stay on for a couple of extra days in Beirut to be treated."

"His clinic is right across from the AUB. I'll go over now and make you an appointment for Monday morning. I hope the clinic's still open. People around here really love their weekends! But don't worry, Baba. You just get some sleep now. What's going on in Damascus lately is enough to wear anybody out, especially if you're a big-hearted person who cares what happens to your country. Just look at what people have been through: the defeat in Palestine in 1948, one military takeover after another, the union with Egypt that split apart, then the internal split between the Nasserites and the Baathists. You helped to build up Syrian autonomy, and you were on fire to see Palestine liberated. All these things have taken a toll on you. But everything's okay, Baba. I'll be waiting for you in the hotel lobby when you come down tomorrow morning."

Gripped with worry, Zain sped over to Dr. Shamma`a's clinic. After parking in front of Uncle Sam's, she walked into the building next door. She'd make the appointment, then go work at the AUB library until it was time to meet her father.

The receptionist, singularly unhelpful, said the doctor didn't have any openings for the next ten days. Zain insisted that her father be given an appointment. As Zain haggled with the receptionist, Dr. Shamma`a walked out with his last patient and was about to leave the clinic. Sensing the urgency in Zain's voice, he asked her, "What's hurting you, Miss?"

Hugging her books to her chest, Zain replied with childlike artlessness, "What's hurting me is the way my father sounds. He's having pain in the chest area, and he's asked me to make him a doctor's appointment to have his stomach checked. He's never been to a doctor in his life."

"I gather from your accent that you're from Damascus," the doctor remarked.

Zain nodded.

"You've got some excellent physicians in those parts. The pioneer in modern laboratory analysis is a Syrian by the name of Dr. Sulayman Haydar. Why hasn't your father consulted him? The pains he's experiencing might be originating in his heart rather than his stomach."

"Well, as a certain Syrian saying goes, 'The church next door doesn't have the cure.' So he wants to go straight to the Vatican!"

After a pause, she added, "My dad's the type that doesn't like to let on if he feels bad, but his trip here seems to have been hard on him. He's never had any health problems before."

Clearly a compassionate person, Dr. Shamma`a said, "Why don't you bring your father to see me right now? I'll wait for him."

"All right, I'll do that! Could I give him a call?"

He led her into his office and, in a solicitous gesture, had her sit down in his chair behind the desk. *A girl beside herself with worry over her father? That's a rare phenomenon these days! I have elderly patients whose grown children I know personally, and who are too busy with their own success stories to take their parents to a doctor, damn them.*

The hotel switchboard operator refused to connect Zain to her father, who had instructed the concierge not to allow any telephone calls through for the next couple of hours.

"In that case," Dr. Shamma`a told her, "just bring him to see me on Monday morning. I'll be expecting you."

She thanked him profusely. As they were leaving, he said, "By the way, what's your name?"

When she told him, he welcomed her all the more warmly, saying he sometimes followed her wars of words in the newspapers. That made her happy.

"You're quite a troublemaker," he remarked, "but when you're worried about your father, you're a tender-hearted little girl."

"Don't tell anybody!" she whispered mischievously.

"Don't worry—I won't!" he obliged with a chuckle.

***

She sat trying to read in AUB's spacious library, but couldn't concentrate. She was counting the minutes till it was time to go see her father. Another hour and a half, and she'd be in the hotel lobby waiting for him. She was happy to know that his colleague Najati would be taking part in the same seminar and that he was staying in the hotel with him. At the same time, she was secretly glad Najati wouldn't be joining them for dinner! When she asked her father why he hadn't invited Najati along, he said, "The truth is, I just wanted to spend some time alone with my girl."

Those words had been music to her ears. She'd agonized over the rift that had occurred between them when she'd stubbornly insisted on marrying somebody he didn't want her to. In the end, of course, she'd admitted her mistake and he'd helped her to correct it. And now, like her, he seemed to hate to remember those difficult days. He was just happy to have his daughter Zain back again. *Or is he happy to have "Zain Al Abideen," the son my mother died trying to give him? I don't want him to love me because I've become the son he never had. I'm Zain, not Zain Al Abideen, and I'm not just the shadow of a son who never came. Actually, though, I know he's proud of me. He's told me how happy he feels when one of his interns asks him, "Is the writer Zain a relative of yours?" and he can say, "She's my daughter!"*

Unable to think about anything but her dad, Zain gave up on trying to read and left the library. She drove over to the hotel and sat in the lobby waiting for him. *I'm not going to mention anything upsetting. I'm not going to talk to him about the past. He sounded so tired when we talked. It's time I stopped demanding so much of the people I love and started sympathizing with them instead. I've got to grow up and stop running around looking for a surrogate mother! When I told Baba I'd made a mistake and wanted to correct it, he was right there by my side, and he told me he was proud of me. At that moment, an unbreakable bond of friendship and human connection was formed between us. He's the dearest person in the world to me. Since I never got to know my mother, I sort of invented her, and then I loved my invention… There he is! He's coming out of the elevator and heading my way.* Running up to her father, Zain threw her arms around him, crying, "Baba! Baba!" like the little girl she was on the inside.

He bent down with difficulty to squeeze into Zain's sportsy little Karmann Ghia. *I wonder if the bright moonlight reminds him of the nights he and I used to spend strolling down the railroad track in Rayhaniya. When we heard a train coming, we'd*

race to see who could jump off the tracks the fastest. It wasn't a
game of chicken. We knew the difference between courage and
foolhardiness. So there was a lot that brought us together. Even my
crazy failed marriage, which had been hard on both my father's
nerves and his wallet, couldn't sever that special bond between his
heart and mine.

Trying to revive his appetite which, as a true Damascene, had
never been in short supply before, Zain sang him a funny song
he'd taught her years before about meat pastries, bulgur and lamb
meatballs, to which the singer could add whatever dishes he was
craving. Then she asked him, "Where would you like us to have
dinner, dearest? At the Seven Seas, where you can see the fish
swimming around under a glass floor? At Al Ajami, where you
used to get together with journalists like Ghassan al-Tuwayni,
Said Freiha, Kamel Marwa, Riad Taha, Rushdi Al Maalouf, and
Badee Sirbiyeh? At the Carlton Hotel? At Faisal's? At Uncle Sam's?
At the Yeldizlar? At Sindbad's across the street from it? At the…"

"Actually," he broke in wanly, still not his usual ravenous self,
"I'd prefer to go to Ghalayini in Raouché by the seaside. I'd like to
go where I took you ten years ago on our first visit to Beirut. You
were a little girl then. I remember having to carry you out to the
car because you'd fallen asleep at the table."

Her father's words stunned her, since she felt a thousand years
old. Had she really been "a little girl" just ten years earlier? What
about all those lifetimes she'd lived through in Damascus, the wars
she'd waged, the experience she'd gained, the sadness she'd endured,
the articles she'd written? Had all those things happened in the
space of ten years? Or had it been ten decades, or ten centuries? She
thought back on her battles with Sheikh Shafiq and the adolescent

minions who had declared open season on her life in the name
of religion. Then there was the war she'd waged on the bourgeois
class that Lieutenant Nahi claimed she belonged to. *He hasn't got a
clue what my father and grandmother had to endure just to survive.*
She'd also been at loggerheads with the Latakian aristocracy on her
mother's side. Nothing in either her conduct or her writing would
have ingratiated her with the Zhdanovists. Both reactionaries and
revolutionaries looked askance at her quest for freedom, especially
as a woman. So she had no intention of pledging allegiance to a
political party as though it were some sort of alternative religion,
and she rejected authoritarian practices of any kind, even if the
people who engaged in them were revolutionaries.

By the time Zain had been a published writer for two years,
Syrian radicals and conservatives alike had decided their country
was in no need of a rebel like her, and society as a whole rejected
everything she stood for. Some expressed their opposition in
shrill, harsh tones, others with a tact and subtlety that left them
a line of retreat. Yet none of this caused her anywhere near the
heartache she'd suffered from her run-ins with her family and
neighbors in Ziqaq Al Yasmin, home to the traditional values
that had so suffocated her mother.

Since coming to Beirut, Zain had carried on with her uprising.
But instead of shunning her, the City of Freedom had embraced
her ideas and supported her in every sense of the word.

Her head still abuzz with all these thoughts and memories,
Zain pulled up in front of Ghayalini's and helped her father out
of the car. *I've never seen him looking this worn out before. But
maybe his condition isn't as bad as it seems. I bet he'll perk up after
we get to a table.*

Gazing at the steep flight of stairs that led down to the restaurant, her father said, "I'm not going to make it down that staircase, much less back up it again."

"That's all right," Zain replied evenly. "I can take you to Maxime's, which is right past Ramlet El Baida and Eden Rock. You don't have to go up or down any stairs to get to it. You just cross the sidewalk from the parking lot, and you're there."

Finally he said, "I don't want to upset you, but the fact is, I'm so tired and my stomach hurts so much, I just want to go back to my hotel room. I think I should just have some light soup and turn in."

"No, that doesn't upset me," Zain said reassuringly. "On the contrary, I want you to do whatever will make you feel better. And I want you at your best tomorrow morning!"

In front of the elevator he kissed her on her forehead. She bent down and kissed his hand.

"Tomorrow we'll go up in the mountains," he said affectionately. "We'll go to Aley, Bhamdoun, Sofar, Shaghour, Hamana, Falougha…"

"We'll go wherever you want to!" she broke in brightly. "And I'll be your chauffeur. What time should I be here?"

"Well," he said wanly, "you know I get up early for the dawn prayer. But could you come at around ten?"

"I'll be here waiting for you when you come out of the elevator," she whispered tenderly.

He disappeared inside the coffin-like wooden elevator, and its doors closed behind him. She walked away happily, daydreaming about spending the next day with her father and reminding herself to set her alarm for eight in the morning. so she could jump up and get ready to come meet him. Little did she know this was the last time she would see him alive.

***

Before her alarm had gone off, Zain was shaken gently awake by a teacher who shared a dormitory room with her. She got up, and before she had a chance to ask what time it was, her colleague told her in a voice filled with compassion, "We got a call from somebody by the name of Najati. He said he was a friend of your father's, and asked for you to come to the hotel right away. Your father is very sick."

Zain nearly asked, "Did he die? Tell me the truth!" But she was afraid to. She didn't know if she could handle the answer.

On her tears' tiptoes she went to the hotel where she received the devastating news. She listened attentively to Najati's account: "We'd agreed to meet over breakfast to go over some topics related to our seminar. I came down to the dining room but he wasn't there, so I went back up to check on him. I found him lying on the bathroom floor. His face was covered with shaving cream that had begun to dry. There was shaving cream on the shaving brush and on his razor. The doctor says it was a heart attack."

On her tears' tiptoes she asked to go up and tell her father goodbye.

"Don't twist the knife in the wound," Najati said gently. "You go back to the school, and I'll call you once I've finished all the red tape. I'll arrange to have him taken back to Damascus this afternoon or evening."

"I'll take him back with you."

"You won't be able to, Zain. You'll be arrested at the Jdaidet Yabous border checkpoint, and instead of visiting your father's grave, you'll be visiting a prison. But you could follow us as far as the Syrian-Lebanese border."

"Please, then," she begged him tearfully, "just let me go up and see him one last time, if even for just a second. Please."

"All right," he relented. "Come with me."

Laid out on a couch, her father was sallow, but more relaxed than she had ever seen him before. He seemed cold, so she took the bedspread and covered him up to his neck.

As she left the room, Najati said to her, "I'll call you when we're about to leave Beirut so that you can escort his remains to the border."

Your "remains"? Oh, God! You used to get mad at me for doing stupid things and not consulting you before I made a decision. And now look at the stupid thing you've gone and done by dying on me just when I needed you the most! How dare you leave me just when I've finally come to see that the only way to live my life right is to seek out your counsel before I act? This world is a brutal place, full of traps and mines, and when you collapsed on that bathroom floor, you crushed my compass beneath you. So what will I do now? How will I go on without your guidance, your support, your affection, your friendship, your love, your forgiveness?

* * *

The convoy started out toward the border. *As I followed the black hearse transporting by father's body to Al Bab Al Saghir cemetery in Damascus, I cried and cried without a sound. The hearse came to a stop in a traffic jam in Dahr Al Baydar, and I stopped behind it. For a moment I turned off my headlights along with everything inside me. My heart stopped beating, and my spirit stood in salute to a man who had fought valiantly for Syria's freedom from foreign mandates and who, by God's grace, had been spared the noose.*

I could hear wind whistling through my lungs and waves roaring off the shores of Latakia where my mother had been buried. I got out of my car and knelt in respect for my father's funeral convoy, which embraced not just his spirit, but the spirits of thousands of freedom fighters I had never known and who, with my father, had bequeathed to me a sense of self-respect and a readiness to stand up against anyone who dared try to rob me of my dignity and freedom. Once, when I was eight years old, I was with my father in a restaurant, and I asked a waiter for a glass of water, saying, "Dakhīlak kubbayat mayy." Hearing what I'd said, my father scolded me, saying, "Dakhīlak is a groveling word. It's a begging word, and I never want to hear you use it again!" But now I found myself pleading, "Dakhīlak, O God, let me have him for just a while longer!"

The funeral convoy set out again, and I set out behind it. During that last visit from my father, he'd told me he was planning to come back to Damascus specially to celebrate my birthday. This was a huge thing for me, since I hadn't been allowed to celebrate my birthday since my mother died. I guess my birthday reminded people of my mother's death for some reason.

As it approached the Lebanese-Syrian border, the hearse stopped. Najati got out and signaled to Zain that this was where she would have to turn around. She pulled over to the side of the road and started to cry without a sound.

I bathed the Masnaa checkpoint and the whole Lebanese-Syrian border with my tears. After training myself since childhood never to complain or cry, I purged my heart of the sorrows I'd hidden in silence all my life.

As the hearse's tail lights disappeared into the distance, the trees stood in mourning for my father. The sunflowers and cannabis plants that dotted the Beqaa Valley curtsied and bowed like willows in his farewell procession, and the forests and fields fell into a reverent silence. All the plants, birds and animals that were so dear to my heart—from owls, sparrows, frogs and insects, to cows and horses—consoled me in my ordeal, and for an entire minute our hearts stopped beating in my father's honor.

For the first time since my mother died, I broke into sobs that brought actual tears. At long last I could cry in the true sense of the word. And with my tears I released curses on those who had prevented me from placing a wreath of myrtle on my father's grave. In fiery agony I whispered, "Without you, Baba, I've got nobody to protect me or hold me up. But I promise to carry on. You taught me how to lose gracefully, and never to give up or lose hope."

The hearse that held the body of my precious beloved stopped at the Masnaa checkpoint. Najati got out, holding the papers that would allow him to take my father home to rest with his forebears.

It was pitch dark, and tears blurred my vision. Even so, the scene before me was clearly visible. I could even see my father's body. His face was at rest, without a trace of the pain, turmoil and conflict that had etched themselves in his features over the years. His placid eyes were devoid of passion, anger and ambition alike. It was all over. He had shed his earthly shell and departed for another planet. So why was I grief-stricken over not being able to go with him to his grave? It was silly to be crying, and I needed to stop. But how?

A fire ablaze in my heart, I prayed for inner calm.

I envisioned myself outside the invisible walls encircling Damascus. It began to rain. I got out of my car and knocked on the gates. "Open the door, Mama!" I screamed in desperation. But there was no answer. "Let me in! Open sesame!" As I stood there in despair before a windowless, doorless wall, I heard a thunderous voice, as if Nahi had installed a loudspeaker in his throat. It said, "If you want to see Damascus, Ziqaq Al Yasmin and Al Bab Al Saghir Cemetery where your father will be buried, get down on your knees and come crawling in!"

"Never!" I shrieked defiantly, up to my knees in mud that felt like quicksand. "I'd sooner die of homesickness than grovel! If I ever come back, I'll do it with my head held high. Never in a million years would I bend the knee for the likes of you and your minions. You're the ones who should get down on your knees and beg my forgiveness!"

Let it be known to Latakia, beloved of my mother, and Damascus, beloved of my father, that I'll never let anybody demean me again. I'd sooner live the rest of my life homeless and alone than suffer a fate like that. And when I die and they take me home to be buried, I want my coffin to be carried upright, with my eyes fixed on Mt. Qasioun. Of course, I'd rather go home before I have to be carried there in a coffin. But there's slim hope of that for a rebel like me who doesn't know how to keep her mouth shut when there's truth to be told, or how to spew hypocritical praise for her captors instead of belting out proud anthems to freedom.

"Quit crying, you stupid idiot!" I scolded myself. "Quit banging on gates you know nobody will open for you. Go find other paths, other countries."

Back in my car, I sobbed for my father, for myself, and for whoever might come after us while Nahi and his clones multiply by the day without anybody daring to call them out.

A voice inside me asked, "Don't you want to go back to Damascus and Latakia and... ?"

"Of course I do!" I said. "There's nothing I want more on this crazy planet. But I want to do it without having to pass through border crossings that strike terror in people's hearts with their 'wanted' lists. A homeland should have enough room for everybody, even for people who have the audacity to criticize Nahi and his ilk, whether in the press, in the workplace, or wherever else. As it is, our coffee shops and restaurants have ears planted in their walls. They're even planted in the walls of our lungs, our arteries, and our fear-sickened souls."

The villain might only exist in our imaginations. But people who've been burned over and over have the right to their paranoia. Is it wise to be paranoid, or is it just a foolish waste of time? I don't know. All I know is that I'm a writer who has question marks running in her veins and who, if she had all the answers, would probably stop putting pen to paper.

I pound on the invisible gates of Damascus in the pouring rain. Sobbing, I cry, "Throughout your history you've stood up proudly to invaders. You've taught me to be proud, too, and not to let myself be degraded by anyone. So why do you want to degrade me now? I should be able to come and go as I please, but instead you want to drag me along by the neck like a little dog. Treat me with love and respect, like the adult that I am, not like a child, or like a criminal who's expected to prove her innocence!

"Hold me up, Damascus. I'm about to fall into the abyss! Hold me up, Ziqaq Al Yasmin, Umayyad Mosque, Church of St. Paul,

Souq Al Sarouja… Hold me up, Mi'dhanat Al Shahm and Ziqaq Al Jinn, Hariqah and Lady Zainab, Qabratkeh, Souq Al Hamidiya, Al Salihiyah Road, Sheikh Muhyi Al Din, Sahat Al Muhajirin, Mt. Qasioun… remember that I'm a boulder that came from you, that's part of you!

"Hold me up, little owl of mine, and we'll go flying together over Qubbat Al Sayyar. The people who've oppressed me, rejected me and crushed me will pass away in the end. But my aunt's house in Al Halabouni and her cat Fulla will still be there.

"True, I'm a crazy woman with a cheery owl flying beside her, and I'll keep on soaring above all my troubles just the way my father taught me to before he died. O God… My father's dead, and here I am ranting deliriously in the rain. It's the middle of the night, but when I look toward Damascus, I can see in the dark."

I climb Mt. Qasioun from Al Rabweh at its base, and I reach the towering boulder where some crazy scribbled way back, "Remember me always!" The day I left Damascus I wrote, "I'll never forget you!" And now I write, "I'll be back." No matter how many continents I fly over, I'll be back! Until then, I'll go flying, orbitless, through space.

I'm no boulder. I'm just a speck of dirt that's been blown away by dark winds. I'm fragile, wretched, lonely, out of my mind.

I'm sobbing, and I hate the way I sound.

Long after the hearse had crossed the border into Syria, Zain sat in her car near the Masnaa checkpoint. She could feel the hearse's huge black tires rolling back and forth over her head, crushing it over and over. How could it be? How could her father be dead?

I kept repeating over and over to myself, my father's dead. My father's dead. My God. My one and only friend is dead. The one real friend I had on this barbaric planet. The one and only creature that knew me through and through but loved me anyway is gone. Gone, just like my mother, who might have loved me once upon a time. I don't remember her face, or her voice. I just remember people telling me she'd been less than thirty years old when she died and that she'd adored me and doted on me. I could tell by looking at my bedroom with all its pink furniture and decorations.

There was no indication in any of her writings that I even existed. That doesn't mean anything, though. After all, the people we love tend to appear in the shadowy spaces between our words, not on billboards lit up with neon.

My father—practically the only person in Damascus who didn't hate me—is dead. Revolutionaries see me as some sort of petty, spoiled girl who, even though she might be a rebel, is still loyal to her bourgeois class, and publishes books as a kind of decorative façade. The bourgeois see me as a dirty radical who needs to be straightened out with a blow to the head. The so-called Muslims want to have me flogged and hanged from their long beards. And as for my family in Ziqaq Al Yasmin, they think I'm a bad example to other girls in the clan. On that point, the folks in Ziqaq Al Yasmin and my mother's aristocratic family in Latakia are actually in agreement. That's a first! They agree that I've got no business flaunting my literary talents. So when I went to that seminar in Latakia, I did it in defiance of everybody who'd tried to crush my mother by depriving her of the chance to write under her own name. They forced her to don a mantle of falsehood, so she donned the mantle of death and left us all behind.

Nobody in Damascus likes me, and rarely was anybody willing to give me a job when I was there. Some of them tried to be polite about it, but the end result was the same. They rejected my applications with a tact and subtlety as sharp as a knife's blade. A half-rebel like my mother was bad enough, and the last thing they wanted was a full-blown insurgent like me.

I'm not even popular with other writers, since I refuse to be tamed, and I'm not interested in playing the "literary call girl."

Some of the people I worked with in my first literary seminars turned against me. Their implicit, male-chauvinist message to me was: You don't write what you want to write… you write what we want you to write. Fall in line, girl, or we'll destroy you. *They didn't manage to destroy me, but they did their best to incapacitate me with their hostile venom. Melancholy woman that I am, all I wanted was a hand to hold in these choppy seas—not to rescue me and draw me safely to shore, but just to keep me company as I battle the waves.*

The storm casts me onto a mountain top, and I find myself standing on a precipice overlooking a deep gorge. As I stand there, I decide that, now that I've lost the one person on earth who knew me inside and out and still loved me, I want to die. I want everything to end. I want to jump into the abyss and leave everything behind. So I hurl myself down. But before I reach the bottom of the gorge and shatter into a million pieces, I feel regretful. I feel genuine, profound, excruciating regret. No. I don't want to die! So instead of hurtling to the bottom of the abyss, I decide to fly. I suddenly realize I have wings, and that I've just got to find them and use them. So, the way I do in my dreams, I move my arms wishing I could fly, and it works! Ecstatic, I see that I can actually fly, and it isn't a dream. I regret the jump I attempted. I don't want to die. I have wings, and I'm soaring.

Zain woke to the sound of someone tapping on her car window. She'd dozed off. She opened the window.

"Are you all right?" a soldier asked her, his accent revealing his Lebanese mountain origins.

"Yeah," she answered groggily. "Thanks."

"What are you doing here?" he asked.

No longer flying in her sleep, she said simply, "I was on my way to Damascus, but some things are preventing me from getting there."

"Yeah!" he laughed. "Like being too sleepy to drive!" Then, suddenly serious, he said, "May I see your identification?"

The first thing she came to as she rummaged through her purse was her AUB photo ID. She started getting out her other identification papers but, satisfied with her student ID, he stopped her, saying, "That's enough. Go find a hotel in Chtaura, get a good night's sleep, and early tomorrow morning you can drive back home."

She didn't say: *Tomorrow is my dad's funeral in Damascus, and when they lower him into the ground, I won't be there. But he'll run in my blood forever.*

Drive back home? Where is home? At the Intelligence Bureau, where Nahi wants to cut out my tongue? In Ziqaq Al Yasmin, where people are demanding my head?

She was exhausted. Half-asleep, half-awake. Weighed down by defeat, her senses were sounding warning sirens. She nearly told the kind Lebanese soldier, "I want to sleep right on the border!" Of course, borders aren't drawn with white lines on the ground the way they are on tennis courts.

She thanked the soldier and closed her window again. As he walked away, she noticed in her rear-view mirror that he was part of a military patrol.

As she drove away in the thick darkness, she thought back on the moment when she regretted wanting to fling herself into the abyss and decided to fly instead. And that's what she intended to do. She'd find her wings and fly… and fly.